How to Seduce a Duke this Autumn

Wedding Fever, Book 3

Sara Adrien &
Tanya Wilde

ARE YOU SIGNED UP FOR DRAGONBLADE'S BLOG?

You'll get the latest news and information on exclusive giveaways, exclusive excerpts, coming releases, sales, free books, cover reveals and more.

Check out our complete list of authors, too!

No spam, no junk. That's a promise!

Sign Up Here

www.dragonbladepublishing.com

Dearest Reader;

Thank you for your support of a small press. At Dragonblade Publishing, we strive to bring you the highest quality Historical Romance from some of the best authors in the business. Without your support, there is no 'us', so we sincerely hope you adore these stories and find some new favorite authors along the way.

Happy Reading!

CEO, Dragonblade Publishing

Additional Dragonblade Books by
Author Sara Adrien

Wedding Fever Series (with Tanya Wilde)
Dare to Tempt an Earl This Spring (Book 1)
How to Lose a Prince This Summer (Book 2)
How to Seduce a Duke this Autumn (Book 3)

Miracles on Harley Street Series
A Sight to Behold (Book 1)
The Scent of Intuition (Book 2)
A Touch of Charm (Book 3)
The Sound of Seduction (Book 4)

The Lyon's Den Series
Don't Wake a Sleeping Lyon
The Lyon's First Choice
The Lyon's Golden Touch
The Lyon's Legacy

ADDITIONAL DRAGONBLADE BOOKS BY
AUTHOR TANYA WILDE

Wedding Fever Series (with Sara Adrien)
Dare to Tempt an Earl This Spring (Book 1)
How to Lose a Prince This Summer (Book 2)
How to Seduce a Duke this Autumn (Book 3)

Ladies Who Dare Series
Almost a Scoundrel (Book 1)
By No Means a Gentleman (Book 2)
A Knave By Any Other Name (Book 3)
A Little Bit of Hellion (Book 4)
Just About a Rake (Book 5)
Only a Duke (Book 6)

The Lyon's Den Series
Beauty and the Lyon

Prologue

One year ago...

WHEN CHARLENE AGREED to meet David in the drawing room that evening, she had been certain of one thing—that he would propose. This was what she wanted. A match with David Cross was sensible, fitting. It would please her family, secure her place, and give her the life of comfort that any woman should aspire to.

Yet now, standing alone with him, that certainty felt like a fragile mask threatening to shatter. The glow of the candlelight did little to soften the sharp edge of his gaze, the quiet force behind his every gesture. A knot twisted in her stomach. She felt as though she had walked into a snare of her own making. This wasn't what she wanted. And it wasn't him. No, the truth was inescapable now. David wasn't the man she had been longing for. He wasn't the one who occupied her thoughts late at night when her guard was down. He wasn't Adam.

"Do you not want more?" David's voice held a note of quiet persuasion, his dark eyes locking onto hers in the flickering candlelight.

Yes. The thought came unbidden, a whisper in her mind, though her lips remained pressed into a thin line. Her hands clutched the fabric of her gown where it brushed her thighs. Warmth rose to her cheeks, though not from the intimacy of his question. It was the weight of expectation, of boundaries she had allowed to blur far beyond what was proper.

David must have taken her silence as invitation.

The corner of his mouth turned up in the faintest smile, confident yet predatory, as if he could read her unspoken thoughts. He stepped closer, the scent of brandy clinging faintly to him, heady and suffocating.

"I've seen the way you look at me, Charlene. You feel it too, don't you? This was always meant to be."

Her lips parted to protest, but no words formed in time. His hand brushed along her sleeve, soft at first, then more insistent as he reached for her waist. She stiffened, her breath catching as he leaned forward, his gaze intent on her face.

And for just a moment, she almost looked into his eyes, almost tried to find the connection that seemed to shimmer just out of reach. But when she forced herself to lift her gaze to his, all she could think of was another set of eyes. Deeper, gentler, and far more piercing than David's.

Adam.

The realization hit her like a crack of thunder. She wanted his brother. She always had. And yet here she was, standing far too close to the wrong man, slipping into a scandal of her own making. How had it come to this?

"Charlene," David whispered, his voice low, his proximity overwhelming. "There is no need to deny what we both know to be true." He leaned in farther as if to claim her lips, his breath warm against her skin.

"David," she said firmly, stepping back with as much measured grace as she could muster. "You've misunderstood me." Although he hadn't. She'd misrepresented. At least to some extent.

The flicker of surprise that crossed his face was brief, but telling. His smile faltered, only to return with a practiced ease. He straightened, unfazed, his hand leaving her waist reluctantly. "Misunderstood? Dearest Charlene, that cannot be true. There is no need to feign propriety when we are practically betrothed. It is what my father wanted."

His words plunged the room into an icy stillness. Her heartbeat thundered in her ears. She'd heard of the dying wish before, of course. David's father's last plea to her own parents that she marry into the Cross family—to one of his sons. But she had never considered what that truly meant until now that the duke was on his deathbed and she on a settee alone with one of his sons.

The wrong one.

"I'm well aware of your father's wish," she said carefully, lifting her chin in defiance of the trembling inside her. "But I do not believe this gives us free rein, David. You and I... nothing has been decided."

David chuckled softly, taking another step toward her, forcing her back against the edge of the settee once more. "Oh, but I think it has been—by our fathers. If not already, it will be soon enough. Why not announce it when Adam returns from university, hmm? We could have the banns posted by winter."

Her chest tightened, her fingers gripping the upholstery of the settee for balance. Adam. It all made sense now. His absence, his long months away, the freedom it had given David to pursue her unchecked. She wondered if Adam had any idea of the situation awaiting him when he returned.

"That is presumptive, David," she replied, her voice clipped despite the tremor beneath it. "I've agreed to no such thing."

David's charm faltered again, just briefly, as another crack appeared in his polished demeanor. His voice dropped lower, colder. "You're being impractical, Charlene. The match is perfect. The entire Ton expects it. Your family expects it. And so do I." The last words came as a growl that made Charlene's blood curdle under her skin.

His candor left no room for misunderstanding this time. She recoiled as his entitlement washed over her, the air in the room heavy and oppressive. This was no courtship; this was an inevitability that he intended to impose.

David's gaze flicked past her, narrowing as something behind her caught his attention. His mouth tightened, his expression sharpening into something dark, almost feral—like a wolf asserting dominance.

Charlene's heart skipped a beat, dread pooling in her stomach. She turned instinctively to follow his gaze, but before she could fully turn, David's hand shot out. His fingers gripped her jaw, angling her face back toward him, and before she could react, his lips pressed against hers.

Ugh!

The kiss was sharp and unyielding, laced with a demand she couldn't abide. Panic gripped her as she placed her hands against his chest, shoving with all her might, but his grip only tightened. The room blurred around her, nothing but heat and the suffocating closeness of him.

"Stop!" she cried, her voice muffled against his insistence. He didn't stop. Instead, he pressed harder, his other hand curling possessively at her waist as if to anchor her to him, to claim her entirely.

Desperation surged through her. Her hand scrabbled behind her, grasping for anything solid, anything that could free her from this nightmare. Her fingers caught something cold and smooth. A vase?

Without a second thought, she gripped it tightly and swung. The crack of porcelain meeting flesh rang out like thunder in the enclosed room.

David staggered backward, a guttural snarl of pain erupting from him as he clutched his face. Crimson seeped through his fingers, where a jagged shard had drawn blood, leaving a small but glaring gash. His eyes blazed with fury, and his lips twisted, revealing the uneven edge of a broken tooth.

Charlene gasped, stumbling back. Her chest heaved as she fought for air, her trembling hands still gripping the jagged remnants of the shattered vase.

David staggered back, one hand clutching his bleeding face, rage flashing in his dark eyes. Charlene barely had time to catch her breath, the jagged edge of the vase still trembling in her hand, when a sharp voice roared through the suffocating stillness.

"Hey!"

The single word struck like a bullet. Charlene whirled, her heart slamming against her ribs as her gaze fixed on the figure in the doorway.

It was Adam.

He stood tall and unyielding, the firelight casting sharp angles across his face. His dark hair, charmingly disheveled even now, shadowed eyes that burned with an intensity that pinned her to the spot. But it wasn't just anger in his stormy gaze; it was disbelief. Shock.

Charlene's stomach twisted.

No. He can't see this. Not like this.

The thought screamed through her head as shame and panic crashed over her. Her lips still burned where David had kissed her. *She was compromised. By David. Oh, please no!*

"Adam," she managed, her voice a hoarse rasp.

His focus didn't waver. His gaze flicked from her disheveled dress and trembling hands to David's bloodied face. And then back to her, as if the answers to his unspoken questions were etched on every inch of her.

"What is happening here?" His voice was like a whip, cutting through the moment. He took a step forward, his broad shoulders blocking the doorway, commanding every ounce of attention in the room.

Charlene opened her mouth, but no words came out. Her knees shook, and she stumbled back, clutching the settee for support, her mind racing but offering no explanation.

David, still clutching his face, straightened just enough to sneer, blood smearing his teeth as he spoke. "A misunderstanding, brother," he said, his tone dripping venom. "No need to swoop in like a knight. Charlene and I were merely... sorting things out."

Adam's expression darkened as his gaze snapped to David, a muscle ticking in his jaw. "Sorting things out? That's what you call this?"

David's smirk faltered, the tension pulsing like a living thing between them. But Charlene couldn't take her eyes off Adam. The man she had longed for, the man she could never stop thinking about, was here. And he'd seen her at her most vulnerable.

Her voice finally broke through, weak and trembling. "Adam, I—"

"Enough." His tone left no room for argument, his eyes locking onto hers with a force that made her chest tighten. "We'll deal with this." He didn't say how, but the promise in his voice was unshakable, lethal.

The room crackled with silence as Adam's presence seemed to suck all the air from it. Charlene couldn't look away from him, her heart hammering as the moment stretched unbearably. Her world had just unraveled, and Adam was the one witness to every broken piece.

JUST OUTSIDE THE drawing room...

Adam stepped into the front hall of the evening's ball, his boots clicking against the polished tiles as he drew in a deep breath. After a grueling year away at university, he was finally home. The calm familiarity of this place should have eased the persistent tension in his chest. But tonight, it didn't.

He had left for university full of guilt and uncertainty about Charlene. Now, he returned with a degree, a newfound sense of purpose, and a single resolve—to tell her the truth. The truth he had swallowed down for years.

I love you. With all my heart.

Always have.

Yet as he arrived, something felt amiss. Mother assured him earlier that Charlene would be at the ball. But there had been no sign of her. Nor David.

David. His brother's schemes always left a sour taste in Adam's mouth. A low dread crept in.

Adam stopped outside the library door. From within came muffled voices, and his stomach turned to ice when he recognized them. David's familiar, mocking tone. And Charlene's voice.

Charlene?

Raised, sharp.

Hope flickered that maybe his brother's target this time was one of the older, more experienced society women. Someone who could deflect David's charm better than a young debutante. But Charlene? No. Charlene deserved better. She deserved everything. *His everything.*

And then he heard her cry out. Not uncertain, not playful. A cry edged with panic.

The dread turned into fury, red-hot and all-consuming. Adam shoved the library door open in a flash. "Hey!"

The scene before him hit like a blow to the gut. Charlene sat on the settee in the middle of the room, cheeks flushed and breathing ragged. Her hands trembled, clutching a jagged shard of porcelain. David staggered a few steps back, blood dripping from a cut on his face as he clutched his jaw, a predatory glint lingering in his eyes.

For a moment, no one moved, the air so thick with tension it felt impossible to breathe. Then Charlene's trembling voice cut through the haze, pleading for an end to it all.

What followed was a chaotic blur. Servants ushering them apart, hushed whispers and judgmental glances from the few who had dared to look inside the drawing room. Adam had shielded Charlene as best he could, helping her gather herself, his touch gentle but firm as he led her from the room. He didn't look back at his brother. He couldn't.

Now, standing on the townhouse steps as the cool night air

pressed against his face, Adam was still reeling. He watched the carriage before him, watched Charlene retreat into its shadowed confines, unable to shake the memory of her broken expression as she whispered her gratitude. She'd been so quiet, so withdrawn, the Charlene he knew buried under the weight of what had just transpired.

The door shut behind her with a finality that made his stomach twist. The carriage jolted forward, its wheels crunching against the gravel, and all Adam could do was watch.

He thought it couldn't get worse.

Thought that the hurt in her eyes, the lifeless way she had clung to his coat, was the worst thing he'd feel tonight. But as the carriage disappeared into the darkness, dread settled deep in his chest.

There were no words, no promises, no actions that could undo what had just happened. David's smirk flashed unbidden in his mind, and Adam's fists clenched tight at his sides. Fury surged within him, an inferno that threatened to consume him entirely. His brother had done this, shattered everything. He swore to himself, then and there, that David would not go unpunished.

But even vengeance wasn't enough to dull the ache in his chest. For all the storms David deserved, for all the retribution Adam promised himself, the one thing he couldn't stop was the image of Charlene's pale face as the carriage rattled away into the night.

Tonight was supposed to be different. Adam had returned from university full of hope and stolen moments of anticipation. He'd imagined a hundred ways he might finally tell Charlene how he felt. How he'd always felt. He'd convinced himself that with his degree in hand and his life's path laid out before him, she might finally see him as more than just a friend. It had been the last thing his father had asked about, whether the Cross and Fielding families would finally join. The logical marriage of two families—yes—but the greatest wish in his heart.

But now, all of it was ash. She hadn't seen him tonight—not

the real him. All she could see was David's brother. His twin. The same face that had brought her shame and anguish, mere hours ago.

"You're all the same!" she'd cried, her mouth wobbling and tears falling from her cheeks down to her chin.

She was right to doubt him. He hadn't protected her. All his clever plans, all his careful thoughts about the future didn't matter. When Charlene needed him most, he'd failed.

Adam exhaled sharply, dragging a hand through his hair. His legs carried him automatically toward his home, the heavy weight of responsibility growing with every step. He'd deal with David tomorrow. He'd make his brother understand how far he'd gone, how unforgivable his actions were. But first, he needed to think. He needed to…

The moment he crossed the threshold, the air shifted. The low hum of peace he usually associated with the house was gone, replaced by a strange tension that tightened the walls and warped the corners of his vision.

And then he heard it.

His mother's sobs.

Adam froze. The sound curdled his blood, sharp and raw. Slowly, he followed the noise to the drawing room, every nerve in his body on edge.

She was there, gripping the newel post of the grand staircase, clutching a handkerchief to her face. Her shoulders shook with every wracking sob. A maid hovered nearby, pale and helpless, unsure whether to comfort or retreat.

Adam's mouth went dry. "Mother?"

She looked up, her tear-streaked face crumpling the moment she saw him. "Oh, Adam…" she whispered, choking on the words.

Panic flared in his chest. He strode forward and knelt in front of her, taking her icy hands in his own. "What is it? What's happened?"

She shook her head, her lips trembling. "Your father…"

The world tilted. Adam barely registered his own voice as it broke. *Father?*

"He's gone." The words tumbled out on a sob, shattering the space between them. "He passed in his sleep, not an hour ago. Oh, Adam, my boy…"

Adam reeled. He leaned back, the weight of her words crashing over him like cold seawater. His hands dropped from hers, limp at his sides.

Gone. His father was gone.

He stared at the plush rug beneath his knees, the colors blurring together as his world crumbled. His father, the Duke of Rotheworth. The man who had taught him everything. The man who had shaped the estates, the family legacy, the expectations Adam had struggled his whole life to live up to.

And now, it was his.

He was the duke.

The weight of it bore down on him, suffocating and unyielding. Tonight, he had lost everything he thought he could hold on to. His hope for Charlene. His brother's respect. And now, his father.

Adam closed his eyes, swallowing back the surge of grief that threatened to choke him. There was no time to mourn. Not yet. There was too much to do, too much to repair.

But as Charlene's face flickered in his mind, pale and frightened, one thought emerged sharp and clear above the chaos.

He would not lose her, too.

Chapter One

London at the Fieldings' townhouse, 44 Portman Square…

It is a truth rarely spoken aloud, yet universally acknowledged, that a lady's life is immeasurably complicated by who she allows to hold her hand. Not in public, of course—that would be ruin—but in private, where the touch lingers a moment too long, or where a perfectly respectable glove is slipped off in reckless abandon. Such trivialities, some may say, but here lies the rub: a single gesture may chart the course of one's entire fortune, be it to bliss… or chaos. And so, dear reader, if your heart must be stolen, in the very least ensure it is by someone you would not mind joining you in the scandal.
~ The Handbook on Seduction and Matters of the Heart

A WHOLE YEAR has passed, Charlene thought. Three hundred sixty-five days. Twelve months. She pushed the handbook away. Such a long time. Charlene perched on the edge of her bed, the muslin of her morning gown clinging uncomfortably to her damp skin. The scent of flowers still clung faintly to her from the bath she had taken earlier, though it did little to wash away the grime she felt on her very soul. It was one of those moments— those moments when her hands trembled as she laced her fingers together in her lap, her gaze cast downward, staring at nothing in particular. She hadn't even lit the lamps, and the morning light filtering through the drawn curtains was subdued, painting the room in shades of shadow. How fitting, she thought, that even the sun seemed reluctant to touch her now.

A year since she'd been almost ruined. Almost because she'd not been caught. Ruined because she still *felt* ruined.

And it had been with a man she had considered her friend at the time.

That was the problem.

However, if a tree fell noisily and nobody heard, the tree fell nonetheless.

Perhaps her "ruination" wasn't evident in the eyes of society, but what did that matter when she thought of herself as damaged? Every part of her body felt ruined, especially her heart. Even a year later, she couldn't wash away the shame—not only of losing David as a suitor but also of losing Adam as her friend. The latter stung the most.

In his year of grief, I haven't caught as much as a glimpse of him.

Her breath hitched as memories surged forward unbidden: David's laughter, the insolence in his eyes, the way he'd carelessly… she squeezed her eyes shut, her nails digging into her palms. No. She couldn't think of it. Not anymore. She needed to move on. But the sharp ache in her chest reminded her that the truth would not be so easily banished. And worst of all, that nightmare had been witnessed—not by some faceless stranger, but by him. Adam. The gravity of her shame pulled at her so forcefully that she felt as though she might sink through the floor and disappear entirely. He'd helped her, but she hadn't even been able to face him in a whole year.

He's a Cross and they're all the same, were they not?
Same faces.
Same blood.
Yes, she shouldn't forget that.
But still, on the one hand, she was relieved it had been him

who walked in when David had... well... On the other hand, it was even worse because of all the people in her life, she cherished how her friends saw her.

He's not my friend anymore.

Urgh! She didn't want to even think about it!

The soft rap of knuckles against her door startled her, and she froze. "Char?" A nickname only her friends and family used. This time, it came from her brother's voice, quiet but insistent.

"I'm not awake," she called back. Her voice cracked on the last word, and she pressed her hands to her face to smother the sound. Maybe, if she stayed silent, he'd go away.

But the door creaked open just slightly, enough for her older brother Waylon's pale face to appear. His brows knit together as he spoke in low, measured words. "I wanted to tell you that Rotheworth, the new duke, I mean, has taken his seat in the House of Lords today. His mourning has ended."

Charlene's hands dropped into her lap, her heart sinking like the air had been pushed from her lungs. "Oh," she managed, her voice faint. "I see." It doesn't concern me anymore... "I'm sorry I can't be—" but she didn't finish, for she swallowed a tear and looked up at her brother.

Waylon stepped inside, his long frame taut with something less than pity but far closer to frustration. "I know. Well, as are we. David Cross might have had Father's blessing, but the betrothal contract had not been signed yet, nor had it been announced, so if we don't go, it will be well. Fortunately, the new duke cleared that up after that night... and none of us have spoken to the Cross family."

Charlene stiffened. She hadn't told Waylon or her father everything that had happened, though they did know something had. Something that had turned her into a sobbing mess on Adam's arm that night.

"He's coming out of mourning and there's a small gathering for him. Again, we won't attend, but I didn't want you to find out from someone else," Waylon finished, studying her the way one might a fragile piece of porcelain, delicate and on the verge of breaking. Perhaps she was exactly that.

Her throat burned, but she swallowed it down. A part of her wanted to be there for Adam, but a part of her couldn't. He was a Cross. David was a Cross. She just... couldn't. "I don't want you to go." *I don't want him to glimpse even a sliver of my shame.* Even though no scandal had erupted, the memories hadn't been erased.

Waylon stepped toward her, placing a hand on her shoulder. "Are you sure you won't tell me what happened?"

She shook her head furiously. She'd sworn Adam to silence as well after he had knocked his brother out cold after she'd refused to... to... argh! This was her secret. And the Crosses'. She didn't want anyone else to know. And she most certainly didn't want to burden her family since the scandal had been spared.

Somehow. Inexplicably so.

"You look serious," Waylon said, his tone light. He tilted his head, craning to see whether Charlene had been crying again. That was typical for her brother: she must laugh if she's happy and cry when she's sad. As if there couldn't be anything in between.

"It's nothing," Charlene replied crisply, though her lips quirked. Her fingers grasped the fabric of her shawl a bit too tightly, betraying her unease. "I am perfectly capable of a quiet moment without complaint."

"Quiet moments, perhaps. But without complaint? I remain unconvinced." Waylon grinned, lounging back in an altogether improper manner. "Tell me, then. What truly has stolen away your usual charm? I miss my sister."

"I'm right here."

"You used to be everywhere. At balls, banquets, and dinners. You laughed." Waylon's voice dropped. "You rarely do now. There's just that look..."

Charlene's hand faltered over the shawl, and she set it aside. She still laughed, she begrudgingly thought. And attended balls and such. Perhaps there was just something *missing*. "You might as well say it plainly, Waylon," she said, glancing at him. His teasing softened slightly; he had always been an astute brother when he chose to be.

"All right," he said, his tone losing some of its prior jest. "I've heard little whispers, you know. That you aren't yourself since that night with the Crosses. That…" He trailed off, hesitant.

"That I long for things I cannot have anymore?" she finished for him, her voice low. A sudden flush swept up her neck, and she clasped her hands tightly in her lap. "I've read enough of their speculation already. Shall we add another chapter to my alleged but unproven ruin?" Her mouth twisted, self-deprecating.

There just hadn't been the scandal that Charlene had expected.

Deserved even.

And nobody had told her what to do with this second chance… it was a secret scandal.

And yet, secrets had ways of getting out.

"You haven't ruined your heart," Waylon said, his brown eyes steady. "The world is unfair. Harsh. But that doesn't mean you're finished."

But my heart feels broken; how can anything else go on?

Her throat tightened. "I want what any woman wants, Waylon. To feel a thrill, a warmth. For love, true love." Her words faltered, her face burning. "It is a cruel twist of fate to still want it when you know you must never dare reach for it. Not fully."

Waylon was quiet for a long moment. Then he offered her a gentle smile, low and familiar. "Only you would make longing seem like a virtue, Charlene. If anyone deserves more than they've been given, surely it's you." His statement was equal parts humor and affection, but his look lingered, steady and kind.

Charlene managed a strained smile, but her chest felt hollow. She could only laugh faintly at his words and turn back to her embroidery, though the thread blurred in her vision, the ache within her far heavier than she dared to voice. "No matter what happens, Char, no matter what you want to do, I'll be here. None of us will turn our backs on you, not even if the truth comes out, whatever that truth may be." His tone was firm, unyielding, his hand briefly squeezing hers as if to anchor her to something more solid than her heartbreak.

"I just want to be alone."

"Very well," he said softly, turning to slip from the room again. The sound of his boots fading down the hall left Charlene alone with the welcoming and supremely oppressive silence that only broke with the ticking of the clock on the mantel.

Alone.

Utterly alone.

Yet, despite the crushing weight of her past pain and her determination to rip that fateful night from her memory completely, her thoughts slipped to the Cross family. She imagined their mourning—once thick as the black wool they must have worn, heavy with solemn silence. Back then, since the late duke had been sick for a while, many would have brushed his death off, but Adam… Adam would have to carry the burden. He always carried more than his share. And now, with him finally taking his seat, the burden was a title. He would never be just Adam again, the boy sitting across the dinner table with a smile at the ready for her. A friendship lost.

Yet it felt like she'd lost more. She pressed trembling fingers to her lips, her remorse eclipsed by an ache she couldn't name. Just a year ago, they might have had a wedding, and instead, there had been a funeral. Had Adam felt heavy stepping into those shoes? To bury a father and become the head of a family and a large estate in the same breath?

But she couldn't ask him.

She never spoke to him again after that dreadful night.

Charlene sucked the air in and pinched the bridge of her nose. If she could shed her skin and become someone else, she'd do it in a heartbeat. But she couldn't. This was her life and a girl of her standing, the daughter of an earl, her reputation felt more fragile than the antique Chinese vases at the British Museum. And yet, somehow, it was intact—even if just on the outside.

Charlene sighed, curling her arms around her knees.

Well, his return didn't change anything. She'd steer clear of him. She'd flit about to her heart's content. And she would *not* get entangled with a Cross ever again.

Not this time. Not even the handsomest young duke.

A few streets east in Mayfair…

ADAM FOLDED HIS apology, slipping it into his pocket. He had rewritten it countless times, stripping it of words and explanations more and more—there was nothing he could say to erase his failure. A mere apology still felt inadequate. He needed a lifetime to live down the shame of that night. Adam was ashamed for his brother. What David had done was inexcusable.

He couldn't blame Charlene for not speaking to him.

And yet, especially on this day, he needed Charlene more than anyone else in the world.

But he didn't know how to go to her.

How do we go back to how things were?

Charlene,

I failed you. I miss you.

Adam Cross, Duke of Rotheworth

The scent of ink wax had long since cooled. A flicker of unease stirred in his chest—not just a dissatisfaction with words, but something far deeper, a clawing awareness that words alone could not repair what had been broken. And on this day, the weights pulling his heart into the abyss seemed unbearable.

And when he stepped out of his study and walked through the hall, even the family chapel loomed, its familiar stillness offering no comfort despite the flowers and respects Mother paid his late father there every day. Beeswax candles flickered in sconces along the stone walls, their flames listless, casting shadows that bled into every crevice. Dampness clung to the air, sharp and tangible, as though the earth itself mourned within these stones—his childhood home had become his responsibility. His burden. He breathed deeply, but the taste of smoke and damp only drove the knot in his chest tighter. A faint prickle settled at his nape, a sense of being watched, though he knew he was alone.

I have to fix this alone, too.

His eyes drifted upward, tracing the muted hues cast by the stained-glass windows. Colors that had once seemed vibrant in his youth now dissolved into pale shards of sunlight across the floor, fractured and distant. His jaw tightened as he dropped his gaze to the limestone beneath his boots, the dull surface cracked in places, worn by years of footsteps far heavier than his own. He shifted his weight, the faint leather scuff breaking the oppressive quiet.

Beyond the closed oak doors came the faint tread of footsteps, distant but deliberate, a sound that set his senses on edge. Movement would not change the truth. Nor would it quiet the growing sense of failure clawing at him from the inside out.

I wish I could speak to Charlene.

But the price of keeping the scandal at bay had been to keep his distance from her.

How cruel, he thought, that he shared a face with the man at the root of this misery. His twin brother, who didn't even have a heart, unleashed such heartbreak.

He closed his eyes, just for a moment, as the weight in his chest pulled, dragging his thoughts into an unfathomable depth he could not name. This was not mere doubt or frustration with poorly chosen words. No matter how well one masked it, this was deeper, rawer, the kind of pain that festered. A lump rose in his throat, unbidden and unwanted, and he swallowed hard against the sensation. The taste of ink lingered faintly on his tongue, a bitter reminder of his morning's toil.

Somehow, he had to make up for his failure to prevent all this.

If only I could turn back time.

And still, the note he'd written to Charlene burned against his chest, its presence more cutting than any accusation. An apology undelivered was no less heartfelt—and yet it was like a spell uncast. Unless he delivered the apology, Adam knew it had no effect. And yet, all year, he hadn't given it to her—for how could mere words grasp what he felt so deeply?

He had drafted so many versions before he finally poured a bare string of words onto its surface, but no flourish, no sentiment could carry the weight of what he meant to convey. Words that could never undo what had already been shattered. They could not rebuild what had crumbled in his hands the day he had failed her. After a year of mourning, a year of carrying the apology with him that he never sent or delivered, the cleft was even larger. How could he approach Charlene and rekindle their relationship?

After a lifetime of friendship, he'd missed her.

More than a friend missed another though…

Despite his brother's transgressions separating them, he longed to know how and where she was. And especially, if she was willing to be with him.

The day wore the trappings of ceremony, but even now that his father's tomb had been erected, nobody from the Fieldings had come to stand with him. It was most unusual—until a year ago—that the Fieldings and the Crosses wouldn't stand together.

The black crepe armband on his coat felt like a stranger's, and he was ready to rip it off already. His father was gone, just like many other things. Adam was Duke of Rotheworth now, at age five and twenty, a title he had not asked for, an inheritance that felt premature and impossibly large.

He adjusted his cuffs, his gaze drifting upward to the chapel's stained-glass effigy of Saint George, sword raised high. Duty.

Honor. These were the virtues his father had prized, had drilled into him. But Adam's chest tightened as he thought of Charlene, no, Lady Charlene Fielding, and the note now tucked away. Those ideals seemed hollow when matched against the confusing mess of desire and shame within him.

Just over a year ago, he had danced with Charlene at a merry gathering before his brother cut in. Her laughter had been warm enough to make his pulse leap in ways it shouldn't have. The same way shivers blew down his spine and he forgot himself whenever her eyes met his across a glittering ballroom. Forgot the discipline, the carefully measured steps he was meant to take. All of which didn't include her. Not in that way. Yet their connection had shattered when he caught his brother, David, with his arm around her waist, while Charlene tried to escape, his intentions unmistakable.

Fury had exploded within him.

There might be some unspoken rules between them as twins, but David had acted rashly, as always—this time, inexcusable.

Adam's jaw tightened at the thought of David's reckless behavior. Charlene deserved better than his brother's schemes. No, she deserved better than any Cross man. Yet here Adam was, holding fast to a thread of hope he could not untangle. At least he had sent his brother away. It had been all he could do at the time. And keep the secret.

Hope, however, was a fragile thing. The Fieldings had been absent at his father's funeral, conspicuously so. Charlene he could understand. But her father and brother should have been present at the cemetery, offering their condolences and upholding the decades-long bond between their families. But they were not. Adam could not blame them either, not after David's behavior, and not after Charlene had so clearly distanced herself from them. Though what she told her family, he didn't know. No one had shown up to demand a duel. Still. The distance between him and Charlene had gnawed at Adam for a year.

Although his father's passing hadn't come as a surprise, the timing of it had, and how deeply affected Adam was struck him to his core in a way he'd never seen coming.

He let out a heavy sigh.

The duties of the day awaited him, but his thoughts stayed stubbornly with Lady Charlene. No title, no inheritance, no oath to his family could root out the memory of her voice, her touch when they danced, or the way her lips had almost curled into a smile when she teased him.

Everything he'd cherished before David had ruined everything.

She's everything I miss in life.

He paused near the corridor, his hand brushing the folded letter in his pocket. Perhaps it was madness to seek her out again. Because, for all his uncertainty, there was one thing he knew with painful clarity. Whatever shame his family had brought upon the Fieldings, he would spend the rest of his days making it right.

And he would start with their friendship.

Chapter Two

One year ago, on the day Adam's father's testament was read to him when Adam became duke...

THE STUDY STILL hummed with the clipped, precise tones of the solicitor's voice, the title "His Grace, the Duke of Rotheworth" ringing out with the gravity of a church bell. The will had been read aloud, every word a decree that carved Adam's future into stone. No invitations for questions, no pauses for grief. Only a litany of duties, each more sobering than the last. Across the table sat his brother, David, a shadow of insolence darkening the room like dusk creeping toward night—especially after what he'd done to Charlene the previous night. And as Adam sat there, the weight of honor and expectation pressed heavy on his shoulders, his resolve bracing against David's presence, an unwelcome reminder of the chaos that loomed at the edges of his newly defined world.

"This is all too hard to believe."

His fists curled against his thighs, the fabric of his breeches straining as David's voice carried across the room, rich with that easy charm Adam had come to resent, a grating reminder of everything broken that David would never care to mend.

"It is, it is." The solicitor's voice droned in crisp, formal tones, moving onto words of duty and legacy, spoken without pause or sentiment. Adam sat stiffly in his chair at the head of the long oak table, the official language naming him duke sinking into his chest like a stone.

Next to his brother, his mother sat shrouded in black lace, her veil concealing all but the pale oval of her face. Her trembling hand moved periodically to her eyes, dabbing at them with a white handkerchief spotted with damp grief. The room, big yet suffocating, bespoke of heavy silences that followed each deliberate word—a burden Adam bore with the same fortitude that had sustained him through their father's funeral the day before. But that resolve threatened to splinter as David shifted lazily in his seat, his boot scuffing the floor in a grating rhythm before he uttered another low insolent remark that sent a ripple of tension through the room like a stone dropped into still water.

"Quite the magnanimous speech for a dead man." David's voice cut through the room, sharp-edged and entirely unwelcome.

Adam's jaw clenched further. He met his brother's gaze briefly, noting the faint smirk tugging at the corner of his mouth, a smirk made all the more damning in the presence of their grieving mother.

"David. A word." Adam's voice was low, each syllable hard as stone. He pushed back his chair with deliberate calm, standing before fixing his brother with a look that demanded obedience.

David arched a brow as though considering defiance but then, with a bored sigh, rose. "Oh, by all means, Your Grace," he drawled, the last two words laced with mockery.

Adam turned, leading the way out of the study. He didn't stop until they were in the hallway, its shallow light heightening the undercurrent that hummed between them like a taut string. Once alone, Adam swung to face David, leveling his brother with a glare that carried years of frustration.

"You will not behave like that in front of Mother again," Adam said, his voice sharp but low. "You should have the decency to show some respect. For Father. For her."

David shrugged, utterly unfazed. "I don't see what you're so angry about. He's gone. No amount of solemn faces or stiff collars will change that. And she"—he flapped a hand toward the closed study door dismissively, as if their mother were some distant acquaintance rather than the woman who had given them life and now sat drowning in sorrow behind that door—"shouldn't expect us to wallow along with her. What I need is a distraction, not another sermon about what's proper."

Adam's composure cracked. His hand shot out, grabbing David by the lapel of his coat, and in one swift motion, shoved his twin back against the paneled wall with a force that made David grunt. Adam kept his grip firm, his face close, every feature hardened with fury.

"You think this is about a sermon?" Adam's words were harsh and pointed. "Do you even hear yourself? Distraction, you said. Is that what Lady Charlene was to you? A distraction when father was on his deathbed?"

Laughter spilled from David's lips, wild and derisive, his head tilting back briefly against the wood before his eyes locked on Adam's. "Since when do you care so much about a distraction?" he sneered. Then, with deliberate slowness, he bared his teeth in a twisted smile, tapping the chipped corner of his second incisor with his tongue.

Adam froze, though his grip on David's coat tightened. The sight of that broken tooth hit him harder than words. Charlene. "She's not a wench," Adam ground out, his voice trembling with restrained fury. "She deserved better than you. Better than anything you could ever offer. You had her fooled, David, but not me. She could have given us something precious, aligned our families, united two great houses. She would have given us her heart, and you tossed it aside like rubbish."

"She was willing enough most of the time," David tsked and arched a brow, implying what Adam didn't believe for a moment about Charlene.

"She'd never... not with you!" Adam snarled.

"Maybe not, but you interrupted us last night!" David gave a laugh that was so sour, it could curdle milk.

"You are rotten to the core," Adam growled.

David shoved against him, breaking his grip and stepping to the side. He smoothed his rumpled coat, throwing a sidelong glance filled with amusement at Adam, but something darker lurked beneath it. "What would you have done, dear perfect brother of mine? Married her yourself? Be honest." He leaned closer, tilting his head. "You never saw her as an alliance, did you? You want her completely, don't you? You're envious of the fun I had testing her temperament."

Adam's fist clenched at his side, but he stayed rooted to the floor, his chest rising and falling unevenly. "More than anything, I want her to be free of men like you," he said, his voice low, raw with the truth.

David smirked again. "And what makes you think you're any better than me? We're brothers. Cross brothers. Two sides of the same coin, duke or not. The same blood that flows through me, flows through you. There's nothing you can do to get rid of me."

Adam forced himself not to react, brushing against the signet ring on his finger, the symbol of his new station. When he finally spoke, his tone was ice. "I'm the duke now," he said, each word measured, deliberate, bearing the weight of his title, his name, his anger. He stepped closer, his eyes locked on David. "Cross brother or not, don't you dare cross me. In fact, it's over. You are over. Before the end of the day, I want you gone from England or else I'll freeze your stipends." It was the very least he could do for Charlene. That and break off any whisper of an engagement that might have existed between them.

"You can't do that," David growled.

Adam took a threatening step forward. "Test me. I dare you."

"Where would I even go?"

How like his twin. He only cared about himself. Never about anyone else, especially not Charlene. She truly deserved better.

"Anywhere but near us or Charlene. Pack your trunks by the end of the day, brother. You are leaving or I will haul you onto that ship myself. And I will do just that."

A flicker of something passed over David's face for the first time. Surprise, perhaps even uncertainty. But he masked it quickly, offering a mocking bow before turning and leaving the hallway.

Adam stayed where he was, his breathing steadying, though the tightness in his chest remained. His fingers curled once more into a fist before finally releasing the tension, staring down the empty hall where his brother had disappeared. The battle between them was far from over. But for now, Adam would do what he'd always done.

Carry the weight.

Stand firm.

And protect what mattered.

Present day...

CHARLENE'S FINGERS WORKED delicately, the small scissors in her hand snipping at the vine of the climbing jasmine as she tilted her head to inspect its stubborn curve. The greenhouse was perfectly damp and just hot enough for the new buds to hopefully open in a day or two. Fortunately, the glass overhead misted faintly despite the late hour and shielded the delicate new leaves from direct sunlight. Every breath tasted faintly of soil and petals, a sweetness that clung to her senses. She often found solace here amid the neat rows of calming greens and the riot of colorful blooms. But today, even the soft scent of roses failed to soothe the ache lodged deep in her chest.

Her hands paused over a cluster of pale pink blossoms.

Adam's name had drifted through her mind too many times these past weeks, like a song half-heard but unshakable. It was only natural to wonder on an anniversary of death if one had done the right thing. Should she have gone to the funeral? Were

David's horrid deeds enough to warrant an excuse to stay away? Would she forever feel this discomfort in her breast like a pebble in her shoe, which no amount of shifting could dislodge?

What's done is done; you can't think like that.

The glass-framed door creaked, breaking her reverie. A gust of cooler air swept in, the movement setting the leaves trembling around her. Ashley appeared, her dark curls gathered loosely, though she fussed with them the moment she stepped through the door.

"It's beastly damp in here," Ashley said, wrinkling her nose as she stepped carefully down the tiled path between the planters. "My hair shall puff like a hedgehog before I've even reached home."

Charlene offered a glance over her shoulder, faintly amused. "You shouldn't have come in, then."

"And leave you brooding alone among your flowers? No, no, I couldn't allow it," Ashley retorted with mock severity, though her tone softened as she produced a folded sheet of newsprint from the ribbon at her waist. "You ought to read this."

Charlene straightened, clipping one last stem before placing the scissors aside. She wiped her hands absently on the apron tied over her gown. "I don't make a habit of reading such things; you know that."

"Perhaps," Ashley said lightly, stepping closer, "but I think you'll want to read this one. Or has avoiding mention of the Crosses become your newest strategy? You decide, you're at a crossroads, so to say." Ashley wrinkled her nose and bit her lip. "Or do you not want to cross any of the Crosses again? Lest you be—"

"All right, let me see," Charlene said as she took the paper.

Charlene's teeth clenched, a small but telling movement. She unfolded the paper and shook her head, resolutely ignoring her thudding pulse. "It is not avoidance of these matters. I simply have better uses for my time." *And I fear being the subject of...*

Ashley's brow lifted, a small smirk tugging at the corner of her lips. Charlene sighed, holding out her hand at last. The rustle of paper was louder in the greenhouse's hush, and though her fingers hesitated only a fraction, it was enough for Ashley to notice.

"I'll just admire the begonias while you read," Ashley chirped, retreating with a sweep of her skirts.

"Orchids," Charlene corrected her. But it didn't matter anymore.

Charlene tried to suppress the faint tremor in her grip. Her eyes had skimmed past the advertisements for soaps and gossip about Lady Hartford's ill-fated hat before falling on the column Ashley must have meant. The ink smudged faintly beneath her thumb as she read, the words forming with deliberate clarity in her mind.

Sources as reliable as the very soil we stand on say that the brother of the new Duke of Rotheworth, Adam Cross, has left the country without further explanation of why he didn't pursue the woman he seemed to have chosen. Waylon Fielding, Lady Charlene's brother, denies all allegations that David Cross had ever asked for Lady Charlene's hand. We are left with a true mystery, and the Ton shall remain unsatisfied with the scandal snatched away from their very grasp. A year, dear Readers, as the mourning period is over, and it's most assuredly too long to wait to find out the truth, isn't it?

Her breath hitched, but she said nothing, only letting the paper fall to her side.

David.

Always David.

The evil Cross brother.

The name now felt more like a thorn than a balm. And Adam? He had become duke while David was gone. Without a word, without anything to indicate why?

I'm the reason.

Her heart gave an unwanted throb, a reminder of all the

words unspoken, all the glances avoided in the weeks since he'd vanished.

"You've gone terribly pale," Ashley remarked gently, moving closer once more. "Surely it's not the worst thing you've read. It was only a matter of time until the sharp tongues would come looking for the scandal."

What she hadn't read was the truth of what happened. The scandal that had never quite bloomed.

And Charlene had the sinking feeling that it would come to a late bloom thanks to one of the Cross brothers.

The question remained, which one?

Charlene managed a shaky smile, though it didn't reach her eyes. "No, not the worst. Only… unexpected." She folded the paper carefully, handing it back. The weight in her chest grew heavier, a silent testimony to the things she could never undo.

Chapter Three

*To attend a masquerade, my dear, is to court the perilous allure
of shadows and whispers. A young lady, once veiled in such
intrigue, may find the delicate threads of virtue unraveling
before society's watchful gaze. Scandal, like a moth to flame, is
ever drawn to the masked.*

~Handbook on Matters of Seduction and the Heart.

CHARLENE SHUT THE book and set it neatly on the low stand beside the raised flower bed. The crisp flick of its gilded edges breaking the silence drew the attention of two pairs of curious eyes. One pair, belonging to Maddie, was wide and a touch aghast. The other shone with a poorly concealed smirk from the recently engaged Ashley who would soon be the Countess of Linsey.

"What dreary nonsense," Charlene declared, casting a glance toward her friends. "Does virtue truly abandon a woman the moment she dons a mask? Or is this merely the invention of someone who never once experienced an afternoon worth writing about?"

"It is not dreary," Maddie said in her usual tone of soft reproach, crossing her hands tightly in her lap. She sat with her back straight enough to make her governess proud, an untouched teacup balanced delicately near her elbow. "It is a warning."

Ashley laughed, leaning back against the settee's arm with the languid grace only the very content or completely shameless possessed. "Or perhaps an invitation to court romance? But for whom, one wonders? The scandal-seekers who haunt balls like carrion crows must be quite pleased with such advice. It frees up all the proper young misses to stay home and read dreary little books, exactly like this one."

Maddie's brow furrowed, and she looked as though she might protest. Charlene, however, grinned. "If this is what propriety requires of us, then I fear I am lost."

"You fear it now?" Maddie said swiftly, wearing such an expression of heartfelt exasperation that Charlene stifled a laugh.

"Completely irredeemable, I'm afraid." Charlene stood, brushing invisible creases from the folds of her breeches which she used for gardening. "And that is precisely why I will be attending the Bennett ball this Saturday evening."

"Unmasked, of course," Maddie said firmly, though her fingers twitched nervously closer to the edge of her teacup.

"Masked, naturally," Charlene replied with mock innocence. "If one is to be irredeemable, one ought to enjoy it thoroughly."

"Charlene!"

"It's not as though I'm planning to abscond with a scandalous rake," Charlene said quickly. "Which I think we can all agree would be the far greater sin." She turned to Ashley then, her curiosity piqued. "Unless, of course, that might be required for true romance?"

Ashley's laugh, rich and full of conspiratorial delight, filled the room. "Romance," she repeated, holding Maddie's horrified gaze with amusement. "My dear Charlene, romance requires risk. And if there is no rake to abscond with, you might still manage to shock someone enough that they think you did. Which is nearly as good."

Maddie buried her face in her hands, muttering something about the fate of her friends being entirely out of her hands. Charlene, however, felt the smallest thrill run through her as she smiled at Ashley in quiet agreement. Masks, after all, were designed to hide what one most feared revealing. What, then, could be more alluring—for the terrified and the fearless alike?

"I want to find a man." *A good one. An orchid, not just a fern. Or someone who can be both.*

Crickets met Lady Charlene Fielding's declaration, and she chuckled, glancing over her shoulder at friends, Ashley and Maddie, who both sat at the central table beneath a canopy of vines that Charlene had strung with lanterns. On the aged wooden surface lay glossy sketches on fine ivory plates—Ashley's wedding dress designs.

So, what if she wanted a man? It wasn't an uncommon request.

Why was her statement that shocking?

The scent of orange blossoms blended with the earthy humidity that clung to Charlene's cheeks. An array of orchids settled in her hands with the hope to bloom in time for Ashley's wedding. Outside the grand panels of glass, late summer leaves rustled violently in the gusting wind, their golden hues whispering the arrival of autumn. Inside was a sanctuary of plants, the air alive with the perfume of orchids in full bloom.

Charlene knelt by a workbench in her worn breeches and carefully worked to pot a type of orchid—a rare Cymbidium she had nurtured for months.

"So, you want to find a man?" Maddie slowly. "May I ask, what for?"

Ashley burst out laughing.

Charlene scoffed. "What could it be possible for? To fall in love with!"

"You don't just find a man to fall in love with, Char," Ashley said. "Love finds you."

"Please," Charlene said. "Did you find your man first and then fell in love?"

"That's a different story," Ashley said. "But I'm pleased as punch that you are ready to find a man. Though, I shall advise to steal a kiss from him first when you do. Kisses say a lot about a man."

"What sort of advice is that?" Maddie said with a frown. "Don't listen to her unless you want to stir up a scandal instead of a betrothal. Those two rarely mix, Char."

Honestly, at this point, Charlene didn't mind as much. She stood after potting the orchid, dusting off her hands on her pants.

"You'll ruin your hands and nails if you keep doing that alone," Ashley remarked. "How will you seduce a man then?"

Charlene glanced at her smudged fingers and smiled wryly. "With gloves."

Maddie chuckled. "Tell her, Char. Besides, a little dirt has never ruined anyone. Just look at you, Ashley."

"Are you calling my courtship dirty?" Ashley scoffed.

"Well, your mind sure had some unchaste thoughts, didn't it?" Maddie put her hands on her hips and arched a brow.

Charlene grinned. "Oh, many unchaste thoughts in there."

Ashley huffed but didn't argue, instead smoothing one of the plates reverently. "Well, if you find a man soon, perhaps you shall have the joy to pick out your wedding dress with me."

"No, thank you."

"You know that is not her style," Maddie pointed out. "She'd probably wed in breeches."

Ashley's wide eyes flashed to Charlene. "Even you would have to admit this fabric design is remarkable. I can almost feel the silk just looking at it."

Charlene wiped her hands on a nearby rag and wandered toward the table, pulled by Ashley's enthusiasm despite her indifference to such fripperies.

The fashion plates were stunning.

Gold thread knitted through the delicate pattern like rivers of light. Her fingers itched to trace the edges, but to her dismay, sudden emotion prickled all over her body. She couldn't place them all at once, but she detected a slice of envy. Charlene swallowed hard, suppressing the incomprehensible sting behind her ribcage.

"Be happy for me, Char. Your turn is bound to come soon. You might be surprised," Ashley teased, her melodic laughter lightening the moment. "But don't frown. You'll alarm the orchids."

I am happy for you. But I want to be happy, too.

"Don't mock me," Charlene replied with a soft smile, even though Ashley's besotted look only clarified the slight ache. Her friend couldn't be a more radiant bride for the Earl of Linsey. "You've chosen well." Now, all Charlene had to do was do the same. "I've no doubt you'll dazzle everyone at the altar."

"It will be a sight, indeed," Maddie murmured with a smile. "I'd imagine the earl will do very much the same."

"Do you mean dazzle? Linsey is far too manly for that," Charlene said with a light sniff as she poured herself a cup of tea.

Ashley poured herself more tea, too. "Speaking of matrimony and matters far-flung, have you read Sera's latest letter? She will be put out when she discovers she missed your wild adventure of finding a man."

"What wild adventure?" Charlene muttered. "I've merely stated an intention."

"But she will still miss you putting it into action," Maddie said with a wink.

Stars, Charlene hadn't even thought as far, yet. She only knew that she wanted what her two friends had found.

Maddie grinned and picked up a letter—probably the sixth of Sera's updates—the only friend absent because she was on honeymoon with her new husband, a prince from Transylvania. "They are in Vienna now."

Ashley made an encouraging motion. "What else does she say? She always has the best stories. Perhaps she has some strategies for Char to find her man."

All at once, Charlene wanted to snatch it up and burn it or possibly devour it. She should never have announced her intention so boldly to her friends! She wouldn't be surprised if they all but paraded a gaggle of men through her family's townhouse later today.

But she knew there would be no strategies, since she'd already read the letter.

Ashley was right.

Sera had the best stories. They came alive on the page. Her descriptions spilled onto the paper in vivid detail. A few weeks ago, she'd written about the lavender fields in southern France, then the fresh air in the Alps, and now this:

"The sweeping countryside of Austria had left her breathless," she wrote, soon leading her to Transylvania's Bran Castle in the Carpathian Mountains, where her prince's parents welcomed her as a daughter.

But more than that, Charlene could feel the love she had for Prince Alex with each and every word. How could she find such feelings before the end of autumn—before Ashley's romantic winter wedding?

"I'm told it once belonged to a great prince whose deeds remain the stuff of legend," Sera had written. "Though something about its austere silhouette on the craggy hills makes me certain such a place could house equal measures of romance and adventure. I can just imagine Alex as a boy here."

Romance and adventure.

Charlene had thought that her heart had long lost its desire for such things after that blackguard...

No.

Do not think of him.

And yet, David Cross had overshadowed it all.

The entire childhood Charlene had spent thinking she'd one day marry a Cross brother. They'd grown up together and then...

But if she wanted adventure and romance, she would have to face the past, right?

"There are no tricks in her letters. Only love," she finally said, rising to her feet, striding over to the greenhouse windows. Beyond the glass, the wind spiraled through the garden, laying the summer asters low with bold strokes.

The sight gripped her.

Change was tangible, brushing against the panes but not yet stepping inside this room of perpetual green.

"Charlene." Ashley's voice softened, laced with a note of concern. "Are you still worried about that wretched rogue, David Cross?"

And a face—handsome, infuriating, unforgiving—seared its way forward from her memory.

Charlene sighed, then turned to send a smile to her friends. "Worried, no." But fear... She knew him.

I thought I knew Adam, too.

And they're both the same, aren't they?

"Well, the minute he shows his face in London again, I'll pummel him." Maddie showed her fists as if a gentle lady like her could ever threaten anyone. Still, the friendship among the girls warmed Charlene's heart.

"Of what I've seen of Adam Cross, he'd even enjoy that, Maddie." Ashley rolled her eyes.

"No need," Charlene said. "I doubt he'll return anytime soon. Though I will not deny the past has made me a touch wary of the future." David Cross had stolen more than her peace. He'd stolen the idea that the world, like the orchids she pruned and nurtured, could grow into something unblemished.

He'd broken her heart.

"You know his brother has returned," Maddie said with a scrunched brow. "He is now the Duke of Rotheworth."

Yes, Adam had returned.

Another face, this one just as handsome but wholly different from his brother surfaced in her memory.

Just as hateful.

Perhaps even more so than his brother. David had broken every romantic dream as a debutante, but Adam, or rather the duke, had cut her to the bone with his scathing words after the fact.

Charlene cleared her throat and strode back to the table. "I wonder what Sera would think of this particular design for your wedding gown," she said to Ashley, drawing the conversation back to safer ground. She'd much rather talk about wedding gowns and baubles with her friends than talk about the Cross brothers.

Once Charlene dusted the soil from her hands, she glanced around the conservatory. Here, it would always be green. Inside these walls, she nurtured life, caring for each plant as if willing them to defy the passage of time. Outside, the leaves would soon yellow, wither, and fall from their branches, surrendering to the inevitable. It was their way, just as it seemed to be with men like the Cross brothers. Perfectly polished, yet destined to disappoint once their veneer faded. The thought settled like a shadow in her chest as she turned back to her orchids, wishing the quiet constancy of her plants extended to the world beyond.

She never wanted to see any of them again.

ADAM SHIFTED IN his chair at the four-story townhouse that had become part of the burden and privilege of his inheritance. The high back of the polished mahogany pressed into his shoulders, and the study smelled of ink and old parchment, reminding him of all the times he spent in this room with his father, listening to his teachings. He'd always meant to take his father's place as the duke, but he had only ever wanted to be a privateer—a man of the sea. Duty had come too soon, and he never had the chance. The solicitor had been droning on for what felt like hours, and Adam could tell by the angle of the afternoon sun slicing through the curtains that it was scarcely just past three. He'd rather be racing through the park on his mare at the moment. Anything, really.

Except for this…

But he was about to fall asleep. Staying awake and thinking of Charlene was taking a toll at daytime.

"It is, as stipulated, that the inheritance now falls under your stewardship," the man said, folding his hands over the ledgers spread across Adam's wide desk. "The estate requires significant attention, given the expenditures of the prior quarter. The tenants are due to pay soon, but it will hardly suffice to cover the current expenses."

Adam set his jaw, a finger tapping on the chair's armrests. This chair had always been a bold feature of the study. Bolder even than the large desk. It was not the first time since he'd been a boy that he sat in his late father's chair, in his place, but it meant more now. It was as symbolic of his takeover as it was tragic. "I'll see it's handled," he said evenly, his words clipped but steady. He kept his gaze fixed on the man before him, avoiding the probing look from his mother.

The dowager Duchess of Rotheworth, Lady Carmen Cross, wouldn't be ignored so easily. Seated elegantly in the corner like a queen surveying her subjects, she sighed softly. "Handled, yes. But when, *hijo mío?*" Her voice always sounded softer in her native tongue since the Spanish words lulled Adam into a sense of comfort. It was why he'd always been the best at school, then at Oxford—Latin was in his mother tongue and in his blood, the foundation for science, law, and even grammar. "These matters demand immediate action."

He finally met his mother's sharp, dark eyes.

Her hair, streaked now with gray strands, remained tied in its customary coiled twist. The brilliant scarlet shawl contrasted with the black mourning dress as if the fire draped around her shoulders spoke louder of her origins than any word she could utter. The corners of his lips lifted. She hated drab-colored clothing. Adam leaned forward, sliding the stack of papers toward him. "I'll speak with Woolridge tomorrow about the accounts. These repairs on the tenant cottages—" He gestured toward the solicitor. "That will begin as soon as the weather allows. And the tenants should be informed."

"Always the responsible son."

The solicitor rose with a creak of stiff joints, murmured polite goodbyes, and left as a servant ushered him out. The heavy oak door thudded shut, leaving an odd silence in its wake.

His mother moved then, rising from her corner with the grace of a woman half her age. She crossed to Adam's desk and placed a thick, cream-colored envelope in front of him. "And now, responsibilities of another kind. You'll make yourself useful to society as well, *mi hijo*. This arrived just this morning."

He glanced at the invitation but didn't touch it. "A ball? Mother, this is hardly the time to—"

"You're wrong," she interrupted, her hands resting firmly on the edge of the desk. Her fingers, adorned with rings of gold, diamonds, and a blood-red ruby, tapped impatiently. "This is precisely the time. Your banquet after confirmation in the House of Lords was too modest. Mourning has ended and your life goes on; you'll not vanish into this study and become a recluse. The estate depends on public perception as much as anything else. You know that."

"I can fulfill my obligations without masquerading at a ball," Adam said, his voice tight.

Her eyebrow arched. "Do you think your father wanted to go to balls? He understood how to maintain appearances." Her expression softened, and her voice, though firm, carried a note of tenderness.

"You must go, Adam. There are alliances to be made, reputations to uphold. And, perhaps, opportunities you would not expect. And let's not avoid the pressing matter that you need to find a wife."

"Do not start with that. I'm not marrying."

"Fine, but you still need to go." She slipped the invitation closer to him. Her movement stirred the faintest scent of citrus, the perfume she had worn for as long as he could remember. Adam sighed and picked up the envelope. He pulled free the card engraved in flowing gold script, reading it with reluctant attention. He set it down again.

"Do you even know who is attending? I've no patience to flatter idle fops today."

"You think I don't know you?" She pushed a long list of names toward him. "The Countess of Worthington is a close friend of mine. She sent me the list of everyone attending. I've marked all the important names, and you'll do well to develop connections with them."

Ever detailed-oriented.

Adam bristled at the idea of spending time among the Ton instead of riding out to the country to look after the estate.

But his gaze flicked over the names to humor his mother. Suddenly, he stopped on one person.

There it was.

Her name.

Lady Charlene Fielding.

The breath he'd drawn caught in his chest. He pushed the list back carefully, as if it might crumble under the weight of his stare.

"What's the matter? You've gone pale," his mother said, studying him intently. "Is something troubling you?"

He shook his head once, his throat dry. "No." He tried to rearrange his expression, but his mother's knowing look cut straight through him. He'd forgotten how little escaped her notice.

"Ah," she said softly, pulling a chair from across the desk and taking a seat. "I see. It has been some time. But there's no harm in seeing her again, is there? Now that your brother has gone to the Continent..."

Adam didn't reply. He didn't trust himself to. Instead, the study's soft ticking clock filled the gap of silence.

You can't even imagine...

He wished he didn't have the urge to kill David every time he thought of how David had hurt Charlene—even if not physically, the wound was deep enough for her family to cut all ties with him. Adam knew his loyalty should be to his brother; they were twins after all. But wasn't there an excuse if one's brother was David? Yet Charlene… She hadn't wanted his pity, his protection, nor his heart. And in the heat of the moment, he had said something he would regret for the rest of his life. That was the last time they saw each other.

She probably hated him as much as she hated David.

His mother leaned forward, her golden earrings catching the sunlight. "You do not have to tell me what happened that night before your father died. But you will accept this invitation. And if I need to drag you there myself, I will."

His thin smile held no humor, but he inclined his head. "If you must," he said dryly.

His mother laughed lightly, as if the matter was already decided. "I taught you how to dance for a reason, *hijo mío*. You'll do me proud yet."

Before Adam could muster a retort, she rose again, brushing an invisible wrinkle from her skirts. She paused at the door, looking over her shoulder with a mischievous gleam that made her seem almost youthful again. "Oh, and be sure to dance with a lady or two. Perhaps even Lady Charlene. That's the thing about life, Adam. You either dance or you sit alone at the edge of the ballroom. I suggest you do what you do best."

Dance. While just out of mourning. It felt abhorrent, a betrayal of the quiet grief that had settled in his chest like an unwanted companion. Yet society demanded appearances over substance, forcing a man to paint over his sorrows as if they no longer mattered.

Why did he have to be born first?

But then, David as Rotheworth? No, it was lucky he had been born first, rather than that do-no-good brother of his.

However, the very notion of waltzing amid the clamor of music and chatter struck him as tasteless. But the mask—at least the mask offered him a reprieve, hiding the truth that his eyes would reveal, concealing the weight of what he refused to speak aloud. Behind its veil, Adam supposed he could be anyone but himself, and perhaps, for one evening, that would be easier.

His gaze lowered to the invitation, his chest tight with something like longing—and something sharper than regret.

You look just like him.

Her parting words of one year ago burned through his gut.

Adam dragged a hand through his hair. Perhaps, just maybe, they could move on from the past?

Chapter Four

Masquerade Ball...

CHARLENE ADJUSTED HER mask for the third time, the satin ribbon refusing to sit comfortably around her head. "I don't want to be here."

"What are you talking about?" Maddie asked, casting her a sidelong glance while ensuring her own mask sat perfectly across her face. "You're the one who wanted to find a man, remember?"

"Not at a masquerade ball." Charlene motioned toward her brother, Waylon, who was loitering a few feet away from them, his arms crossed and his gaze vigilant. His fiancée stood at his side, her elegant figure draped in a gown that practically sparkled like glitter under moonlight. Well, for a moment before he slipped away like a true gentleman who had no intention of torturing himself with feminine shenanigans.

"This is still the perfect place," Ashley countered from the side. They had all dressed at Charlene's house and set out together. "Consider it a trial endeavor."

Trying, yes. But a trial? Could a woman's reputation ever survive a trial?

Truth be told, she neither wanted to be there nor did she think it wise.

Still, she wasn't going to leave.

Charlene broke into goosebumps at the thought of the scandal that night might have unleashed.

Oh, the Cross brothers. Or at least one of them.

"For what is this trial, exactly? Looking beyond the masks in the ballroom?"

Ashley chuckled, lowering her voice. "Flirting, dancing, and stealing kisses. Masquerade balls are the playground for romance and adventure. Practice!" Ashley winked at her.

Aha! Certainly not something Charlene felt her reputation could survive. And even that was an understatement!

Charlene almost groaned. She wanted to find romance and adventure, yes, but she wasn't sure that was the way to go about it. Stealing kisses? That would mean being alone with a man she didn't know, and given what had happened a year ago with a man she *did* know…

No, she couldn't do it.

"I might just try all that," Maddie said with a laugh.

"Can you two be serious?" Charlene tried to hide her exasperation. Fighting back a smile, Charlene bit her tongue. She was forever grateful for her friends and wanted them to be happy. But she also wanted to be happy. Not merely wed. Not merely shelved. Not merely anything, no! She didn't want to settle for anything less than bone-melting kisses and adventurous romance that was the material even most naughty books left out. And yet, her heart wasn't complete.

"Oh, I'm very serious," Ashley replied, her grin widening. "The men in disguises are your playground. You're here to find one, aren't you? What better place than a room full of masked ones to consider which traits you cherish the most?"

Anonymity was on the top of that list.

"Besides their faces, you mean?" Charlene asked.

Ashley shrugged. "This is the only way to be excused for considering the other qualities of a gentleman," Ashley said as she twirled and flipped her hips.

"I can't believe you just said that," Charlene muttered.

Ashley leaned in, her voice brimming with mischief. "One

never knows. Your gallant suitor might be standing just beyond that potted plant. Would that not be the very height of perfection?"

Maddie laughed and covered her mouth with her fan as she blushed. "You two are a scandal; no men are needed."

"Many orchids are potted but not every potted plant is an orchid." Ashley arched a brow. She ought to know, Charlene thought. Considering that she and Thomas... but well, that was another story entirely.

"You know," Maddie murmured. "Rather than orchids, all you need to do is search for your rare fern, the steady and humble kind. Or perhaps flirt with some regular orchids and avoid all potted plants."

See the men as plants? She could do that. Potting was the problem—and not merely metaphorically speaking.

"But there is a glaring problem. Orchids are rare and distinguishable. With men, it's the exact opposite."

"You are taking this analogy far too seriously, Char," Ashley muttered. "Take your enjoyment. Don't think, act. We are here. We have our eyes on you." So history won't repeat itself? Charlene thought bitterly of that night.

Perhaps she was thinking more than acting, but the more she thought, the more she wanted her rare orchid.

Maddie nodded. "You may rely upon our steadfast support. And you are allowed to amuse yourself again. On your terms. But given all of that, now I don't even know where to start looking for my future husband!"

Charlene laughed. "He'll breeze into your life sooner or later."

"Or sneeze into it," Ashley muttered. "What? Don't look at me like that, Char. Maddie's the queen of potions in her travel apothecary. Hidden potions and such..."

"Not hidden," Maddie denied.

"Well," Ashley said, grinning at Charlene, "needless to say, orchid or potted plant, just do what you do best with them. You kiss them, I mean, water them, plant them in different soil, and all those things you gardeners do. Go do that."

Charlene raised an eyebrow. "So, you're telling me to go around watering men?"

Or were they supposed to pot her, take her away from her family, and set her aside in a forgotten corner or household while they were off gallivanting like the Cross brothers?

No, thank you.

Speaking of garden, how far can a woman go without giving them her flower?

"Precisely," Ashley said with a nod. "And while you're at it, plant a few and see which ones thrive. It's all about the effort, my friend."

Charlene shot her friend a flat look. "Like your revenge effort with Linsey?"

"It all turned out for the best, didn't it?" Maddie flicked open her fan and waved it lazily in front of her face. "Ashley's gardening advice might be the butchering of plant comparisons, but it's not that bad of an idea."

Charlene sighed, a reluctant smile tugging at her lips. "Fine. I'll water a bit. But if I have only a dead fern, or worse, it's on you. You shall find the wrath of my brother."

"Oh, don't worry," Ashley said, looping her arm through Charlene's. "I'll be here to prune your scandals."

Charlene laughed. "Why, thank you."

Maddie let out a sigh. "I'm starting to feel the heat with all this talk of plants," she said, glancing around the room. "Then again, with all these masked shrubberies, you have your work cut out for you."

Charlene raised an eyebrow. "Should I be worried about you?"

Maddie shook her head. "I haven't caught the wedding fever yet."

"You might catch it tonight," Ashley pointed out.

"No, tonight and the nights to come are all about Charlene

and her man she wants to find."

Yes, she should never have made that declaration. "We can all find someone."

Waylon appeared then with the typical scrutinizing look of a brother, his imposing frame interrupting their fun like a general inspecting his troops. His dark eyes swept over the three of them, his brow furrowing. "What are you plotting over here?"

"Why would you believe we are plotting anything?" Charlene asked, turning to her brother with an arched brow.

"You have that look of plotting women."

"Oh," Ashley murmured. "And what does that look like?"

"Like this." He gestured at them with a quizzical look. "Danger. I can feel it."

Maddie waved her fan a bit faster. "And what does that feel like?"

"Like a shiver down my spine."

"The best kind of shiver," Ashley countered with a grin.

Waylon turned his attention to Ashley. "And you," he added. "Don't encourage my sister with reckless antics."

"Who, me?" Ashley said, placing a hand on her chest. "I would never."

Charlene bit the inside of her cheek to keep from grinning.

"Oh, stop, Waylon." His fiancée stepped forward and smiled at them. "Let the girls have some fun."

"I'm their chaperone."

"Are you?" his fiancée asked. "Or are we? So long as they don't leave the ballroom, give a lady some space."

"All right."

But Charlene wasn't hearing her brother anymore. Her eyes had caught sight of a man. A man in a black mask casually speaking to another man... A man she had hoped she would never see again.

What was he doing here?

WHAT *WAS* HE doing here?

Adam's gaze raked over the ballroom, filled with pretentious faces behind even more pretentious masks. What felt the worst was that he was one of them. Every polished detail about him bespoke an air of artifice. He hated cravats. And what was with all this layering of clothes? Not even to venture into colors. His mother didn't enjoy drab, but he preferred it. He didn't belong here. "I don't want this; let's leave."

"Have you seen your mother's hawk eyes on us? Leaving is not an option without dancing. And stop scowling," Jack Cavendish, wealthy, a hotelier, and the sort of acquaintance who showed up when least expected and vanished just as easily said. "You're here, I'm here, and let me tell you, I'd also rather be at home with my wife."

"Your wife? She hasn't agreed to marry you yet."

"She will."

"It's been two years."

"I'll wait a thousand; I'm patient."

Adam's lip curled in disdain. "I cannot believe her brother is allowing you to live in scandal with his sister."

Jack waved his comment aside. "Stop diverting the topic that's really on your mind. She is here. You have a chance. And your brother is on his way back."

Adam's blood froze, his head whipping to his friend. "Say that again?"

A sigh. "I just received the news myself. It's ten percent accurate. The spare has boarded a ship back to England."

"Ten percent? Why even mention it in the first place?"

Jack shrugged. "As duke, you should know this. This is why you should act ten percent faster to secure your love."

"She is not my love." Not yet. Not anymore.

There was that sharp pain in his chest that surfaced every

time he thought of Charlene.

"You cannot still be denying this? But you love her."

Adam scowled. "Don't speak of love so casually. She chose my brother."

"And how did that end?"

Adam cursed, glaring at his friend. Horribly. It bloody ended horribly.

You are all the same.

That one sentence would probably haunt him forever. "We are not compatible," he simply said. They were not, no matter what the feelings. They were one-sided anyway. And she thought him the same as his brother. No, whatever may be his dreams at night, they could never be his reality in the day.

That sunny chance of love had set forever. Every sunrise that followed was subtly different, for no two suns or sunsets are ever the same. Unless, of course, one was to stand in the exact same spot for an entire lifetime.

And what human could do that?

He felt a hand on his shoulder.

"Come now, old friend, let's make the best of this, eh?" Jack made a sweeping motion over the crowd. "You're not going to stand here all night, looking like a masked statue. Not that I mind. I don't care for this sort of affair either, but your mother will skin us both alive if you do."

True. "She might. She might not. What the eye does not see, the heart cannot fuss over."

"You believe she doesn't have eyes and ears everywhere?"

Oh, she most certainly did. He couldn't refute that either.

Adam sighed. His gaze was locked on the dancers gliding effortlessly across the floor. The kind of life that never seemed to touch him. So poised, posh, and pompous. At least that was what he had thought while growing up. He much preferred the open seas. Vast. Raw. True beauty.

"Go on," Jack prodded again. "Pick a woman. Ask her to dance. You'll forget all about your brooding by the end of the waltz. Also, it should get your mother off your back."

"She wants me to engage, too. Form connections."

"I'll introduce you to the Duke of Mortimer later. That should please her. You dukes should have some influential friends."

"Much obliged."

Jack gave Adam a friendly shove. "Now, go dance with someone so we can get out of here quicker."

Adam sighed. "I don't know who." The last thing he wanted was to give any woman here the wrong impression.

Jack's grin widened. "It's a masquerade ball. Everyone's wearing a mask. Half of them are strangers. Who's to say who's who? Just ask one of them. Dance with her. Well, ask three if you must. You know as well as I do that women can't resist a man who looks like he doesn't care. And frankly, if you are recognized, I'll jump into a bush of thorny roses completely naked."

Adam smiled at that. "I feel like a fraud asking anyone to dance. I don't belong here."

"You do belong here," Jack said, his voice firm. "Whether you like it or not, you have a place among all of them. If you want to nitpick, I'm the one who doesn't belong."

"The difference between you and me is that you don't care."

Jack chuckled. "True." His friend clapped him on the back. "So, stop looking so miserable. Your mother and I are the only ones here trying to get you out and into Society. Be grateful to us."

Sometimes he wondered how they became friends in the first place. But that was one of the things he enjoyed about the man and why he didn't mind his friendship. His mystery. That, and he never once judged Adam on any score. In fact, if you don't want to talk about duty, and family, and David, Jack was your man. But Adam barely registered his friend's words. His gaze had locked on a group of three women. One in particular.

Charlene Fielding.

He knew it as he knew the sky was blue.

Well, black in the darkness of night, but still... She'd illuminate the night as her sight made his pulse quicken.

Of course, it shouldn't.

But it did. She did.

Every time.

The only woman capable of truly making him question everything.

Adam drew in the sight of her, his chest contracting. She wore a green dress with a sparkling green mask, and he just knew her eyes sparkled the same green. Still not able to catch his breath at the mere sight of her, even after one year.

For a moment, Adam stood there, torn between thought and action.

His mother's words, his heart, and his head all collided at once.

Without thinking, and then, before reason could hold him back, Adam moved. It wasn't a conscious decision—more like an instinct, a pull he couldn't resist.

"Adam?" Jack called, but he ignored him.

He couldn't think about why he was approaching her or what he would even say. It didn't matter; his feet carried on, every nerve in his body on edge.

She turned slightly, her profile illuminated by the soft glow of the candles.

So beautiful.

Could he be so lucky and remain hidden or would she recognize him if he asked her to dance?

Chapter Five

"CHARLENE?"

Charlene blinked, glancing at Ashley, who gave her a probing look.

"Did you see something?" Ashley pressed.

"I don't know," she murmured offhandedly. She didn't want to ruin her friend's mood, but was David Cross truly here? She didn't know why her thoughts went to him first. Perhaps it was just pure instinct. Yet, Charlene's blood froze at the thought. She glanced at the spot where she had seen the men, but they had both disappeared. She didn't even know why her thoughts went to him first. Perhaps it was just pure instinct.

Her gaze flicked over the crowd, searching.

No, hunting.

On the dance floor, masked figures twirled like brushstrokes on a canvas, each gown a splash of color set against the gleaming expanse of the ballroom. She tugged at the silk of her gloves, a small motion to steady the restless energy coursing through her, but in the end it did nothing but make her more anxious.

If he was here, she'd leave.

She wouldn't be able to survive another encounter with David Cross.

But the embarrassment tasted bitter as if it had been only

yesterday and not a year ago… Charlene wished she'd never laid eyes on the man.

She couldn't stand being in the same room as that man. She just couldn't. Of course, she wanted to find adventure and romance, but was this truly the place for her to find it? Her gaze drifted over the crowd, the sea of feathered masks and glittering jewelry. Everything appeared rehearsed, although she knew that wasn't the case. But there was a pattern to it all, a choreography that felt as predictable as the steps of the quadrille the dancers were enjoying. And then her eyes stilled, once again fastening on a figure cutting through the smoky glow of the room as he danced.

Her eyes briefly rested on his hair. Dark.

A breath of relief escaped her, but just momentarily, because she hadn't been wrong. She had recognized him. He was a Cross. Just not the Cross she thought.

He stood apart from any other man, not in defiance of the crowd but as though the space around him bent to accommodate him. His hair gleamed under the flickering light, each step drawing reflections from the polished marble beneath his boots. The line of his broad shoulders shifted with a kind of quiet intensity that struck her like a chord struck true.

Charlene blinked, unsure why her breath had hitched.

Adam Cross.

Here, in the flesh.

The new duke, not the boy she'd called her friend as a child—Adam.

The one who'd come to interfere when his brother had… well… and yet, Charlene didn't quite manage to give either of them credit—not even when it was due.

It wasn't that he was like the other gentlemen. He didn't have their polished air, their effortful refinement. Rather, he carried himself with a rhythm and force that felt utterly untamed.

Especially when he was near his twin brother.

His movements weren't like the dancers', who flicked their

arms and arranged their feet in deliberate, practiced poses. No, his body moved as if the steps answered to him instead of the other way around. His strides, even off the dance floor, were deliberate but fluid, each one falling with a precision that seemed to echo some unheard drumbeat. He didn't need music to guide him—he was the beat, the pulse of energy threading its way through the crowd.

Maddie's head suddenly pressed close. "At whom are you gazing so intently? Has some gentleman managed to capture your attention after all?"

Yes.

"I wish to know the same thing," Ashley piped up.

Something stirred inside Charlene, unfamiliar and unwelcome. Her pulse throbbed faintly in her ears as her fingers curled at her sides, her nails brushing the fabric of her skirts. He turned then, not sharply but with a natural grace that made the layers of his dark coat ripple faintly.

"Rotheworth," was all she said.

Her friends gasped. "The Rotheworth?" Maddie asked.

"Well, we always knew he might be here," Ashley said. "He's staring this way and patting something in his coat."

"His heart?" Maddie asked.

"His pocket." Ashley tilted her head in an effort to see better.

For a moment, the crowd surged around him, blocking Charlene's view. But she didn't look away—not even when the heat of watching him made her cheeks prickle beneath her mask. When he reappeared, the light caught the edge of his jaw beneath his mask, the curve of his neck above his cravat. There was nothing exaggerated in him, no artifice. And still, he stood out in a room full of opulence and feathers and gold. Her heart gave a small, unsteady kick as he moved again, cutting through the throng with simple, quiet purpose.

He made the rest of the masquerade feel like hollow decoration, as though, without him, the chandeliers might as well have burned out and the music fallen silent. She swallowed hard, ignoring the flutter low in her stomach. No matter who he was, whatever spell his presence had cast over her, she couldn't quite convince herself to look away.

Her brother and friends told her but still, some part of her hadn't truly believed it.

He really was back.

And it seemed this time, for good.

"Are you all right?" Maddie asked. "We can leave if you want."

"No, I'm fine," Charlene said. "It's not like he will recognize me or we'll cross paths."

If he was aware of her scrutiny, he didn't show it. Yet Charlene couldn't shake the growing sense that the pulse driving his steps was the same one now thrumming faintly in her chest. Some untamed rhythm—irresistible, unrelenting—that she had been swept into without even realizing.

"Your brother won't be happy," Ashley said.

Charlene grimaced. While she'd narrowly escaped that fate worse than death, she couldn't hide her swollen eyes or her torn clothing from her brother. He still didn't know what had happened, but he did know David and Adam Cross had been involved. "He will be fine, just like me."

Charlene adjusted the edge of her mask, suddenly conscious of the press of people around her. The masquerade had drawn half of London, it seemed, and yet the sea of silk and champagne barely touched her mind as her attention snagged on the figure at the far end of the room.

A fan snapped somewhere nearby, startling Charlene enough that she realized her lips had parted slightly. She dragged her gaze down, heat developing low in her chest, and smoothed her skirts, though nothing about her gown required adjusting.

She inwardly cursed.

Don't forget who that man's brother is, Charlene!

"Well," Ashley said. "I must admit, the duke dances quite splendidly."

"Forgive me for agreeing," Maddie murmured.

Indeed, he danced as if he had been perfecting the art for a thousand years.

I can't dance that well.

Charlene felt her heartbeat quicken, her cheeks flushing. There was surely something unrefined, almost untamed about his dancing—a shift from mechanical precision to something instinctive. It left her throat dry, a strange sensation that she had stumbled upon something she wasn't meant to witness.

I want this.

Adventure. Passion. Grace.

Dangerous love.

Charlene shifted, her feet half-turning as if some deeper instinct urged her to either draw nearer or flee completely. She remained rooted in place. And then, mid-turn, he stopped. He didn't hesitate; the pause was intentional. His gaze swept across the ballroom—dark, searching—and fixed directly on her.

Her breath hitched.

Caught. But Charlene didn't look away. Couldn't. She swallowed hard, her fingers pressing into the smooth silk at her sides. He inclined his chin ever so slightly, the barest acknowledgment, before turning his attention back to his partner and guiding her through a final flourish of steps.

It wasn't merely a greeting, nor a fleeting glance. Charlene felt it—just as surely as she felt the thrum of violins vibrating through the ballroom. The tilt of his head, the weight of his gaze, promised there would be more to come.

HER MASK, EDGED with silver, lent her an air of daring that she likely required to extend her hand and propose a dance. He hadn't demurred. His hesitation would only have invited attention, and tonight he wanted none of it. Besides, at that moment, he'd welcomed the interruption more than he cared to admit.

The whole room hummed with the notes of a lively quadrille; the violins pulling the couples on the floor into sweeping arcs. The chandeliers overhead flickered with too much light, glinting off the endless sea of silk and satin. Yet Adam's focus wasn't on the spectacle swirling around him or even the woman he was dancing with. All his attention was entirely on her.

She'd lingered earlier at the periphery of the ballroom, half-obscured by the towering potted palms. From afar, she'd seemed almost ethereal—slender but striking, inconspicuous yet somehow unmissable. The curves suggested by the gown only stirred the corners of his imagination. But it was her eyes that undid him. They had locked earlier. Briefly. Bright, perceptive, and utterly arresting beneath the delicate lines of her green mask. He could feel their pull even now, following him like a challenge he couldn't resist.

Had she recognized him?

Would she even be looking his way if she had?

The dance finally came to an end. Unhooking himself smoothly from his current partner's hand, Adam offered the woman a brief smile and murmured his goodbye. He couldn't hold back anymore, his course unwavering as he strode across the marble floor toward the girl who had refused to relinquish her hold on his attention.

Their eyes locked again, and his stomach lurched.

He could instantly tell she was caught somewhere between retreat and uncertainty, her eyes darting to her left shoulder, then her right, as if seeking someone to carry her away from this moment. So, she had recognized him. And yet, she didn't run. He felt it then—that connection that thrummed through his blood and never seemed to leave him.

He wouldn't hesitate or be side-tracked this time. He wanted her back in his life. It didn't matter which way or how; he'd do anything to reclaim a spot at her side. Even if just as a friend.

His mother had been right.

The dance goes on.

But he didn't want it to go on without her.

Stopping just two feet short of her, he cast a brief glance at her friends before meeting her gaze again. "My lady. Would you do me the honor of the next dance?" Adam extended his hand, palm up, his smirk laced with both confidence and promise. "Yes," his voice dropped low, intimate, meant only for her. "I've come for you."

Her hesitation spread like ripples across water, visible only for a breath before she lifted her chin and placed her gloved hand in his. Without a word, Adam led her to the floor, trying hard not to grip her hand tightly and run for the doors. It was all he could do not to groan at her fingers' light pressure and the faint lavender wafting from her skin.

Oh, how he'd missed her scent.

He turned to her, offering her an assured nod as they positioned themselves for the music. The first strain began, a waltz that swelled with lush, lilting rhythms, and they moved.

She still hadn't said a word.

Actually, thinking of it, Adam had never danced with Charlene more than once before. They'd been at countless gatherings together over the years—at least before this past year. And then he had taken a step back when she showed interest only in his brother.

It was clear within the moments that the waltz started that she was no trained dancer. Her body fought against the natural fluidity of the steps, as though coiled too tightly to give over to the music. She moved stiffly, her feet catching now and again on imaginary threads of the polished floor. The awkwardness should have annoyed him—it usually did—but instead it fascinated him.

She was a blank page with uncharted potential.

Was she really not going to utter a word to him?

He could tell that she was trying very hard not to, just as she was trying hard to keep up with him in the dance. The verbs of

Latin, Adam thought, biting back a smile. *She's dancing like I once conjugated amicus, amica, amicum.* Painfully methodical.

He couldn't take it anymore. He chuckled.

Her eyes instantly shot to his, narrowing beneath her mask.

She was endearingly full of contradictions. Her dress—scandalously cut compared to the sea of pastel silks and cream flounces surrounding her—suggested she knew how to play the dangerous game of allure. The deep-green fabric hugged her waist, flaring to emphasize the tempting length of those legs hidden beneath layers of skirts. The mask, though simple, framed high cheekbones and a soft mouth that Adam couldn't help but notice as her lips pressed together. It prompted the urge to tease her, to get her to respond. To say something. Anything. "I would have thought that a woman dressed so strikingly," he mused, "would be able to dance well."

She arched a brow, her lips curving in a faint, almost teasing smile. "I dance tolerably well."

He chuckled low, the sound warm enough to brush against her skin. "And modestly, too, I see."

"Why did you ask me to dance, Lord Rotheworth?"

"Ah," he said lightly, though his gaze lingered on hers a heartbeat too long, "so Lady Charlene recognized me after all."

"It's difficult not to," she replied, just above a whisper. Then, after a pause, she added, "You knew me as well."

"As you pointed out," he said, his voice softer now, "some things are impossible to miss." Then, almost imperceptibly, he pulled her closer. She stiffened at first, but when her eyes searched his with a flicker of surprise, the corner of his mouth lifted in quiet amusement. "Although it seems your dancing could use some refinement."

She averted her gaze, clearly intent on masking the sudden flush at her cheeks. "Flawless footwork has never been my ambition."

"Allow me, then," he murmured, his tone touched with mischief, "to instruct you."

Her head angled sharply in his direction, her eyes narrowing as though seeking to uncover the hidden motive in his words. "And why," she asked cautiously, "would you do such a thing?"

For a moment, he faltered, his usual easy confidence slipping into something unguarded. "Perhaps," he said finally, a softness entering his voice, "I miss what we once had."

"What was it?" she asked without looking at him, and her mask didn't hide the blush creeping up her face.

"Friendship. Trust." Adam swallowed hard. "Perhaps a past strong enough to warrant a future?"

"Is this what you call a polite gesture, Your Grace?" she asked, her voice low enough to keep their exchange from curious ears. "Forcing your company upon me under the cover of civility?"

"A truce, perhaps?" *Was there such a thing as a truce for avoiding one another?* He tilted his head just slightly, drawing her close as they began to move. "Would you rather I called it an honor, instead?"

Honor?

Charlene narrowed her gaze, but he smiled—she could tell even under the mask, from the way his mask shifted, and his forehead wrinkled.

Her heart skipped a beat, though her steps were seamless. "I would rather you hadn't called it anything at all."

"Perhaps," he murmured, his tone unreadable, "but then I would have missed the pleasure of this moment."

Charlene bristled, her fingers tightening against his shoulder. "Do not mistake this for some act of pleasure. I am here only because decorum demands it."

His lips curved faintly as they turned with precision, the whisper of her skirts brushing against his leg. "Then allow me to thank that ironclad decorum of yours. It does me a great service."

Her frown deepened, though it only made him smile more. Her cutting glances might pierce others entirely, but Adam seemed to be made of steel. "For a man who claims to wish for peace, Your Grace, you do seem intent on stoking the fire."

He leaned a fraction closer, his voice now edged with something more dangerous. "And for a woman who declares herself indifferent to me, you seem determined to keep striking the match."

Her breath hitched at his words, the precision of his steps never faltering. Her annoyance rose with every beat of the violins, her pulse matching the tempo. "Do not insult me with these games, Your Grace. I know what lies beneath the surface of your words."

"Enlighten me."

She fixed him with a glare that could have frozen fire. "A Cross man polished to perfection, charming everyone until his way is secured. But beneath it all? Empty words and empty promises."

Adam's jaw tightened, but he remained steady, his grip resolute. "You may have me confused with my brother," he said at last, each word measured. "But if all I am to you is a reflection of his sins, then I will do whatever it takes to shatter that mirror. Charming as I am." A glimmer of mischief lit his gaze as he inclined his head just so, the faintest wink escaping unbidden. It was an instinctive gesture, born of years entwined in shared confidences and easy familiarity with Charlene, a deeply rooted bond that required no words.

"You overestimate your ability," she retorted coldly, spinning gracefully under his hand before returning to him. "There is nothing you can say or do that will undo what has been done."

"And yet you still dance with me," Adam replied, his voice just low enough to cut through her resistance. "If my cause were so hopeless, would you have granted me this waltz, even for appearances? Or is it that some part of you remembers me before that night, Lady Charlene?"

Her breath caught. The question struck deeper than she cared to admit, but she masked her reaction with a sharp laugh. "What I remember, Your Grace, is that some lessons are learned only once. Do not test my memory."

His gaze softened, almost imperceptibly, though his tone remained firm. "Then know this. I am here. Not as him, not as the man you believe me to be, but as the man who will spend every day proving otherwise. If you'll only look hard enough to see it."

"That is your burden, not mine, Your Grace."

Adam's gaze stayed locked on hers, unwavering. "A burden I will carry gladly."

"Then enjoy carrying it," she returned softly.

And he would. He would also keep holding his breath in her presence. She felt wild and untamed beneath the exquisite surface polish. Whatever sophistication this girl had cloaked herself in, it had gathered cracks—but that didn't matter. Each of her flaws, each unstudied movement, pulled at something deep within him, a curiosity and a lust to unravel her further.

"Is that a position I can never hold again, Char?"

She stiffened. "Don't call me that."

Adam tilted his head and leaned close, nearly brushing the shell of her ear. "Relax," he murmured, unreadable but charged with intention. Her breath hitched, an audible draw of air that made his grip on her waist tighten slightly. He adjusted their step, guiding her more assertively now, his hand firm against the curve of her back. "Just feel my body."

And for the briefest heartbeat, she yielded. Her body softened against his lead, her movements trusting for just a measure before the tension crept back in again. But Adam didn't mind. That brief moment meant everything to him.

Perhaps he had a chance after all.

SHE'D VOWED NEVER to give a Cross brother the time of day again.

Then what was she doing here?

Charlene's steps faltered slightly as Adam guided her into a wide turn. She caught herself, adjusting her footing with a sharp intake of breath. Her gloves felt too tight on her hands; the pressure of silk against her fingers made her all too aware of the firm warmth of his grip. The room seemed to sway with the music, violins filling the air with a lilting elegance she could not seem to match.

"I should warn you, Your Grace," she said, her chin tilted high even as her words were clipped. "It's better to stop distracting me with senseless platitudes. I am not an accomplished dancer. This requires my full attention."

"Does it?" he replied, his tone maddeningly light as he adjusted their course with a gentle flick of his wrist. He led her through a backward glide. "You seem to be managing… just fine."

Charlene scoffed. Her slippers brushed faintly against the marble with every step, and it took all her determination to keep her movements in rhythm with his. "I am managing, yes. But that does not mean I wish for conversation."

Adam's gaze rested on her, steady and appraising. The amber light of the chandeliers above reflected in his eyes, softening what might otherwise be a too-direct stare. "I can give you lessons to improve your dance," he said smoothly.

She snapped her head up. "I beg your pardon?"

"Lessons," he repeated, the faintest hint of amusement curling at the edges of his mouth. "Should you wish to ease your difficulty, I would be glad to assist." She wasn't sure if he winked at her and barely had time to complete the thought when he added, "To maintain the truce, of course. Nothing else."

I don't believe him.

Charlene's pulse quickened, but not from surprise. Her cheeks felt hot beneath her mask, and she counted every delicate footfall as though it might disguise the sharp anger twisting beneath her ribs. "How very magnanimous of you, Your Grace, but I would rather endure my shortcomings than accept your tutelage."

"We don't have to make our interaction a battleground, you know." His voice softened then, carrying just enough intensity to pull her eyes back to his. "What I mean is simple—I wish to help. And to encourage something I daresay would suit us both." He paused briefly, then added with a clarity that made her wish they weren't crossing the center of the ballroom. "I want to be friends again."

Friends. The word hung in the air between them, incongruous in its simplicity. Charlene's gut twisted, though not in the way she might have expected. She averted her gaze, watching how her skirts brushed against her feet, the hem threatening to catch in the delicate arches of her slippers. A thousand retorts swirled in her mind, yet none seemed sufficient for the weight behind his offer.

"I am not certain what you expect of me," she murmured at last, just above the swell of the orchestra. "Friendship under these circumstances feels unsuitable. And unwelcome."

He didn't release her hand, didn't falter in his steps. "Then consider it patience. I'll wait until it becomes welcome."

"Why?" she all but croaked.

His mouth twitched as if he were suppressing a laugh. "My mother said these balls are to forge connections. Let's connect."

She tightened her grip on his shoulder. "You misunderstand me, Your Grace. What you ask is not merely unwelcome. It is impossible."

Charlene was glad her mask offered her a layer of protection from the heat she glimpsed in those eyes. They had no business looking so sincere, so utterly determined. The realization chilled her more than she wished to admit. And when the violins began to ease into the final stretch of the waltz, and he steered her into a graceful turn, she counted the seconds until she could slip free of his touch.

"I hope you don't think these dances will soften my resolve," she said stiffly as the music slowed, her curtsy already forming in her mind. "Whatever lesson it is you imagine teaching me, Adam,

I have no interest in learning."

He bowed as their movements came to a natural end. "Perhaps not yet," he said softly, his gaze lingering on hers. Then, with a bow sharp enough to suggest he meant every word, he stepped aside, leaving her with the space she had craved.

Charlene clenched her gloved fingers at her sides, standing tall even as her breath wavered. She refused to look back at him as she turned and moved toward the edge of the floor. But his words lingered behind her, daring her to dwell on them. Friends. Lessons. Patience.

Impossible. And yet somehow, impossibly tempting.

Chapter Six

CHARLENE GROANED WHEN the music stopped, and she made her way back to her friends in a daze. They stared at her wide-eyed, Maddie fanning her face furiously. This time, she did groan. She'd practically fled the dance floor the moment the orchestra's last note struck.

Just feel my body.

Her heart hammered within her breast, her breath coming out short. The heat of his hand on her waist lingered, a strange, discomforting feeling.

Relax, his soft timbre whispered in her head.

Why was he so nice to her? She'd distance herself from him and hadn't even been there for him with his father's death, and also… the same blood that pulsed through his hateful brother pulsed through him. That could never be changed.

She had not forgotten the promise she'd made to herself—never again, she had sworn, would she entangle herself with a Cross. So, why had she agreed to dance with him?

They were all the same.

He wasn't her orchid.

He was just some plant in some pot.

No steady fern.

Her hands shook as she adjusted her mask again, praying it

concealed the heat radiating from her face.

"Char," Maddie said, her gaze flicking beyond her before meeting her gaze again. And then she felt it. His presence. She didn't need to glance over her shoulder to confirm.

He had followed her.

She turned, her eyes locking with his.

"It's only proper to escort a lady back to her friends," his gruff voice came. "Also, let me know if you wish to continue our discussion." And with that, he turned and disappeared into the crowd, leaving her to blink after him. Continue their discussion? What discussion? A personal affront, perhaps. An embarrassing offer.

And the worst part, it was awfully tempting, too.

I can give you lessons to improve your dance.

Oh. That discussion.

I want to be friends.

"Proper. Pah!" Ashley muttered. "He didn't escort his last dance partner off the floor. He left her in the middle of it and came straight to you!"

Charlene blinked. *He had?* She hadn't even considered it.

"Tell me I'm hallucinating," Maddie said. "You didn't just waltz with him, did you?"

Charlene groaned, running a hand over her forehead. "I did. And no, you're not hallucinating."

Ashley raised a questioning brow. "And how was it to dance with the devil? Was his dancing just as devilish?"

"It was dreadful," she admitted. One might even say it was a little corner of Dante's *Inferno*. "I was terrible."

Ashley waved her comment away. "Don't worry too much about it. You never excelled at dancing. And he seems to excel at it a bit too much."

Still… did the blackguard really have to point it out?

Charlene's cheeks burned as the entire dance flashed through her mind.

Just feel my body.

Those four words…

Why did they make her body feel so hot? And why did they replay in her head like a careless whisper that wouldn't die down? Hah! It was a careless whisper from him! One laced with wickedness and sin.

She had felt his body, every inch of it. Broad shoulders, strong hands, and eyes that burned with something unfathomable. In fact, now that she thought about it, he moved like a predator on the prowl.

Gah! Charlene! Haven't you learned your lesson with those Crosses before?

"Why?" Maddie asked, her fan snapping shut. "Why would you dance with him?"

"Do you think I had a choice?" Charlene muttered.

"Well, yes, we do think that," Ashley said slyly. "You could have said no. Yes. No. Choice."

"Don't look at me like that," Charlene said. "Even I don't know why I said yes."

Ashley chuckled. "Is he your rare orchid?"

"Of course not!" Never.

"Then perhaps you shouldn't look so enchanted."

Enchanted? "Don't jest. I look nothing of the sort!" The word grated against her pride. She wasn't some wide-eyed debutante swooning over a rogue. She knew better. She had been burned before, had vowed she would never be burned again.

But there was something about him she couldn't ignore.

"All right then," Ashley concurred. "I was just jesting."

And then it happened again.

Her eyes found him.

He stood near the refreshment table, his tall frame cutting an imposing figure. He spoke to the same gentleman as before, his expression composed, but he sported a smile that was both faint and dangerous.

As if sensing her gaze, he turned his head. Their eyes met again across the distance, and Charlene's breath caught. His smile deepened, a slow, deliberate curve that sent a shiver down her spine.

Her fingers clenched around the edge of her skirt.

She averted her gaze before she did or said something horrifyingly embarrassing.

"Shall we step outside?" Maddie asked, her tone gentle. "You look like you could use some fresh air."

"No need," Charlene said quickly. "I'm going to look for a gentleman to dance with." She would practice. But who said it had to be with him?

Also, she needed to escape those burning eyes.

And stay far, far away from him.

"WHAT ARE YOU grinning about?"

Adam's smile slipped as he turned back to Jack. "Nothing."

"That didn't look like nothing," his friend said. "So, the woman you danced with right now…"

"Yes, Lady Charlene."

"Are you sure that is wise, given what happened a year ago?"

Adam didn't know. That night had been scorched into his brain and was a standing nightmare for him. However, he didn't want to let that night define him, or her. He didn't want to relive that night forever in his dreams. He wanted to create better memories. With her.

They had been friends once. No matter the discomfort he had felt, no matter how much he'd longed for more, he was happy to just be in her life.

I want to get back to that.

"It's best to keep your distance from her."

Adam scowled. "Why?"

Jack shrugged. "If my source is correct and your brother is returning to England, it would be best to have her far removed from your family."

Adam clenched his fists at the mention of his brother. The idea of Charlene becoming tangled up with David again made his stomach churn. Surely David had other interests while away and had forgotten about Charlene.

I can't even stop thinking about her.

But he didn't want to admit that was reason enough to keep his distance. What if Jack's sources were wrong? What if his brother never returned? He'd already lost too much of her; he didn't want to lose any more. Besides, he could handle his brother.

He had once before.

"She might not want to be entangled with the Crosses either," his friend pointed out.

Oh, Adam knew she didn't. He wouldn't have wanted to, either. But the thought of Charlene being lost to him forever had left a bitter taste in his mouth. It was downright unpalatable.

As duke, however, he had more power.

Perhaps even sway.

That ought to count for something. Even if it was just a little something.

He sighed. "She's not the type to hold grudges," he muttered, more to convince himself than to argue with Jack. But he knew, deep within, this wasn't about grudges.

Jack raised an eyebrow, clearly unconvinced. "Is she not? You think it's that simple?"

Adam shifted uncomfortably. "It's not about simplicity. It's about—" He broke off, not sure how to finish that thought. What could he say? But damn it, he didn't have any experience mending such broken fences.

Jack didn't seem to need any more prompting. "Adam, my friend, in my experience, when a woman has been hurt to that degree, you should either let it go or be prepared to grovel for the rest of your life, and in your case, you'll be groveling in your brother's stead. Do you really want to do that?"

Adam paused.

"Let's not forget," Jack went on. "You share the same face."

"And that's all we have in common." Adam's jaw tightened, the familiar ache of frustration gnawing at him. True. No matter how much he wanted to, that was one thing he couldn't change. "I don't want it to be easy." He let out a slow breath. "But I can't let it end like this."

"It ended a whole year ago."

"Exactly," Adam said. "So let's start something new. Something fresh."

Jack was silent for a long moment, studying him.

"I'm not saying you can't try. But you have to be prepared that she may not want anything to do with you. You may be hitting your head on a brick wall with no result."

"Then I'll hit my head against a brick wall. But I won't stop trying." Adam reached into his waistcoat pocket. The faint crinkling sound reassured him. The apology he'd written for her was still there. And perhaps he could finally deliver it now. "I need to speak to her again." Adam let go of the paper. He'd carried the burden of the unspoken and undelivered apology for far too long. He'd allowed too much to happen before his eyes, but as duke, he wouldn't be so lenient with David. And he'd most certainly protect Charlene from him. He'd find David and send him away. Most importantly, he'd speak to her again.

"Well, don't look now, but your little bird just fluttered off to another man."

Adam's head whipped around, his body stiffening as he watched Charlene smile up at another man. The man smiled back and held out his arm, which she took before he led her to the dancefloor.

It's just a dance.

A dance didn't mean anything. Nothing more than a polite social ritual. Liar. It didn't mean something until it meant something. Then a dance was the most intimate thing in the world. The way she met his eyes, the way she let him take her hand, the way her body swayed…

Adam cursed.

Her dancing with someone else after being with him stirred something deep inside Adam that he had no desire to confront. A primal, almost instinctual possessiveness that would serve no purpose or benefit. So, he shoved it back into its cage.

"Not looking too well there, old chap."

"Be gone," he muttered under his breath, his jaw tightening as he stood rooted to the spot, watching her glide across the floor with another man. Blast it. It was merely a dance. She had every right to enjoy herself.

But the damn thing gnawed at him. No dance was ever just a dance, even if it meant nothing. It was at least a fleeting moment of flirtation. He knew that much. He sensed it with this dance. He could see it in how she held herself and allowed that man to guide her with an ease she hadn't permitted with him.

"Is that Henry Grafton?"

"Her brother's friend from Oxford, yes." Jack's voice broke through the haze of annoyance building in his mind. "Don't cut in."

"Cut in? Don't talk nonsense. I would never do that." *I would take over.*

"Tell that to the look on your face."

"I'm wearing a mask."

"You still have that look," Jack said with a shrug, his tone dry. "It's bleeding into the very air around you."

Adam wanted to argue, but there was no denying it—Jack was right. Again. His legs were practically wired to spring into action at any moment. But damn it, watching Charlene smile and dance with another man, all while the same feelings of longing, guilt, and regret twisted in his chest, made him want to pummel something. He wanted to be the one to hold her, to share the intimacy of a dance, to be near her again.

"Patience."

Adam stiffened. "What?"

"If you're going to try to walk the path of establishing a relationship again, be patient."

He snorted.

"I am patient, thank you very much."

"Doesn't look like it from where I am standing."

Well, being patient and feeling patient were two different things. But Adam didn't respond. He couldn't. Because in that moment, as he watched Charlene, he knew the truth. Patience was a trait for the calm. He didn't have any calm at the moment. Not in his head. Not in his heart. Nor did he know if he could drag some forth from somewhere much deeper within. And that might just be the very thing that would break him.

Chapter Seven

The M-Press, April 17, 1819

Dearest readers,

It would seem that last evening's masquerade ball, already destined to be the jewel of the season, delivered enough intrigue to occupy even the most jaded tongues across Mayfair. Amidst the sea of silks, satins, and anonymity, one could hardly miss the fairer of a certain pair of ducal twins, whose commanding presence still managed to shine through the disguise of his black Venetian mask. What drew this humble observer's keen eye, however, was not the duke himself or his fetching Spanish elegance, but the daring creature who positioned herself at his side with rather striking boldness of conversation rather than elegance in quadrille.

This mysterious lady, her identity concealed yet her intentions powerfully laid bare, danced perilously close to a certain duke. One cannot help but wonder how this audacious woman has succeeded in standing between two brothers who, by all accounts, are not known for sharing anything so willingly— even their affections.

And yet, where there might be embers, fire surely had burned. How, pray tell, does one court such mysterious entanglements and yet maintain the appearance of innocence? A trick of the masquerade, no doubt—but masks eventually fall, my dear readers, and this one will be no exception. Rest assured, my quill is poised, and I mean to uncover if this lady's charm is strategic brilliance or merely a reckless wager soon to come undone.

Until the truth emerges, I advise the lady in question to tread carefully.

After all, secrets are never safe from the M-Press.

Charlene had barely been able to sleep last night. Soon, Ashley and Maddie would arrive for tea in the greenhouse and let her know if the society papers or gossip had anything of importance to say. But for now, Charlene couldn't help but think of him.

She had danced with Adam and was almost giddy with excitement—that is, if she allowed herself such silliness.

Which she didn't, of course.

Thus, after contemplating the matter instead of sleeping, Charlene grew restless. And as soon as the house finally awoke with servants bustling downstairs, she left her chambers. The soft murmur of household activity greeted her as she descended the sweeping staircase, her hand trailing lightly along the polished banister. The familiar scent of baked bread and lemon polish wafted from the dining room below, yet it did little to ground her thoughts. Her mind still lingered stubbornly on the events of the masquerade, where mystery had danced far too closely with temptation for her comfort. And what bothered her most was that she'd recognized the feeling at all.

No Cross brother should have such an effect on me.

She had barely slept, her dreams tangled with indistinct figures in masks and whispered words that faded before she could grasp them. Yet one sensation lingered, vivid and unshakable, like a shadow cast by firelight. It was the way he had felt—so unwavering, so utterly inescapable.

Adam Cross.

His presence clung to her thoughts, a quiet, insistent pull that made her chest ache with something she dared not name. She wished she could dismiss it, yet even now, in the fragile light of morning, the memory of his touch and the way his gaze held hers refused to fade.

At the bottom of the stairs, the butler, Mr. Aldridge, waited with his customary calm, a silver tray balanced in one hand. His expression was as neutral as ever, though Charlene noted the tiniest arch of his brow. He held out the tray as she approached, a single folded letter resting upon it.

"Good morning, Lady Charlene," he greeted, his deep voice as steady as a hearth's hum. "This arrived only moments ago. The courier left no name."

Charlene paused, her fingers hovering just above the paper of the folded note. "No name?" she echoed, glancing once at the butler's composed face, as though he might betray some hidden knowledge. "Did he say nothing of its origin?"

"Only that it was urgent and meant for you alone." Mr. Aldridge's tone betrayed neither interest nor concern, though Charlene imagined it might take much to surprise him after years of service.

"Hm." She picked up the note, her fingertips brushing the embossed edges of expensive paper. Without another word, she turned toward the drawing room, already feeling the curious weight of it in her hand.

"Shall I bring breakfast to you, Lady Charlene?" the butler inquired before she could retreat.

"No, thank you. I'll come to the dining room shortly," Charlene replied without looking back. Food was the last thing on her mind.

Once seated near the window in the privacy of her orangery, with sunlight splashing through the windows, she unfolded the note with equal parts hesitation and anticipation. Her breath caught as her gaze fell upon the scrawl, each stroke of ink as deliberate and bold as the figure behind the mask the night before.

For the Lady who hides nothing and everything all at once. Meet me...

She caught her breath. With trembling fingers, she closed it and unfolded it again, as though reading the words a second time might change them. It didn't. Hides nothing? What did he mean by that? And the invitation? The audacity!

She traced the edges of the note. Even with his boldness, he was not wrong. About the hiding. Only he would know, wouldn't he? The paradox of those words unsettled her. Had Adam seen her so clearly—or had he hoped she would see herself?

A warmth kindled in her chest and spread with slow, beguiling insistence. She tried to temper it with reason, ticking off his flaws in her mind. He teased too much. He smiled too often. And yet... it had been so long since she'd been something other than a title, a person altogether apart from a daughter, a niece, a name attached more to a dowry than to an independent soul.

The words bespoke of a lovely lie, a dangerous truth.

What game was he playing?

What role was she about to step into?

And did she want to lose that sense of being wholly, completely known? Her stomach flip-flopped; her heart betrayed her with its quickened pace. She pressed the note closer to her skin, a tiny smile tugging at her mouth.

Perhaps, just this once, she would play along.

What did he say? Meet him at the park? She tossed the note aside. Why did he have to send that? Did the man think to mock her? How infuriating!

Man. Duke.

Fern. Orchid.

She couldn't trust her own senses when it came to the Cross brothers.

Charlene scowled and poked at her ghost orchid. They weren't exactly the prettiest in comparison to others, and they tend to grow on the bark of a tree in the darkest part of the wild, but they were still rather rare. And some were even very funny-looking.

They did, however, never fail to make her smile.

They were leafless.

They hovered.

They only bloomed once a year.

She traced its stems with her fingers and thought it wouldn't be enough all her life, would it? Well, on the more positive side, they had scales instead of leaves. And roots, of course. They also smelled of apples. And, while they hovered, they gave off the appearance of floating. It wasn't easy to mimic their preferred environment. They were stubborn and difficult to cultivate.

But they appeared the loneliest of all of her rare ones.

Unlike Adam.

What are you thinking, Charlene? You can't compare this beautiful, floating orchid to that man. Well, perhaps only in the fact that she wished he was still a ghost in her life. But he was determined to re-enter her life as though his brother hadn't torn it apart. Urgh! They were friends once. But friendship… Some friendships weren't meant to last. And as her brother so often pointed out, a woman can't just be friends with a man. Such things did not exist. She hadn't listened to him in the past.

Perhaps it was time to do so now.

But what was she to do about his improper invitation? She should ignore it, right? She peeked at the discarded note.

She had read the thing a hundred times already, and it made less sense each time. Meet her in Green Park. At dawn. To practice her dancing. Was he serious? Or sarcastic. He was a duke now, for stars' sake. She should show some sense! They might have been friends once, but this man was a stranger to her.

The memory of their dance the night before flared in her mind—the way he had moved so effortlessly, so maddeningly, told her to relax.

Hah! She was relaxed. Very, very relaxed!

Charlene balled her fists so hard, her nails dug into her palms.

And he wanted to be friends again. Friends. As though one year of silence and—Charlene's chest tightened—everything else could be easily swept away.

Well, it couldn't.

And she was most certainly not meeting him in the park. The last time a Cross had extended an invitation to somewhere private, it had turned out disastrous. He should know better than anyone that this was the worst way to approach her.

Her lips pressed into a thin line as she picked up the note. Well, she had to admit, looking at the thing did send a small shiver down her spine. "Does he honestly expect me to meet him?"

"Meet who?" Waylon's voice came from behind her.

Charlene's head whipped around so quickly her neck protested. Her brother appeared in the corner of the orangery, one brow arched, and he strode up to her, swatting away the branch of a fern.

She scrambled to fold the letter and tuck it into the folds of her skirt, her movements far from subtle. "No one in particular," she said, forcing a casual tone.

"You expect me to believe that? Because you're hiding that letter like it's a state secret."

"Well, I wouldn't want to burden you with my secret affairs," she said drily.

He didn't press. Most likely believing it was some nonsense scribbled by Maddie or Ashley. She turned back to her orchid. "Shouldn't you be busy tormenting someone else?"

"I was on my way to do exactly that when I remembered something," he said, stopping a few feet away. His expression shifted, losing its teasing edge. "You danced with Cross last night."

Charlene froze. It wasn't a question. She should have known he would notice. Her brother noticed everything. "Oh, so you recognized him, too."

"Hard not to," her brother said, his tone darker now. "He hasn't changed much. Except for that ugly mask, of course."

There had been nothing ugly about it. "It was just a dance."

"Now that Adam Cross is duke, he'll have his pick." He

wagged his index finger in the air. "And the woman Rotheworth picks will be the reigning queen of the Season." He nodded as if he couldn't help but agree with himself. "Perhaps of the Ton."

Charlene tasted acid. The woman he picked…

Somehow, the scandal with David paled at the thought of what Adam Cross had to offer.

But was he truly that different?

"Nothing is just something when it comes to that family. You didn't think to mention it?" he pressed, stepping closer. "The man appeared a year after disappearing after that night, and you just… waltzed with him?"

"It was a masquerade," she shot over her shoulder. "I saw no harm."

"No, harm? Char, what happened a year ago wasn't 'no harm'."

"That was a year ago." Why was she defending the man? She shook her head. "And he's a duke. It would do no good to have him as an enemy. Besides, nothing happened."

"Look at me, Char."

She sighed, turning to her brother.

His gaze searched hers. "I don't care whether he is the king of England. If you hurt my family, you are my enemy."

"Stop," Charlene said, rubbing her temple. "He didn't hurt me." Not with actions, anyway. However, sometimes words stung more than any thorn could. "He didn't prevent it either."

Her brother's jaw clenched, but he didn't argue. "Fine. But if he does anything I don't like, I will set that family ablaze, duke or not. Just look at today's M-Press and you'll understand why I am so worried about you."

"I don't need to read that. If there's anything noteworthy, Ashley and Maddie will inform me." Charlene smiled at that. "Plus, he won't. Besides, we don't have that sort of relationship where he could hurt me." *Not anymore. I'm tainted already, and he's the only one who knows it.*

Her brother stared at her for a moment longer before nodding once.

"Very good." He glanced at her orchids. "Then I shall leave you to your plants." He mumbled something about infernos among the Ton and shades in the damp greenhouse as he left, but Charlene paid him no heed.

Neither did Charlene watch him leave before returning to the ghost orchid, pulling the letter from her sleeve. She stared at the bold handwriting once. Friends... She could barely recall anything except that night a year ago. It's as though it eclipsed all the good ones that came before.

Just as well.

There was only one path to walk, and that was forward. Not backward. She crumpled the letter in her fist, frustration bubbling to the surface. "The nerve of the man to send me such an invitation. Let him stand in the park alone to all eternity for all I care."

But even as she said it, a tiny spark of curiosity flared. And against her better judgment, she found herself wondering what would happen if she did accept.

No.

Charlene. No!

She was most certainly not meeting him.

ADAM CROSS SAT in his study, the soft crackle of the fire in the hearth doing little to thaw the chill that had settled in his bones. A ledger lay open before him, columns of figures neatly inked in black, but he wasn't seeing them. His pen hovered over the page, motionless.

He was dreaming, right?

Adam hadn't sent a note to Charlene asking to meet him at dawn, alone, in a damn park, to practice her dance? Jack's mocking laughter filled his head. Yes, he would laugh exactly like that if he knew what Adam had done. That little word *patience* came back to haunt him tenfold.

He leaned back into his chair with a groan. He had sent the letter that morning, and now his whole body was restless with regret.

Should he not have done it?

Should he have waited for the next event to ask her to dance? Perhaps. Perhaps he should have done anything but send that damn invitation. But he hadn't been thinking.

Charlene might laugh in his face or, worse, ignore him altogether.

The latter was almost assured.

She was more guarded now. Her defenses might as well be as high as the sky. Fortunately, Adam enjoyed reaching for it. Unfortunately, his lack of patience might just push her even higher. Beyond his reach.

No, he shouldn't think like that.

She might be guarded, but she still possessed the same fire.

And that fire was one of the reasons why he couldn't walk away. He wanted it to blaze hotter than the sun.

But would she come to the park? He had no idea. If she did, she might be accompanied by her brother. Or a pistol. But doing nothing felt worse than taking the risk. He would send her an invitation to the park forever if there were a single, minuscule chance that she would accept.

The door to the study cracked open, and Adam's mother glided in. Ah, he would recognize that purposeful walk anywhere.

"You've been hiding in here all morning," she said, taking the chair opposite him, her eyes studying him like a hawk just about to lunge for its prey. "Have you read the M-Press?"

Adam sighed. "Good morning to you, too, Mother. No, I haven't." *I would never.*

After a pause of her scrutinizing stare, she broke the silence. "You looked troubled," she commented. "Did you find the ball that taxing?"

"On the contrary," Adam said. "It was tolerable enough."

"Only tolerable?" she asked. "Didn't you dance with two

ladies? A feat, considering your usual aversion to such things."

Ah, so this was her purpose. "Your eyes and ears never cease to amaze me."

"Nor should they," she said simply. "They are quite impressive."

"So, I danced with two ladies," he remarked dryly, reaching for the quill to fiddle with. "Hardly something special."

"That depends," his mother said. "Who are the two ladies?"

Adam shrugged. "Does it matter?"

"Of course it matters! They are the ladies you chose. And one of them sent a note that she'd like to call on me."

"Well, one chose me," he muttered offhandedly. "I can't answer that question, Mother, since they were masked." And why would Charlene come to see his mother?

Her eyes narrowed on him, something no man wanted from their mother. "You didn't ask for their names?"

"That would defeat the purpose of a masquerade, would it not?" *I live and breathe the only name that matters every moment of my life—Charlene. Nobody else holds any sway over me.*

His mother studied him for a short, but severe moment before she leaned back in her chair. "Very well. Hold onto your stubbornness, Adam. But you cannot hide behind your ledgers indefinitely."

"Is that not the very definition of stubbornness?"

His mother's lips twitched as though suppressing a smile. "You've inherited your father's penchant for deflecting. He always thought he was terribly clever at it, too."

Adam arched a brow, leaning back in his chair. "Is that so?"

"Quite," she replied smoothly. "But I always knew when he was hiding something. Just as I know with you."

"I'm not hiding anything," Adam said, his tone flat.

"Then why do you look like you're debating whether to blurt something out? The quill will snap if you keep toying with it like that."

Adam glanced at the quill in his hand, realizing he was pressing the thing into the desk. He set it aside. "I'm not in the mood for this discussion."

His mother laughed, a soft sound that softened the usual sharpness of her gaze. "Men usually aren't."

He debated whether to tell his mother about David but thought better of it. He'd only be sullying her mood and might cause her unnecessary concern for something that might not occur. Given the beating and warning he'd given his brother never to set foot in England again unless he wished to die, the man shouldn't dare disobey him.

However, David had more courage than sense.

"Wife aside, the estate won't perish if you leave the study occasionally. At the very least, go have a bit of fun."

"I believe our definition of fun is different."

His mother pointed to the ledger. "I know this is not yours."

"I've changed since I was a boy."

She inclined her head. "Indeed, boys do change, but some things remain ever constant—such as their penchant for keeping secrets from their mothers. Now, what is it you are concealing?"

He hesitated, his thumb brushing the edge of the desk. "Nothing of consequence, I assure you."

"Nonsense," she said firmly. "That answer alone is trouble enough as it is."

"Only because your curiosity knows no bounds," he countered, a faint smile tugging at his lips.

She laughed lightly, the sound warm and teasing. "That much is true. I do delight in unearthing secrets, particularly those that leave you brooding so. Mark my words, my dear—I shall uncover it. I always do."

Ah, the delight of meddling mothers.

He didn't reply, and after a moment, his mother rose gracefully.

"I trust you will do the right thing," she said, moving toward the door. She glanced over her shoulder, adding, "And try not to brood too much. It's unbecoming."

When the door clicked shut behind her, Adam exhaled and leaned forward, resting his elbows on the desk. Despite his mother's nagging, despite whether his brother would be returning, he couldn't stop thinking about her.

Would she come?

Chapter Eight

THE NEXT MORNING at dawn, she found herself in Green Park, where the crisp breeze nipped at her cheeks and tugged at the edges of her cloak. She drew it closer, the heavy folds of wool warding off the chill. But the shiver running through her wasn't from the cold. It started somewhere deeper, stirred by the mere thought of Adam and the quiet intensity he carried, a presence so steady and unshakable it seemed to linger even in his absence.

He'd already been waiting for her.

He grinned at her, a smile that had a mix of surprise, elation, and something else so sincere that she forgot why she doubted whether she should come.

"Charlene. You came."

"Adam," she returned. "Curiosity won. After all, we haven't seen each other in all this time and then you send me a rather scandalous invite to meet you here."

"Well, I'm glad your curiosity led you here. Come." He motioned ahead.

Well, I'm here already. So Charlene followed him.

He walked a step ahead of her, his casual stride outpacing the brisk crunch of her boots over the dried leaves. Dark tendrils of his shiny black hair curled around the edges of his collar and stuck out under his top hat, the damp morning air teasing them loose.

Charlene wished he would turn around.

She wanted to read his face.

But would that give her insight into him? This? She didn't know. But she still wanted to inspect every line, every crinkle when he smiled.

She pulled a face at his back, wondering why he'd insisted on meeting her here in Green Park, of all places. The fog clung to the edges of the park like a half-drawn curtain, softening the world into layered shades of gray. Almost eerie. No, most certainly eerie. Dew glistened on the skeletal branches of various types of trees, their leaves littered in fiery reds and burnt orange.

And then, just as they crested a small rise, Adam stopped. "There," he said, his mouth curving in a satisfied grin. "What do you think?"

At first, Charlene wasn't sure what she was supposed to think. She also wished to unravel the meaning of his smile.

She stepped up beside him. In front of them, a massive pile of leaves rose from the earth like an autumnal monument. It was absurdly large, almost unbelievable. "You brought me here to see… dead leaves?" She shot him a skeptical look. Was there some symbolic meaning to this?

He turned to face her, his grin unfaltering. "Not just any leaves." His hand swept over the scene. "These are your leaves."

"Mine?" Charlene blinked. "How so?"

"It's my gift to you. As a friend. You love plants."

Was he mocking her?

"Really? Leaves?" She honestly wanted to pry his head open and have a look. She gave a snort. "Most girls are presented with emeralds or diamonds—or at the very least, a bouquet of roses. But leaves?"

"You're not like most girls, are you?" His tone was light, teasing, but the edge of sincerity could not be mistaken.

"I'm not," she agreed but curled her lips.

He stepped closer, and in the thin morning light, she glimpsed the expectation in his dark eyes. Like he wanted to be praised for bringing her to this spot.

"Besides," he added. "Jewels shatter under pressure. Leaves… they are softer."

"Are they? They are certainly crunchier."

"Only the dead ones."

"Come." He led her closer to the pile, then stooped to scoop one up, holding it between two fingers before letting it flutter back to join its comrades.

"You do realize that I like plants. Leaves attached. Not leaves piled like this."

Adam straightened, his grin sharpened by the faintest hint of detectable mischief. "Well, you'd hardly grow to love them standing there like a skeptical schoolmistress. Come closer, and I'll show you."

Grow to love…

Against her better judgment—or exactly in line with it, she couldn't tell anymore—she stepped forward. The cool morning air swirled around her feet, catching the hem of her skirts as she stopped just before the riotous mound. They smelled like autumn and dirt. That she did love. The smell of soil. And for a moment, she almost forgot the absurdity of the situation.

Adam held out his hand. "We're going to try the jump."

"The what?" Charlene's voice lifted, incredulous.

"You know," he said, tilting his head. "A lift. Like in that Spanish-style dancing. Bolero, it's called. Very dramatic. Very impressive." He clapped his hands once, the sound startling in the stillness. "And very fun."

Charlene arched a brow.

"If you master this, Charlene, you can master any dance."

"A shortcut to mastering rhythm then?" She narrowed her gaze and considered the matter.

Adam's eyes lit up as he began to explain. "It's a Spanish dance that my mother taught me when I was a boy. Lively, full of rhythm. You've got the dramatic arm movements, quick footwork, and sometimes they use castanets to keep the beat. It's as if..." He paused, swirling his free hand in the air as if summoning the spirit of the dance itself. "Elegant, but with a fire underneath. Quite theatrical."

Charlene cocked her head, intrigued. "And they do lifts in it?"

"Well, not always," Adam admitted, grinning. "But I think we can make our own version, to round off the dance lesson I promised you?" He held out his hand again with a playful flourish.

She stared at him. "Please tell me you're not serious."

"Completely serious." He gestured to the pile again. "That's why I raked together the leaves. They're for you... to be safe. Should you, you know, misstep."

"Is this what you meant with your goading to practice?"

"Practice starts with fun."

Fun.

Was this fun? And safe? "It's like you know I always misstep," she muttered. In life and otherwise... "I always do."

"So, I'll keep you safe when you misstep again."

Again. There it was. She was a clumsy dancer, and the leaves were to cushion them from her missteps. The entire charade at the park was a misstep. It would be better to return home, would it not?

Charlene opened her mouth, then closed it again, at a rare and temporary loss for words. "Adam," she managed finally, "if anyone saw us out here..." If she gave in...

"They won't." He glanced at the leaves, his grin spreading. "The Ton's still asleep. It's just you, me, and, well, an impressive half-crackle underfoot."

The half-crackle inside her chest grew into a rolling thunder.

Very well.

She wanted to jump.

"You're impossible."

"Leaves are meant to be impossibly jumped into when raked into this fabulous mattress."

Impossible.

Charlene shook her head, biting her lip to keep from laughing as he flicked the leaf from his finger. Very well. What was a jump into leaves? It certainly wouldn't hurt. And for whatever reason, he equated this to her missteps.

So he remembered that they jumped on mattresses as children—all those years ago seemed like yesterday when he smiled at her so.

"Two…"

Charlene placed her hand gingerly in his, feeling the warmth of his skin, so sure, so steady. He guided her other hand to rest on his shoulder, his fingers brushing the curve of her wrist with an ease that felt practiced, intimate. The slight pressure of his palm against hers anchored her while the back of her neck prickled with awareness.

"Three," Adam said softly, though he didn't move right away. Instead, his gaze dropped to her feet, then flicked back to her face. "Feet first. Always the feet."

"I see," she murmured, though her pulse betrayed her calm.

He shifted closer, the hem of her gown brushing against the polished leather of his boots. "Watch me," he said. His voice was low, his words crisp, as if they were discussing something far more mundane. Yet his nearness turned the moment electric.

Adam stepped back and tapped the damp ground lightly with his foot, a deft, sharp rhythm that struck her as unexpectedly graceful. His movements were quick, deliberate, and somehow impossibly smooth. The shift of his narrow hips as he angled toward her caught her attention, the movement fluid and deliberate, as if every step had been rehearsed a thousand times. His broad shoulders spread like a promise as he lifted his arms to guide hers, filling the space between them with a quiet power that made the air feel impossibly thin. She could sense his warmth even through the layers of fabric separating them, an unspoken pull that left her rooted to the floor. His strength was undeniable—not just in the firm press of his hands, but in the steady calm that seemed to radiate from him, anchoring her against emotions she couldn't yet name.

"This"—tap, pause, sweep of his foot, retreating again to a poised stillness—"is how the bolero begins. It's not merely about rhythm. It's about control, about anticipation." His dark eyes lifted to meet hers, and Charlene forgot what breathing felt like. "Think you can do it?" he asked, his tone teasing.

"I… suppose." She hesitated, then mirrored his movement, her slipper brushing softly against the ground. Her first attempt was clumsy, her foot skittering awkwardly.

"That was terrible."

Charlene startled, glaring at him. "You could at least pretend I'm not hopeless," she shot back, but the humor tugging at his lips suggested he was enjoying this immensely.

And just like that, they were like childhood friends again. Just like a lifetime before last year.

And yet different.

"Hardly hopeless," he replied. "I've always had hope for you." His voice gentled as he leaned slightly closer. "Try again. Slower this time."

Charlene straightened her spine and focused. Tap, pause, sweep. Her heart thudded with an odd mix of determination and self-consciousness.

"Better," Adam murmured, his tone low and approving. Suddenly, his hands were on her waist, firm and unyielding. She froze.

"Relax. Just trust me," he murmured, his fingers spreading slightly, his steady grip both grounding and—for reasons Charlene could not articulate—wildly unsettling. He pulled her gently forward, aligning her movements with his. "The steps should… flow," he said, his words washing over her like a current, enticing her to follow.

Their feet moved in tandem now, her slipper alternating with the sharp tap of his boot. The sweep of his coat brushed against the fabric of her skirts, and she could feel the faintest pull of them together, like the rhythm demanded it. The tension between the precise staccato of the movements and the softness of his voice sent a quiver up her spine.

"You see?" Adam said after a beat, his hands still anchoring her. "Not so hopeless."

Charlene shot him a look, but there was no sharp reply ready, only her pulse quickening at the satisfaction in his tone. He stepped away—not far, just enough for her to feel the absence of him as glaringly as his presence.

"Now, the arms," he said. One of his hands left her waist to take hers, his fingers curling delicately around hers in a way that sent a flicker of heat to her cheeks. He lifted her hand, guiding it in an arc, and her breath hitched as her arm obeyed his gentle pressure. His movements were impossibly smooth, but hers wavered, her instincts caught between the rhythm of the dance and the silent tension filling the air between them.

"You've done this before," she said quietly, half teasing but wholly curious.

"I've been known to pick things up now and again," Adam replied without breaking their measured steps. "Though I'll admit... this is my first attempt with someone quite this unsteady."

That's why I need a steady fern.

Charlene felt the sting of his words, though the glint in his expression softened it into something bearable. The corner of his mouth quirked, the faintest suggestion of a smile that left her breathless despite herself.

She lifted her chin and quickened her steps, surprising even herself when her foot struck the ground in perfect cadence with his. His brows rose in response, only for his lips to part in a quiet laugh.

"There it is," he murmured. "Better than I expected, Charlene."

Her name on his lips anchored them both in the moment, a tether neither of them acknowledged outright. For a brief second, they seemed to forget the nature of their arrangement, the lives that waited just beyond these walls. But the bolero demanded their attention, a discipline of rhythm, touch, and unspoken trust. For now, at least, they gave in.

Charlene's breath came out in pale, fleeting wisps. Her pelisse, buttoned snugly to block the morning chill, weighed lightly against her shoulders, the hem swaying with each tentative step. Adam, his tailored coat wrapped close to his form, cast an impressive figure against the mist, his dark silhouette cutting cleanly through the hazy light.

"Trust the rhythm," he said, his voice low and steady, breaking the quiet like a warm current.

There was no music! Did he mean trust him?

His gloved hand closed around hers, a light, guiding pressure that belied the firm strength beneath the leather. With his other hand, he held her waist, just above the cinched fabric of her pelisse, a touch that seemed both careful and possessive.

Charlene moved with him, her slippers brushing against the moist path as they turned in synchronized steps. The fog swirled faintly around them, cloaking them in a cocoon of muted light. She swayed instinctively under his hold, her movements slowly meeting the rhythm he set, the stitches of her nerves beginning to loosen.

"Good," Adam murmured, his words intimate in the quiet. His breath scattered faintly against her temple, close now, closer than she'd realized.

The hand at her waist adjusted slightly, anchoring her firmly as they stepped together again. Yet as his pace quickened, her footing faltered. Charlene wavered, the damp ground beneath too slick to hold her easily.

And then she tipped forward, her momentum pulling her straight into him.

Adam caught her, his arm locking around her back with startling precision, pulling her flush against his chest. The crisp wool of his coat pressed against her bodice, his warmth leaking through the barrier of fine fabrics. The air was suddenly different, charged with a current she couldn't name, and for an endless moment, she could hear nothing but the faint whisper of his breathing as it fanned against her hair.

She froze, every inch of her acutely aware of where they touched, of the controlled strength in his hold. He seemed equally affected, the tension in his body apparent as he kept her close, his gloved hand splayed firmly over her back, the leather cool but his grip unwavering.

Charlene lifted her gaze, and Adam's eyes caught hers, dark and searching under the veil of the lingering fog. A flicker of something unknown passed between them, unspoken but undeniable, threading through the closeness they shared.

"You're heavier than I expected," he murmured, breaking the spell—but the rasp in his voice sent heat curling low in her stomach.

"And you're insufferable," she whispered back, though her tone lacked any bite. Her hands were braced against his chest, fingers curling slightly against the fine weave of his coat. She could feel the strength beneath, the steady rise of his breath. Without thinking, her fingers smoothed over the fabric, more to steady herself than anything else, but the movement felt… daring.

Adam's lips tilted, the faintest hint of amusement curving his expression. "Careful there," he said, his voice softer now, the words balanced between teasing and something more intimate.

She started to pull away, to step back and recompose herself, but his arm tightened, holding her for just a moment longer. His thumb brushed absently against the curve of her waist. "You're not running off after one misstep, are you?" he asked softly, his tone laced with something oddly coaxing.

Charlene swallowed hard, her pulse thrumming wildly. "I… believe I prefer to be upright," she managed, though her breath hitched as she realized he still hadn't released her fully.

His fingers eased their grip slightly, but the touch lingered as he finally looked away, tilting his face toward the fading path ahead. "Then we'll try again," he said easily, though his voice had a new roughness to it. He stepped back, his absence jarring as he reclaimed the space between them.

Charlene couldn't speak for a moment, her lips parting faintly as she struggled to break through the haze of awareness that clung to her. She adjusted her pelisse, fingers trembling slightly as they worked the folds of fabric.

Adam's hand was out again, steady and sure. She hesitated, then placed her hand in his, unable to ignore the faint quiver that rippled through her as his fingers curled over hers with controlled firmness.

"One more time," he said with a faint smile, though there was a glint in his eye that unsettled and steadied her all at once. "Are you ready?"

"Let us do this, then."

"On three," Adam said, his tone suddenly serious, though the humor still danced in his eyes. He nodded. "One…"

Her skin tingled as his hands grazed her waist, steady but never lingering.

"Two…"

The fog lifted slightly, the morning creeping forward without fanfare as the park began to glow faintly gold.

"Three."

And then she jumped with him, a laugh spilling from her lips unbidden, her skirts swirling like the disturbed leaves below. The air zipped past her face, cool and exhilarating, and for one suspended moment, she felt weightless—untethered and entirely free.

When he set her down again, the world reassembled itself, but Charlene's laughter stayed, bubbling as his grin widened.

"See?" he murmured. "Better than diamonds, chocolates, or flowers."

That remained debatable.

ADAM GAZED AT her, momentarily taken by the sweet shriek she'd let out when she fell and as he tried to reach for her, she gave him a tug. It wasn't strong, but he'd been caught off guard by her beauty, mesmerized by the light in her eyes.

The world shifted, a blur of damp earth and crumpled leaves rushing up to meet him. His hand reached out instinctively, but instead of catching something solid, his fingers grazed the soft fabric of her sleeve. And then, with a graceless thud, he landed beside her, the sharp scent of wet foliage filling his lungs.

She came to me.

He almost still couldn't believe it.

Music soared in his mind as though her presence alone gave him the rhythm he'd dance to.

For a moment, Adam simply lay there, stunned by the absurdity of it. The firmness of the ground beneath him, the cool bite of a stray leaf against his cheek, and the faint, joy-ridden notes of Charlene's laughter pierced the haze of his shock. He turned his head, her bright face now just inches away, framed in wild strands of hair and specks of leaves.

"You've really mastered the art of the bolero," she teased, her voice light but just low enough to unsettle him.

Adam exhaled, the corner of his mouth twitching despite himself. "And you've mastered falling," he replied, though he didn't move to rise just yet. He wasn't entirely sure he wanted to.

His eyes met hers just for an instant, wide with surprise as she put her arms in the air and let herself fall into the massive pile of leaves behind. For one fleeting second, time seemed to linger, suspended in her trust, in the unshaken bond of her laughter even as she fell. And then the weight inside him came crashing down—an unfamiliar, undeniable pull that made it hard to breathe, even harder to think.

"I give up!" her voice came from the leaf pile.

Where did she fall? The weight in Adam's arms vanished before he could register what was happening. He looked up first, expecting to see her still there, her smile lit by the amber glow of the rising sun. But she wasn't. She was already gone. His breath hitched as his gaze snapped downward.

There she was, a tangle of skirts and curls half buried in a cascade of damp leaves. The rich brown of her pelisse blended with the autumn debris, her laughter spilling out in soft, breathless bursts that caught him unprepared. His boots slipped on the uneven ground as he tried to step forward, the sudden give beneath him stealing his balance.

"Charlene?" he called, his voice breaking through the thick morning mist. He spun around, only to find himself staring at an unsettling emptiness. The pile of leaves—once towering and triumphant—had swallowed her whole. He stared, heart hammering, the cold biting down his spine. "Charlene!"

A faint cough rose from the jumbled pile.

He exhaled sharply, relief flooding him in a heady rush. Without hesitation, he dropped to his knees, hands tearing through the leaves in a frenzy. Each swipe brought crunching sounds, the earthy scent of dampened foliage twisting into the foggy air.

"Hold on, hold on, I'm coming," he muttered, fingers brushing deeper into the clinging dampness. It smelled like rain-soaked earth, like the dying flames of autumn, like something ancient and alive all at once. The cool air masked his breathing, turning it into fleeting clouds of mist, but all he could hear was the dry shuffling of leaves until finally—finally—his hands found her.

The sight was almost his undoing. She lay there, half-buried, her petticoat bunched and askew like the petals of a flowering carnation, her legs exposed to the morning air, pale and graceful as though they belonged to a porcelain doll rather than the woman who moments ago had been airborne. Her chest rose and fell in sharp, rapid breaths. Her cheeks were flushed, burned with warmth betraying the chill around them. Wisps of brown curls clung against her brow and leaves clung stubbornly to the curves of her hair. Her lips parted, expelling quick wisps of steam that mingled with the fog.

And she was smiling at him.

Minx!

He groaned, brushing a hand over his face before leaning forward to clear the rebellious leaves still stuck to her hair. His fingers threaded carefully, and as they pushed damp strands from her brow, he realized how close she was. Too close. His hand froze before he brushed one more stray leaf from her cheek. It was soft, impossibly soft, and so warm he withdrew his touch like it burned. But his throat was dry, and everything about Charlene—her breath hitching, the color blooming in her skin, the line of her exposed calf—had him pinned.

"You're a sight," he said, his voice rasping, barely audible over the crunching as he finished unearthing her. "Are you hurt? Do I even need to ask?"

Charlene looked up at him through thick lashes, her voice high but colored with amusement. "This is quite fun." She shifted awkwardly, her skirts tangling around her hips as she tried to brush herself off, but she had fallen on her back like a turtle that couldn't turn around—not with a petticoat of that size.

Not with such gorgeous lean legs.

Not on my watch.

"Here, stop moving—I've got it," Adam said quickly, his words tumbling out as he reached to fix her skirts, only to snatch his hands back. His neck heated under his cravat, imagining how improper—how utterly mad—this all was. But then there she was again, laughing softly, unbothered. She was gorgeous, so stunning it made his heart clap unsteadily against his ribcage.

She caught him mid-thought, her fingers brushing his, her touch so light he barely felt it. "Adam," she murmured, her voice teasing yet quiet enough to undo him entirely. "You've gone redder than the maple leaves."

He opened his mouth, but words failed.

The surrounding air thickened, though whether from the cold fog or the twining heat low in his belly, he couldn't tell. Her petticoat was still improperly shifted, and her skin, pale and smooth as winter's first morning, seemed to sear its imprint forever onto his… let's call it memory. He darted his gaze back to her flushed cheeks, yet still—somewhere lower, the tension burned, too raw and too sharp.

Her breasts rose and fell with her breathing—quick and uneven—and that damned flushing color in her cheeks only spread. Every breathless puff from her lips mingled in the air until Adam thought he felt steam in places he shouldn't.

The world narrowed to only her for a moment—the tangles of hair and leaves like a misplaced crown, the breath escaping her lips, the faint smile pulling at her mouth. "You should've caught me," she teased, though her tone was lighter than it could rightly be considering her state.

"I—" His mouth worked before some deeply buried fragment of composure found him. "I did catch you," he replied lamely, jerking his chin toward the leaves. "Sort of."

"Was that before you slipped and fell?"

"You pulled me!"

Charlene laughed again, tossing him a wicked smile despite her thoroughly disheveled state. "If this was catching me, I'd hate to see what missing looks like."

For a reckless heartbeat, he wanted to lean closer, to say something equally sharp, something that would make her laugh again.

Instead, he mumbled, "Horrifying, I'd imagine." And then fell back onto his heels, running a hand down his face as he worked to steady his breathing. Charlene might've been half-smothered by the leaves, but he was the one suffocating.

The world seemed to close in around them, muffled by the leaves and the persistent fog. Adam leaned forward, bracing himself with one hand against the damp ground as he hovered over Charlene. His other hand instinctively reached out, brushing aside a stray leaf clinging stubbornly to her calf. Her skin felt impossibly soft under his fingers, chilled by the morning air but warming beneath his touch. She shivered, a subtle tremor running up her leg, and his jaw tightened.

She didn't move away.

Was this permission?

Adam's eyes flickered to her face. Her lips were slightly parted; her breath came out in shallow puffs of vapor against the cold air. Her gaze locked with his, a mixture of heat and vulnerability that rooted him to his spot. His fingers hesitated at her ankle before curiosity—or something much deeper—urged him onward.

"Charlene, stop me."

But all she did was give a faint shake of her head.

Slowly, deliberately, his hand trailed up her lower leg. His thumb brushed the delicate curve of her knee, then higher, the fabric of her petticoat bunching beneath his exploring palm. The warmth of her skin seeped through his skin as his fingers roamed, passing her knee. Each inch brought more heat, more tension, and his heart thundered like hooves on cobblestones.

I have to stop.

By the time he reached her thigh, her breathing had quickened. A soft gasp escaped her lips, faint but deafening against the silence. Her cheeks flushed a deep crimson, but she didn't pull away. If anything, her body seemed to edge closer. Adam swallowed hard, his focus darting between the inviting curve of her leg beneath his hand and the undeniable invitation in her gaze.

"Charlene..." he murmured, his voice rough, unintentionally betraying the low burn smoldering beneath his control.

She didn't respond with words. Instead, her hand came to rest lightly atop his, her fingers trembling as they curled around his palm. For a moment, she merely held him there, her grip steady despite the way her chest rose and fell in uneven rhythm. And then, gently—hesitantly at first—she guided his hand higher.

Adam's fingers trembled where Charlene's hand rested, her touch light yet searing against his skin. Her chest rose and fell unsteadily, and despite all the promises he'd made to himself, he couldn't pull away.

"What are we doing, Charlene?"

"I don't know," she whispered. "Show me!"

"I must not go further than this, Charlene." The words came out ragged, a thin thread of resistance barely holding him back. He felt the tension within him coil tighter, threatening to snap, every thought centered on where her trembling fingers met his.

She didn't answer, not aloud. Her hand simply curled around his, her grasp growing steadier even as her breaths hitched. And then, with a boldness that left him utterly wrecked, she guided his hand, inching it higher.

"Charlene," he began, his throat dry, "it's always been you. Only you."

Her lips parted, as if wavering on the verge of protest. "What? What do you mean?" Her hand went slack, and his heart twisted as he watched her fold inward, retreating.

He couldn't stand it—not her hurt, not her doubt. "I've held you above everything, Charlene. I put you on a pedestal so high, I couldn't even reach you. And I've hated myself for it every day since because it was my fault that I was out of reach and I didn't protect you from him."

Tears slipped past her lashes, and she quickly swiped them away. "You've always been my closest friend, Adam. Always. But then..." She faltered, dropping her gaze.

Then it all went to blazes.

She suddenly turned her head sharply, her eyes locked on something just beyond him. Her lips parted in shock.

Adam followed her line of sight, his blood running cold when he saw the silhouette. A movement. Almost imperceptible at first, drifting at the edges of the fog-draped park like a shadow given form.

Adam's thumb grazed Charlene's knuckles, his heart hammering against his ribs. Her trembling fingers curled tighter around his hand, a whisper of breath escaping, "Adam..."

"Someone's watching us." Her voice faltered, barely audible.

Her eyes opened wide. Uncertainty. Fear.

"Stay still." Adam's eyes never left the stranger.

"Who are they?"

"I don't know."

The figure stood just beyond them, where the tree-lined path blurred into a haze that sent goosebumps through him. It was a woman. She wore a hat, its wide brim failing to mask the air of mystery that clung to her like the swirling mist. Her shape was slight, draped in hues dulled by the gloom. Adam couldn't make out her features, for the fog seemed to cling to her, rendering her ghostlike.

The woman didn't move. Silent. Ominous. And then, with an eerie grace, she turned. The mist shifted with her, swallowing her form as though she had never been.

Adam's heart thundered in his ears. His experienced mind urged reason, logic, yet no explanation fit the chill that gripped him now. Beside him, Charlene's hand slipped from his as she scrambled to her feet.

"Do you know her?" she asked again, her voice threading with concern.

"No, I couldn't tell." Adam couldn't look away from the space where the figure had stood. The chill of her presence still clung to the air, as heavy as the questions she left behind.

The moment between them had splintered, the fragile magic of it now lost. And yet, Adam felt a new current shiver through his chest, tangled in confusion and unease. Whoever she was, her arrival had changed everything.

Chapter Nine

LATER THAT DAY, back home, Charlene plopped into a chair in her greenhouse, the welcome scent of fresh leaves wrapping around her and calming her racing heart. But unfortunately, not enough to stow the flashing images of Adam in her head.

She had gone to the park.

I confessed my love. She slapped her hand on her forehead.

She wasn't a fern; she was a weed. Clover at best.

She had met Adam. And worse—so much worse—she had played with him in the leaves like a child, letting laughter slip past her lips as though the past did not weigh upon her like an iron shackle! They had almost... She didn't even want to think about it. It was just too embarrassing. And that woman! Who had she been? Had she recognized her and Adam? Or was it just some stranger who had happened upon them?

I need to think about other things.

Like how was she ever going to look at an autumn leaf again? The colorful hues, the slight indication of decay—once symbols of change and beauty—were now tainted. Very well, perhaps tainted was too strong a word. But it was something! Every rustling leaf would remind her of him. Of the way his eyes crinkled at the corners when he laughed, the warmth of his hand as he pulled her up from the ground, the way the world had fallen away in those fleeting moments of reckless abandon.

She had tried to loathe him. Hadn't she? His bloodline, his very existence—everything about him should have been an affront to her. And yet, standing in the park, covered in leaves, breathless from laughter, she had felt none of the anger she had so carefully cultivated.

That terrified her.

"You cannot forget the past, Charlene," she whispered to herself, fisting her skirts as though she could hold onto her grievance with that alone. No, she couldn't forget. Forgetting meant that she might relive it. Forgetting meant she might make the same mistake again.

Forgetting meant… letting go.

And letting go… that would be like it never having happened at all, would it not?

She couldn't accept that.

But wasn't she already letting go, little by little? Hadn't she let go the moment she met him in the park? The moment she let herself forget who he was—who she was—and simply existed in that autumn-filled moment?

That was the most dangerous part, wasn't it? Not forgetting the past but remembering how it felt to be unburdened by it. How easy it had been, how natural, as though she had been waiting all along for someone like him to remind her what joy was.

She dug her nails into her palms.

No, Charlene! What was she doing? What was she thinking?

She had spent a year rebuilding the foundation of her heart, and a wall for good measure, brick by painstaking brick. She had told herself she was safe behind them, untouchable, immune to the whims of foolish, reckless temptations.

But Adam had walked right in, hadn't he? No chisel in hand, not forcefully hacking anything down, just a smile and a pile of dead leaves, and suddenly, she was slipping.

And if she slipped too far?

She might fall. Forgotten!

And this time, there would be no getting up.

No, she had to stay away from him.

Charlene exhaled sharply, as if she could force the very thought of Adam from her mind with one breath. She leaned back into the chair, staring blankly at the glass panes above, where the morning light filtered through in beams. She needed to think of something else. Anything else.

A rustle.

She jerked upright. The orangery was hers alone—no one ventured here unless she was here, which meant someone entered while she was away. She twisted toward the sound, calling. "Who's there?"

For a moment, there was only silence. Then, another shuffle, the faintest scuff of a shoe against the floor. A shadow moved between the leaves. Charlene rose swiftly, snatching up a small garden trowel as if it could be used as a weapon, absurd as the thought was. Who would break into an orangery!

Then, a head popped out from between two large potted ferns, dark curls tumbling into view. "Oh, you're here," Maddie said, blinking as if she weren't the one caught somewhere she shouldn't be.

Charlene dropped her trowel with a huff. "Maddie? What are you doing here?"

Maddie stepped fully into view, brushing soil from her hands. "Looking for some herbs for my medicine."

She crossed her arms. "In my raised beds? Shouldn't you go forage in the park or something?"

Maddie smiled, entirely unrepentant. "Yes. You never know what gems you might find." She gestured around as if she had full claim to the space. "Also, you let me plant some here."

She did? Well, she probably did.

Charlene sighed, pressing her fingers against her temple. "You nearly gave me a fright."

Maddie studied her for a moment, tilting her head. "Were

you lost in thought?" A pause. "Why do you look like that?"

Charlene stiffened. "Like what?"

"Like you've just crawled from the barracks of trade ships," Maddie said, arching a brow. "Or lost some great battle, perhaps?"

Charlene scoffed. However, thinking back—which she refused to do!—she did do some crawling. At least, a near form of it. "Don't be ridiculous."

Maddie stepped closer, peering at Charlene as though she were inspecting a wilting plant. "I don't think so. You look positively wrecked."

Charlene turned away, fussing with a nearby sprig of lavender. "I do not." And what's with that word wrecked? Did she look wrecked? Well, her thoughts, if she were to admit, might be a bit wrecked. Urgh.

She was not wrecked!

"You do," Maddie countered. "And since I know you haven't been dueling in the garden—unless you have?—that leaves only one possible explanation."

Charlene refused to take the bait. "I daresay there are a thousand different explanations?"

Maddie grinned. "A man."

Charlene's hands froze mid-motion. Maddie let out a delighted gasp. "It is a man! Oh, how thrilling! There can only be—"

"No one," Charlene cut in swiftly. No. One. To admit to her friend she'd been frolicking in the park would be like admitting her worst failure, would it not? She plopped back down into the chair.

Maddie hummed, entirely unconvinced. "No one, you say. And yet, here you are, looking as if you've been emotionally trampled." She leaned in. "It wouldn't happen to be a certain Cross brother?"

Charlene shot her a glare. "Please don't say his name."

"Well, according to the M-Press this morning, the twins may be reunited after all." Maddie bent down and inspected some plants. "Is this digitalis?"

But Charlene couldn't focus on the seedlings. "What do you mean the twins reunited?"

"Oh, you know those gossip columns. One day they say David Cross is back and then they say he's gone forever." Maddie waved in the air.

"Oh, David," Charlene said, curling her lip in disgust. "But Adam is… Adam is…"

Maddie's grin widened. "So, it is the duke. Finally, you admit it?"

Charlene groaned, rubbing her hands over her face. "Don't you have herbs to forage?"

"Oh, absolutely not." Maddie plopped onto a nearby bench. "This is far too interesting. Weren't you finished with the duke's family? Though, if you ask me, the duke is far from his brother. He's more handsome, better-educated, more eloquent, and such a good dancer. I saw you two at the masquerade."

Charlene turned, exasperated. "It's not interesting. And they might not be the exact same, but they are twins, and they share the same blood."

Maddie tapped her chin. "And yet, I find you here, sighing like a tragic heroine, looking haunted by the mere thought of him."

Charlene's lips pressed into a thin line. "I loathe him." *Because he doesn't feel about me the way I feel about him.*

"Do you, though?"

"I am not discussing this with you."

Maddie's voice followed her as Charlene stormed away. "You can run, darling, but you cannot hide from that man. He seems determined to rekindle your friendship."

Charlene groaned.

Charlene sighed. She was beginning to think she couldn't hide from Adam, either. However, what if she did let him into her life again? If he ever betrayed her, hurt her, wouldn't she be the only one to blame?

Maddie watched her carefully, a knowing glint in her eye. "You're thinking awfully hard over there."

Charlene shook her head. "I'm thinking that you should mind your own herb-like business."

Maddie grinned. "Oh, but your business is so much more interesting than mine. But I'm more than happy to use my potion business to help you out. Just tell me what you need."

Charlene huffed a reluctant laugh, but her thoughts still swirled. What if Adam was different? Not his bloodline, not his past, not the history between them, but him? The man he was now. What if he was not the villain she had painted in her mind?

Hadn't she felt it herself—the warmth in his laughter, the steadiness in his presence?

But there was risk in letting him in.

Charlene exhaled, long and slow.

Some risks were just not worth taking.

ADAM FELL DOWN onto the settee, throwing an arm over his face. He had gone to the park with the intention of seeing her, yes, but not like that. Whatever you could call "that" was. Not touching her before he could stop himself. Not by pushing his luck. Not by making a fool of himself.

He had raked those infernal leaves for her. He hadn't thought so at the time, but he felt like a fool. A besotted fool. What madness had possessed him, he didn't know.

Charlene was not a woman to play around with. She possessed a soft heart, sharp-tongued, stubborn nature, and she had made it exceedingly clear that she wanted nothing to do with him.

And yet—

Yet, she had laughed today.

A true, unguarded laugh. And save him, he had lived a hundred lifetimes in that sound.

Ah yes, he was a fool. An absolute, irredeemable fool.

Because he wanted to hear that laugh again.

No, not just hear it—he wanted to be the reason for it.

And that? That was the most dangerous thought of all. Given their history, and her reservations toward him and his family, it might end only in torture for him. Because if he wanted more, if he let himself believe, even for a moment, that she might let him in—

Then there would be no coming back from it.

And then there was that woman.

It was probably nothing.

"Ah," his mother's voice carried across the room. "There you are, dear." He turned his head slightly to see her standing in the doorway, her gaze assessing. "You were out early today."

"Riding," was all he said.

His mother arched a brow, gliding into the room. "Ah, riding. You never go riding so early in the mornings. What changed today?"

She changed everything.

The world changed because she loves me.

He swallowed back the words and let out a slow breath instead.

His mother was not easily deceived. She had a mind sharper than most men he knew and an intuition that was even sharper. He would have to tread carefully.

Lowering his hand from his face, he sat up and studied her. "How would you overcome an obstacle in your path?"

She arranged her skirts as she sat across from him and replied without missing a beat. "I would trample on it."

Adam snorted despite himself. "I can't do that."

"Then ignore it."

"Can't do that either."

"Challenge it, then," she said, her eyes narrowing with interest. "That is your only recourse."

Challenge it.

That was what he was doing, right? However, he didn't know if he was going about it the right way or the wrong way. Instead, he was just going with his heart. He didn't know how else to do it.

His mother was watching him closely, her keen gaze unwavering. "You are troubled."

"I am not troubled," Adam muttered. "Merely…" He trailed off, unable to find the right word.

"Vexed?" she offered.

"Not quite vexed, either."

"Bewildered?"

He huffed a short laugh. She wouldn't give up. "I suppose that is a bit closer."

Her lips twitched. "Ah. Then let me guess—there is a woman involved, then. A particular one?"

Adam tensed.

That was answer enough.

His mother's expression turned knowing. "Who is she?"

"No one."

"No one has ever made you look like this, my dear."

He sighed, rubbing his temple. "It is complicated." Too complicated for words.

Her expression softened, but there was amusement there, too. "Is it not always the case? I have yet to meet an uncomplicated matter when it comes to the two sexes."

Adam leaned forward, bracing his elbows on his knees. "She dislikes me. Strongly. She has reason to."

His mother tilted her head. "And yet, you do not wish for her to dislike you."

A muscle in his jaw ticked. "No."

"Why?"

The question was deceptively simple.

Adam stared at the patterns on the carpet, his thoughts tangling together like a knotted rope. Yes, why? Because Charlene made him wish to feel like his old self again. Because she also challenged him. Because the thought of walking away from her left a hollow ache in his chest.

Instead of saying any of that, he exhaled sharply and murmured, "Because I'm an idiot."

His mother chuckled. "That is a given. All men are idiots when it comes to any matters that are not from the head."

He shot her a dry look. "Who said anything about it being anything but?"

She merely smiled. "No one had to."

Adam groaned, dropping his head into his hands. "This is why I never speak to you about these things."

"Oh, my dear, if you did, your life would be infinitely easier."

"I rather doubt that."

His mother nodded thoughtfully. "Perhaps that is where you must start, Adam. This doubt of yours. What is it that you truly want from this woman?"

The answer should have been simple.

And yet, it was anything but.

He wanted her forgiveness.

And especially her trust.

Most of all, he wanted the chance to see if they could be something more than enemies.

His mother must have read the conflict in his face, because her expression softened. "If you seek to change her heart, Adam, then you must be willing to risk your own in the process."

He swallowed.

Risk.

He had never been afraid of it before. But this? This felt like a battle he had no armor for.

His mother rose, smoothing out her skirts. "Well, I can introduce you to a lady or two if you wish?"

"Please don't."

She chuckled. "Well, perhaps after your duties."

Suspicion instantly rose. "What do you mean?

She turned toward the door but paused before exiting, glancing back at him. "Why, you need to do the rounds of the family estates."

Right. He had forgotten about that.

Bloody ducal duty. This almost made it seem like he couldn't be with the one who was perfect for him because his brother did, in fact, ruin it. Her and Adam's chances with her.

Except if he could undo that somehow… remedy the situation—avert the crisis?

Adam didn't want to leave right now. Every nerve in his body resisted the idea. He had finally—finally—moved an inch with Charlene. And now, just when he needed time to think, to strategize, to act—he was being dragged away by obligation.

He let his head fall back against the sofa with a groan.

It wasn't just a formality. These visits were necessary. His tenants depended on him. There were leases to review, accounts to settle, disputes to mediate, roofs that needed repairing before winter settled in.

But the timing—the timing could not be worse.

His mother watched him struggle, amusement flickering in her eyes. "It won't take more than a fortnight."

A fortnight.

Fourteen days away from Charlene.

Away from that sharp tongue and heated gaze. Away from any opportunity to close the impossible distance between them.

He clenched his jaw.

He didn't have much choice. If he stayed, his mother would hound him relentlessly.

Perhaps this was for the best.

Perhaps distance would bring clarity.

Or perhaps it would drive him mad.

TWO WEEKS HAD passed, and Charlene had not heard a word from Adam.

Not even a note.

Why hadn't he?

The drawing room at Ashley's townhouse glowed with a serene charm, soft light spilling from the chandelier. A subtle honeyed candle scent fused with the earthy bitterness of sealing wax melting on its silver spoon, balancing the faint metallic tang of fresh ink spread in delicate loops across the wedding invitations. The warmth of the fire crackled faintly behind the three women, its waves of heat brushing against their ankles despite the slight chill carried in from the cooler autumn air.

Charlene sat beside Ashley at the table, smoothing her skirts each time the paper crinkled beneath her hands. Even the velvet upholstery beneath her, paired with the comforting pops of chatter from Ashley and Maddie, couldn't halt the restless pacing of her thoughts. Her hands, usually sure and steady, fumbled as she folded an ivory sheet for yet another pristine envelope. The fibers of the paper stung after sliding against her fingertips for what must have been the fiftieth time that afternoon.

"Ouch." The word escaped under her breath, sharp and sudden.

Ashley's head whipped toward her. "What happened?"

Charlene stuck her fingertip into her mouth instinctively, the sting of the paper cut small but sharp. The taste of salt met her tongue as she winced from the tender ache flaring across the small slice in her skin.

"Is it bleeding?" Maddie peered over from her place on the other side of the table, where she had given up on ribbons in favor of arranging the paper slips into neat stacks. "Should I fetch my apothecary bag?"

"No, not yet," Charlene murmured, withdrawing her hand from her lips to inspect the thin, faintly red mark trailing across her index finger.

Ashley shook her head with a sympathetic cluck of her

tongue as she warmed yet another stick of wax over the flame. "Paper cuts. Nasty hurts, those. Remember when I jabbed myself in the palm folding programs last Yuletide? Awful."

Her words might have drawn a wry smile on another day, but at that moment, Charlene felt emotion rise unexpectedly, catching her off guard and forging a hot sting in her throat. She dropped her gaze to the table, her shoulders falling even as her nervous fingers traced the edges of the envelope resting before her.

"What is it, Char?" Maddie teased lightly. "Has it gone deep?"

Her laugh was quick and bright, but it trailed off when Charlene didn't respond.

Deep, yes. Like cupid's arrow to her heart.

Ashley had paused mid-movement, her brow furrowing as her friend sat silent, shoulders hunched.

"Charlene." Ashley's voice dropped, the warm companionable tone shifting to one of concern. "Surely it doesn't hurt that badly. By all that's certain, I've seen you give yourself worse cuts in my mother's greenhouse with those pruning shears."

It was meant to soothe, to draw out the ghost of humor between Ashley's words, but Charlene just swallowed hard, her chest tightening as tears unexpectedly slipped over her lower lashes. She turned instinctively toward the window, ashamed of the weakness surging forward so unbidden.

Maddie placed the papers in her hand atop the others, leaning back in her chair to give her full attention. "Char?" Her tone, lighter moments before, softened with the tender prodding of a sister's patience. "What is the matter?"

Ashley set her wax seal down with a small tap on the wooden table and turned fully in her chair toward Charlene. "It's him, isn't it?" Maddie's sharp gaze flicked to Ashley. "It's the duke."

At this, Charlene stiffened, her throat closing further under the weight of their attention. She shook her head, though her hands had grown as cold and bloodless as the paper they rested on. "It's nothing," she murmured. "Nothing at all." Her gaze dropped to her hand. No blood. That, at least, was lucky.

"That doesn't seem like nothing." Maddie's expertise in wheedling wore patience like a well-tailored sash. She folded her hands in her lap and tucked one slipper under her chair, an image of innocence gilded by determination. "Whatever it is you're holding in, it won't give you rest to sit in it."

"And if it's about him…" Ashley's voice braced, rich with the tone of a loyal knight unsheathing her sword. "If something has happened, say the word and I'll see to it."

The warmth of their support, though well-meaning, only threatened to shatter her already fragile resolve. Charlene straightened her shoulders, seeking composure as her trembling fingers brushed back an unruly curl behind her ear. "He hasn't sent word," she admitted quietly. "Not once."

Maddie tilted her head as Ashley's eyebrows rose indignantly. "Why," Maddie asked pointedly, "should he send word? Have you done anything?"

A faint blush rose up Charlene's neck. Before she could respond, Maddie's eyebrows shot upward in realization. "You did, didn't you?" Her tone carried an elegance laced with jest, tempered only slightly by her affection. "Did something, I mean."

"Oh, Char," Ashley said, placing her seal aside to focus entirely on Charlene. "What have you done now?" She frowned, then added in a softer voice, "You know we are your friends, dear. If you must unburden yourself…"

"Or," Maddie cut in with a teasing grin, "who?"

"Maddie!" Ashley swatted her arm, shooting her an almost real glare behind the red creeping along her cheeks. "Honestly."

"It's not funny," Ashley said sharply. "The city thrives on gossip worse than dogs to a bone. The *M-Press* already threatens fire for the Cross brothers alone. Adding you to that would fuel an inferno."

"What gossip?" Charlene interjected, gripping the arms of her seat as her pulse quickened.

Ashley hesitated, her lips pursed under Charlene's urgent

stare. "Rumors," she admitted cautiously. "A Cross brother in Green Park. Masquerade dances are more scandalous than secretive. Pall Mall carriages sweeping blinding beauties…"

"Stop," Charlene whispered, her voice low but heavy. Her chest tightened to bursting under the weight of a question begged first softly, then roaring angrily within her rib cage. Something about those rumors set her shoulders tight and her palms cold.

Ashley's next words came faintly to Charlene, muffled as though through a fog. She caught fragments of her friend's voice, scattered and broken. "Some unknown woman… Said to be quite beautiful… That hat of hers, it's become infamous now, if whispers are to be believed."

The warmth of the room seemed to recede abruptly, her senses clouded by the icy grip of fear clutching at her chest. Maddie laughed lightly, a sound meant to tease, but it cut sharper than Charlene expected. Each note seemed like a soft chisel against her composure.

"Charlene…" Maddie's voice was less distinct now, though her persistence prickled like a persistent drop of rain sliding down the back of her neck.

Charlene's hands trembled as she pushed the curling edge of a ribbon aimlessly across the table. Her knuckles brushed against waxy drips hardened like tiny monuments of productivity, but her mind was far from the present. The possibilities surged in her thoughts, all unwelcome and none clear.

Her throat tightened as she lowered her gaze to the ribbon, willing herself not to break. Could it be true? Her pulse quickened at the thought, her worry blooming into an ache more cutting than any paper's edge.

Had Adam replaced her so easily? Had all those years of longing, of quiet patience, meant nothing to him after all? It couldn't be and yet, why had he vanished after that morning at the park?

Chapter Ten

F*INALLY. BACK HOME.*

Adam sighed with relief.

The soles on his boots were still smeared with mud from the estate roads, despite the valet's earlier efforts to clean them. How he loathed when the smell of damp leather clung to him as he paced the length of the library, a stack of correspondence balanced in one hand, untouched. Although the fire crackled cheerily in the hearth, its heat did little to ease the bone-deep weariness that clung to him after nearly two weeks of relentless travel.

He'd thought he'd get it all done sooner.

That hadn't happened.

Two days of riding and twelve days of work.

Twelve days of riding from tenant to tenant, inspecting fields, touring cottages, shaking hands. And so many new names to remember while there was only one on his mind—the one that ought not be. Two days' hard ride to return, only to fall straight into more obligations, more hours spent proving to everyone— even himself—that he deserved the title he hadn't asked for. His shoulders ached from the strain of sitting in the saddle and keeping his back straight during every overly polite conversation. But his physical discomfort paled in comparison to the gnawing unease that had been with him every step of the way.

Charlene.

No matter how exhausted he was, he couldn't seem to push her from his thoughts. She owned them. Left him with no respite. When he'd finally fallen into his massive bed at Rotheworth Manor, pillows perfectly fluffed by the housekeeper's staff, he'd expected to black out with the kind of sleep only true fatigue could warrant. But instead, he only saw her face. The way she looked at him. The way fire would light up in her eyes. And even the way she'd swallowed a retort when he struck too close to her heart.

He groaned, running a hand through his hair as he leaned against the heavy desk.

Adam hadn't wanted to leave her like that.

He wanted to spend more time with her. He wanted to deepen the frayed connection between them. Strengthen it. And for that, he needed time. He needed proximity. He needed to show up wherever she was.

He raked his hand over his face.

He wanted to see her. Badly.

Charlene was on a pedestal of female perfection, and he felt as though he could only ever roll a rock to her like Sisyphus up the mountain—she was so much better than him in every way, he'd never truly reach her, no matter how much he tried to touch her. But he wanted to try. Had to try.

He patted his vest pocket. There it was, the apology he'd never delivered.

I have to go to her.

A knock creaked against the study doorframe, interrupting his brooding.

His mother swept in, the light-gray sheen of her silk gown catching the firelight with every purposeful step. Her smooth and commanding expression reminded him that no matter how high his shoulders stood, hers bore decades of practice above his.

"You're not dressed," she stated flatly, her gaze dropping to his mud-dusted coat.

Adam gave her a curt nod. "I've only just returned."

"And yet society doesn't pause." Her tone was crisp, the voice of a woman who'd run one of the country's largest estates by her strength of will—and expected him to do the same. "The Guy Fawkes Fair is scarcely an hour away. You'll join us at the square. This is not an invitation, Adam. It's part of the role your father left to you."

His jaw tightened. "I'm exhausted. The tenants—" And he wanted to hunt down word of Charlene.

"Have occupied you for twelve days. Society deserves the same attention as your fields do. Or will you allow the gossips to write you off as too aloof for the Ton before the year's end? You'll attend, and you'll smile. That is the duty of a duke."

And then what? Adam wanted to snap, but swallowed the retort.

He stared at the fire for a moment, jaw flexing as he weighed his reply. But there was nothing to weigh. She was right. She always was, and it grated on his fraying temper—even when, in this case, it was his conscience that agreed with her. Shallow as it might be, he was at the very least duty-bound to attend events. He'd reserve his opinion on the smile. Unless Charlene was there. Then he'd smile all night long.

"Very well," he bit out. "I'll dress and inform the footman I'll need the carriage ready within the hour." He'd go to this blasted festival or whatever it was. Then, he'd hunt down Charlene.

She gave a small nod of approval and turned without another word, leaving him to collect himself. The second the door clicked shut behind her, Adam slouched against the desk with a sigh.

One more obligation. One more night of appearances, of playing the part the world demanded of him. And no matter how short the fair might prove, no matter how many smiles he offered to the Ton beneath the fireworks sky, he wouldn't rest tonight either—because she would still be there, lodged in his mind.

And like everything else, this would need to be dealt with

eventually. The harder truth was that the matter with Charlene couldn't be ignored—and he didn't want her to be.

November 5th, 1818

GUY FAWKES DAY had come and gone, and the celebrations of the night became louder as the hour of the fireworks loomed.

Charlene might as well have been a wisp of smoke among the guests at Cavendish House but Ashley and Maddie had joined forces with Waylon, so Charlene had to bow to them and come along. Below the balcony, the crowd swelled, their voices a lively chatter woven through the crackle of roasted chestnuts and the bite of gunpowder in the crisp November evening air. She adjusted her spencer jacket against the bite of the autumn chill, her eyes drawn to the sprawling bonfire being built in the center of the square. Bundles of wood stacked high, glowing in the golden light of dusk, gave the promise of warmth that the breeze denied.

From her perch among nobility, she should have felt grand. Instead, loneliness curled around her like a shadow, unseen yet inescapable.

Even accompanied by her dear friends, she couldn't quite evade the feeling.

Charlene glanced over at Ashley, who clutched her doting fiancé Thomas's arm and leaned toward the rail, her cheeks pink with excitement. "Look at this view! You always think of everything."

"Spectacular, right?" Thomas said, but his eyes were on Ashley, his hand lightly covering Ashley's where it rested on his sleeve.

Charlene almost rolled her eyes at the pair; at the same time, she also felt a pinch of envy.

"It's almost time for the spectacle," Thomas added. "Let me

fetch some ratafia before it begins."

The moment he left, Maddie nudged her shoulder. "Why are you so quiet?"

Charlene pressed her lips together, her gloves twisting in her hands when she noticed that Ashley was now also scrutinizing her.

Should she tell Maddie? But once spoken, it would no longer be hers alone. Did she even want it to remain a secret? Or was she simply afraid of what saying it aloud would mean? On the one hand, keeping it to herself felt safer, but on the other, these were her friends. If anyone could help her make sense of this mess that warred in her head and heart, it was them.

Well, there was nothing for it, then.

She would tell them.

"I…" Charlene began, her voice faltering. How was this so difficult! She sighed and lowered her gaze. "I shall admit, I did something shocking, and now I don't know what to do."

Her friends exchanged quick looks.

"Shocking?" Ashley whispered, her tone a mix of curiosity and alarm. "What happened?"

Charlene hesitated, color rising to her cheeks. "I went to the park," she said finally. "Alone. To… to meet Adam."

"When was this?" Maddie asks.

"About two weeks ago."

Two delightful weeks of agonizing over the man.

Ashley gasped, covering her mouth with her gloved hand. "Char! Alone? With the duke? Do you have any idea how dangerous that is?"

Oh, she did. "I wasn't thinking," Charlene said, her voice barely a notch above the clamor in the square. "The man just makes me so furious!"

"Oh?" Maddie murmured. "And how did he do that?"

"He sent a note after the ball," Charlene said flatly. "Practically goading me."

"And you fell for it," Ashley said with a nod. "Of course you would."

"Of course I would? What does that mean?"

"It means," Ashley said with an arch of her brow, "You have unfinished business with that man."

Charlene felt her pulse quicken, felt the heat rising unbidden to her throat. Unfinished business? It felt rather finished to her. Or it had, before he returned. Since his return… Perhaps Ashley wasn't wrong.

"Yes," Maddie said thoughtfully. "Because goading aside, why else would you need to meet the duke if not for a sense of unfinished business?"

"However," Ashley said. "I'd caution you, Char. A new duke, handsome and unattached? People will notice. People will also talk. You should be careful not to put yourself in a position where you cannot get yourself out."

"Well, there were certain positions, for sure," Charlene muttered. But none too scandalous.

Ashley's eyes bulged. "What are you saying?"

Charlene laughed. "Wait, what position do you think I—what are you implying?"

Maddie scoffed. "Any position with you in the park, alone, would be improper."

"Well, I, for one, am glad you chose any position at all," Ashley said with a grin. "You've been far too busy pruning your orchids lately."

Charlene rolled her eyes. "They require a lot of attention."

Maddie chuckled. "Hah! Does the duke know he is competing against plants for your attention?"

"There is no competition," Charlene argued. The orchids would win, however. Besides, Adam seeking her attention? He wasn't even in London.

Would he return soon?

The first streak of light cut across the dark sky above them, bursting into gold as the fireworks began, drawing her attention. But as the light flared, a tightness gripped her whole being, and she quickly lowered her eyes, turning her focus back to the bonfire below, its crackling flames far less chaotic than the turmoil she wished she could smother under the crush of the crowd.

Honestly.

Why did it feel like her heart might explode for that man?

Just like those fireworks.

Chapter Eleven

ADAM ENTERED CAVENDISH House with a scowl.

He'd rather be caught in a storm in the middle of the ocean than be there to watch fireworks. Completely different sorts of explosives raged within him, but he couldn't act unless he could speak to her. And that was a slim possibility this evening, if she were in attendance, too. He shouldn't lament his fate, but his skin itched with irritation. He had no desire, no patience for polite, insipid conversations, which seemed to be the turnout for every event where she wasn't.

And she wouldn't be here.

Not at Cavendish House.

The sound of the fireworks exploding outside annoyed him even more. If he were to see the fireworks, he wanted to see it with her.

He had no friends. Well, he had one. Jack Cavendish. A businessman. Also, the owner of this house. The man of questionable birth, filthy rich, and a mysterious magnet to the Ton. They'd met after Jack helped him out of a scrap years ago, but his friend had yet to show his face since Adam's return to London.

He scoffed.

And Adam had a sinking suspicion that even his host wouldn't be around tonight. The man had been tamed by his woman. Something he had never thought would ever happen. But then, he'd never thought he'd have a true chance at love with Charlene Fielding either.

The house was still a crush.

His mother would probably scold him for choosing this particular event, but since he had yet to learn Charlene's whereabouts, he felt more comfortable here. And he'd hoped, the smallest of hopes, to see his friend, too.

A good night was something to hope for as well.

Adam searched the room. To his surprise, in the back, he caught sight of the Earl of Linsey, the fiancé of one of Charlene's friends, attempting to balance four glasses of wine in two hands.

His mood suddenly cleared.

Did that mean Charlene would be there, too?

He didn't delay; he made his way over to the blond earl. "Linsey, how unexpected. Can I offer you some help?"

"Rotheworth," Linsey said in greeting, allowing him to take two glasses. "Thank you."

Adam gave him a nod. "No problem. I'm surprised to find you at Cavendish House."

Linsey nodded. "Because of Cavendish? I agree, but the women argued it has the best view."

Indeed.

"The view or the host?"

The earl scoffed, then let out a chuckle. "Both, I suppose, though they've only been greeted with the sight of one."

"That's Cavendish for you, absent at his own party," Adam said, his gaze sweeping the room for that extremely familiar beautiful face.

His eyes found her, out on the balcony, her elbows leaning against the balustrade, facing her friends.

She was there.

So blindingly exquisite.

Linsey, catching his gaze, followed his line of sight. "Shall we?"

"Of course."

Linsey led the way toward the women, Adam staying just a step behind him. He hadn't seen her in fourteen full days, fifteen counting this day. And he couldn't tear his eyes away. She suddenly glanced up, their eyes locking.

The breath knocked from his lungs.

A flicker of something—relief, maybe? Though he couldn't be certain whether that was what he wanted to see—passed through her features before she masked it with an arched brow.

"I've brought the wine, ladies," Linsey said. "And the Duke of Rotheworth."

Adam handed off one glass before handing the last one to Charlene, who accepted it with a soft thank you. The moment she took the glass from his hand, her fingers brushed his. That small contact, a touch too brief, sent a shock through him. The jolt of awareness made his skin tighten.

She tipped the glass to her lips and took a small sip. "What a surprise, Your Grace, meeting you here."

"It can't be that much of a surprise, can it?" he countered. Three sets of eyes bored into him, but he ignored the burn. "After all, you are here."

Her gaze held his. "True. But I rather thought you'd be somewhere else, raking the leaves of your estate."

Adam's lips quirked. "And yet, here I am, trying to rake in something else."

"Oh?" She tilted her head, studying him. "It seems you have come to the right place, but the wrong group."

"Have I? I don't think so."

A slight cough came to his left, and he pursed his lips, eyes never leaving Charlene, who flushed.

He let out a quiet laugh. "Forgive me, I find myself bewitched by the sight of... fireworks."

She arched a brow, swirling the wine in her glass. "Fireworks?"

He nodded toward the sky beyond the balcony. "Yes. They

are quite an exquisite sight, wouldn't you agree?"

Her lips parted, as if ready to challenge him, but she hesitated. Then, ever so slowly, she turned her head just enough to glance at the distant bursts of color. "Hmm. I suppose they do have a certain charm. Bright. Bold. Impossible to ignore."

Adam tilted his head. Was that directed at him? "Sounds familiar."

"Are you suggesting I am bright and bold, Your Grace?"

"Not at all. Merely that, like fireworks, you seem to have a way of drawing my attention."

"Oh, dear Lord," a female voice muttered from the side, but Adam ignored it.

Charlene let out a soft laugh, the sound rich with amusement. "Is that an attempt at poetic flirtation? I hadn't taken you for a man of such sentiment."

"I have depths, my lady," Adam murmured. "I had hoped you would know that by now."

Her gaze flickered over him, assessing. "Perhaps. But even the ocean has depths, and one can drown rather easily, as you know."

"I recall you to be a good swimmer."

She didn't answer, merely stared at him. A sudden burst of fireworks momentarily bathed her in a soft light, stealing his breath. Then, she drained her glass in a single gulp, setting the crystal down with a soft clink on the balustrade.

She smiled at her friends. "Excuse me for a moment; I'll be back in a jiffy."

"Do you need company?" Lady Madeline asked.

She shook her head and quickly stepped through the doors.

Adam's brows furrowed. For a moment, he stood frozen, watching her retreating figure. He couldn't bring himself to move. It was as though his body refused to obey him, too confused and baffled to act.

He cursed.

"Please, excuse me, too." Without another glance at the group, Adam turned and followed her.

THE DEAFENING CRACK of fireworks rattled the windows, slicing through the muffled shouts of delight from the ballroom. Charlene winced and tightened her shawl around her. She had hoped that slipping away would give her a measure of peace to calm down her heart, but her thoughts swirled restlessly.

Her pulse still continued to race—how could it? He had returned. And his eyes, oh, those eyes, once they had fallen on her, they hadn't left. Ashley and Maddie may not as well have existed!

Her friends' earlier words rang in her ears. About competing. The duke competing for her attention? Adam?

No.

Surely not.

He only wanted to… rekindle a broken friendship.

He had, after all, not even called on her in two weeks. Not even a note.

She slipped down the hall and found an open door. A small study with some ledgers on a big desk beckoned, and the window overlooked St. James' Park. If not for the spectacle of fireworks, the room would be shrouded in darkness. She probably should not tarry too long. The thud of footsteps made her pause.

She turned abruptly to face the door.

Adam stood there, filling the space as if daring it to contain him. His silhouette was sharp against the glow of firework flares—brilliant reds, greens, and golds flickering over his face. His eyes gleamed, catching the light like chips of amber, and something about the way he stared at her made her breath seize.

"Spectacular view this evening," he said.

"Oh, the fireworks, yes." Charlene didn't dare meet his eyes.

"No, you."

Her stomach did something and her palms grew clammy.

"Silly to think that gunpowder is part of a celebration, considering it was the problem to begin with," he said with that maddening calm, his voice carrying easily over the next crack.

"Ironic, isn't it? Almost an homage to Guy Fawkes rather than a criticism of his shortcomings."

Adam stepped farther into the room, closing the door softly behind him. "So you don't think we're celebrating the escape? We're admiring the attempt, are we? How interesting."

"Only you would find much of my thoughts interesting," she said archly, though the corners of her mouth twitched upward despite her heart-pulsing state.

He'd followed her.

You had hoped he would, her inner voice whispered.

His eyes crinkled with humor, and he stepped closer. "Or perhaps you're too clever for the others."

"Tell me, though," he said softly. "Why do you think this odd mix of powders is so celebrated?"

Charlene tried to ignore how close he was. "Because they're harmless here, I suppose. Pretty in the sky. Predictable, tidy explosions. Nothing unpredictable. Except," she paused, eyeing him, "perhaps when men are involved."

"Are we still talking about gunpowder?" Adam's grin widened. "And here I thought you'd credit the salts."

"The salts?"

"Yes," he said, leaning even closer, his voice dropping slightly. "They're what give those pretty, tidy explosions their color. Without them, all you'd have is dull flashes of white and gray." His fingers idly brushed the desk's edge. "A pinch of strontium makes red, barium makes green, sodium makes yellow. Simple, when you think about it."

"And you know this why?" Charlene retorted.

Adam smirked. "Because I was a boy once. Science was… useful for mischief. And such knowledge is always useful in foreign lands."

"I would never have guessed," Charlene said, her tone dry.

"About the mischief? I rather think you enjoy my mischief," he said, his voice teasing now, edging farther into her space. His words hung in the charged air between them. She could feel the faintest warmth from him, and her breath caught as his eyes flicked to hers.

Another burst of light filled the room—green this time—and the duke smiled again, softer this time, as if he were just as aware of how close they were.

"Why are you standing so close?" she asked, her voice quieter, though firm, refusing to back down even as her pulse clawed for attention.

"Because," he said, his tone low, "you haven't asked me to leave. Neither have you run."

His eyes bored into hers, and she couldn't look away—she didn't want to. Lord, her heart pounded so furiously in her chest that she half-worried he might hear it.

"I thought you lost interest in teaching me to dance," Charlene muttered.

"I'd never lose interest in you. And even though I'd love to dance, this moment calls for something else, Lady Charlene."

"Just Charlene. We're alone, Adam. Just call me—"

"*Charlene.*"

"You were away for a long time. Without a word."

He tilted his head. "What?"

Her eyes locked with his.

And there, he saw something other than reproach. That glimmer of magic he'd seen in her eyes before.

Oh, she should really run.

Before Charlene could consider doing so—she wouldn't—Adam closed the inches between them. His lips caught hers, his tongue sweeping into her mouth. Every thought slipped from her mind—words, logic, all of it vanished.

Oh dear!

A PROTEST SHOULD have formed, some logical rebuttal against this madness, but none came. Instead, she wound her arms around his neck to steady herself. Or was it to lean into the kiss? Both, perhaps. Both, most certainly. His hands found her waist, pulling her close, and she took that as an invitation to lean into him. He tasted of something unmistakably, maddeningly him even though they had never kissed before. She tasted him in a way she hadn't expected—a faint trace of mint, the undercurrent of some type of brandy—rich and warm. It was strange but intoxicating, and her head felt light.

Charlene trembled as his mouth moved against hers, unhurried but purposeful. The friction, soft but steady, sent ripples up her spine. And behind her, somewhere, the fireworks blasted into the air as if they tried to shine as brightly as the feeling blooming in her chest.

She didn't know if she was doing it right. The kiss was a language she had never spoken, but she wanted to learn, wanted to understand every word, so she mirrored as best she could. The sensation deepened even more, if that were at all possible. A spark ignited—sharp and startling—and a soft gasp broke free, though she wasn't sure if it came from her or him.

Adam's hands shifted slightly. One moved from her waist to her lower back, while the other hand brushed the curve of her jaw. His thumb made the lightest pass over her cheek, and she leaned into the touch without thinking, feeling her breath quicken. His hand on her back pressed slightly, holding her as if he feared she might slip away.

I'm kissing Adam.

Of all the things she thought she'd ever do, this never even reached her list! It was so... so... unexpected it almost felt as though she had entered a dream. Were all kisses like this? This deep? This exploratory? The man kissed her as though tasting her, as though he had all the time in the world to learn the shape of her mouth.

Charlene's head swirled with sensation. She felt everything in sharp relief—the pull of his lips, the slight intake of his breath, the charge from where they touched. Her pulse raced, her body humming with some unfamiliar, thrilling spark that made her toes curl. It was a collision of want and recklessness, a breathless unraveling that left no room for sense or second thoughts.

No room for doubt.

Only want.

Her hands wound around his neck, drew to his chest, her fingers brushing the fabric of his coat. The wool was smooth under her touch, and she gripped it, pulling him closer. And she realized, with no small shock, just how much she didn't want this to end.

And just like that, he broke the kiss.

He eased back, enough to breathe, her eyes fluttering open. Her lips felt flushed, tingling from his kiss, her senses racing to catch up.

"Charlene," he murmured, his voice rough, almost hoarse. Her name on his lips sent a shiver skimming down her spine. "I don't know what happened, but I did send you a note before I left. I don't know why it didn't reach you."

He did? She could tell he wasn't lying. Tension seeped from her body. So, he had sent a note but it hadn't reached her? She shouldn't be feeling so relieved, but she was. She couldn't even summon words—none seemed adequate. Instead, her lips curved faintly, and her fingers stayed curled against his coat. Whatever this was, whatever came next, she only knew one thing.

She didn't want it to stop.

Which was exactly why it had to.

Chapter Twelve

THE NEXT MORNING, Charlene had no appetite. Nor thirst. She stared at the cup and saucer on the small table in her parlor.

The tea had cooled in Charlene's cup, though she held it steady, vainly pretending to sip. Instead, she stared into the soft amber liquid, her mind tangled and heavy. The pressure of her teacup's delicate handle reassured her fingers, but her thoughts were far from orderly.

The kiss.

She could still feel it, could still summon the faint warmth of his lips against hers.

Adam Cross.

She barely needed to close her eyes to remember how he'd looked at her, how the world had gone achingly quiet in that single moment despite the blasting cracks of the fireworks outside. It was the light inside her chest that he'd kindled, and it brightened her every thought—even though it shouldn't.

Because he was a Cross, of course.

No, Char, rein your nerves in, it couldn't have been that good a kiss.

And yet, it was.

"Charlene. Did you hear me?" Ashley broke through her thoughts.

"Yes, yes." Charlene blinked and looked up.

Ashley sighed and set her cup down with an air of exasperation. She leaned forward, the light catching the small emerald ring on her left hand—Thomas's most recent token of affection. "Honestly, my dear, you've been away in your thoughts since you arrived. I was simply asking what on earth has you so distracted?"

"She's been distracted since she walked in." Maddie arched one brow, her eyes faintly narrowed. "It's quite the sight to witness, since you are usually so clear-headed."

Charlene sighed. Both women watched her expectantly, and Charlene realized there would be no slipping past their inquisition today. "If you must know, I... kissed him," she said bluntly. Her hand lifted to her mouth as if she could catch the memory of the kiss.

Ashley's face split into a wide, delighted grin, and she clapped her hands softly, barely managing to contain herself. "Oh, that's utterly smashing! I told you there was something between you and that duke of yours."

"He's not mine," Charlene snapped, her face heating.

Maddie's lips pressed thin. "You kissed him?" Her voice dropped low, as though the very notion might summon scandal to the room like a ghostly specter. "How improper. What could have possessed you to allow such a thing?"

"Possessed me?" Charlene sat up straighter, the heat on her cheeks now prickling into irritation. *I wish he possessed me as I wish to possess him, but that's unfortunately not the case.* "I don't know. It simply... happened. He was there, and then suddenly..."

Ashley leaned closer, her eyes alight with interest. "Did you like it?"

"That's hardly the question she ought to answer," Maddie interrupted, looking between the two of them as if scandal might burst through the door at any moment. "What matters is what will be done about it."

Ashley waved her hand dismissively. "Oh, Maddie, don't be

such a bore. She liked it—I can see it written all over her face. Didn't you, Charlene?"

Charlene opened her mouth, but the words couldn't seem to come. Did she like it? Yes. No. Perhaps. Could she admit how much she'd liked it, even to herself? "It doesn't matter. It was a mistake. All of it."

Ashley leaned back, blowing out a breath. "He's kissed you once. I'd wager my emeralds he plans to do it again."

Maddie's eyes widened in horror. "You cannot encourage this! She'll be compromised! Like you almost were! Like Sera almost was!"

"Keyword, almost," Ashley muttered.

Maddie pushed her chair back and stood, walking with her usual precise steps to the writing desk in the corner of the room. Charlene's brows furrowed as Maddie, the picture of propriety, opened a drawer and retrieved a slim, well-worn book bound in faded green leather.

Maddie's cheeks flushed the faintest pink as she turned back to the group, the book clutched tightly to her chest. "If we're to discuss such impropriety," she said primly, though her voice faltered just slightly, "Did you consult the handbook?"

Charlene's breath caught. Not that book. The one whispered about among her friends, passed along with furtive glances when they were alone. A compendium of advice, as it was euphemistically called, though everyone knew it to be far more daring.

"The book doesn't know everything." Ashley waved grandly in the air as if she didn't need any advice.

"And yet there is a section on kissing, isn't there?" Maddie said almost proudly as though she'd found the only collection of maps to matrimony, even though the book was something else entirely.

"Well, I never needed the book to know how to kiss Thomas," Ashley said.

But I don't know what to do about Adam. "What does it say indeed?" Charlene pressed on.

Maddie was already rifling through the pages. "Let me find a passage that suits the facts. Fans... balls... masquerades... neighbors... ah!" She turned the open page over to Charlene. "Kisses!"

> *A kiss is no trifling matter for a lady. It signifies courtship, a binding promise of intent, and, in most cases, a scandal of the highest order. Such an act, even in private, is fraught with peril and must be approached with the utmost caution or not at all until after an engagement is secured. To steal away for such an intimate gesture is a bold and reckless endeavor, one that may ignite the fires of gossip or, worse still, lead to legal repercussions should the union fail to materialize.*
>
> *~ Handbook on Seduction and Matters of the Heart*

"So don't do it!" Maddie poked at the book as if it laid down a law she'd obey at all cost.

Charlene pinched her lips into a flat line. "It says caution—"

"Courtship. Engagement. Scandal. That's what I read." Maddie nodded gravely.

And Charlene didn't know what to say. It was too late now. And honestly, courtship, engagement, and all that wasn't so scary if Adam was in the picture.

"I agree with that pause," Ashley chirped. "I encourage love, dear Maddie. Forget the book, Char. Follow your heart."

There was nothing to follow! What did her heart know? Cross brothers were scandal, warnings, and ruin. But Adam was a temptation. She wanted to do what Ashley suggested; she just didn't know if it was her heart she was heeding. Or something else.

"And a lady waits to be followed in this book." Maddie opened it to what seemed a random page and handed it to Charlene. "Take a look if there's a cure for your ailment or else I'll go to the apothecary for you."

Adam followed her. And then he kissed her.

Charlene sat frozen under their watchful gazes. "I don't want a cure!"

"Oh, so you do like him!" Ashley clapped and smiled with the knowing way of a blushing bride-to-be madly in love.

She wasn't!

But... Something had changed. Charlene knew that much even though she had no words for the way she felt, nor could she look them up in something as grounded and trivial as a book. Cherubs in butterfly wings should let down lovely scrolls of declarations with the fanfare of trumpets to even slightly begin to describe the fireworks Adam had placed in her chest—since the kiss during the fireworks.

What a kiss!

Oh, how confusing everything had become. Still, she hadn't felt like herself since it happened, and some small part of her dreaded and longed for it in equal measure.

The door opened. Charlene exhaled in relief at the distraction and turned to find her brother, Waylon, stepping inside.

Charlene's relief drained away the moment she saw Waylon's face, his mouth pulled into a grim line and a folded piece of paper crushed in his hand. His boots scuffed against the polished floor as he shut the door firmly behind him. "You won't like what I've just discovered," he said, his voice low and weighted as he handed it to her.

Charlene unfolded it and her heart sank as soon as she recognized the header of the M-Press.

At Cavendish House's Guy Fawkes revelry, one scarcely knew where to train their gaze, with the newly betrothed Earl of Linsey and Lady Ashley garnering much attention. Yet, it is not glowing sparks that linger in this observer's mind, but rather the peculiar absence of Lady Charlene Fielding and the Duke of Rotheworth during the fireworks. What pressing matter, one wonders, could draw them from such a spectacle?

Charlene swallowed hard and looked at her brother. There was just a moment that was so intense, panic rose to her throat. Ashley tapped Charlene on the arm and took the paper, skimming it as Waylon seemed to keep up appearances.

"Ladies," he said, inclining his head. His tone was heavy, as his olive-green coat caught the muted afternoon light. Behind him, a stranger followed. A young man, clean-shaven and impossibly poised. His light hair was cut crisp, and his well-fitted coat suggested wealth—but it was the effortless ease of his smile that softened the space between them. Why did he seem familiar?

"This is Henry Grafton," Waylon said. "A friend from Oxford. He's to stay with us for the week." Her brother turned to her. Waylon spoke politely but Charlene knew that it didn't escape him when Maddie now took the M-Press paper from Ashley and gasped. "I trust you'll make him feel welcome," Waylon added.

He trusted her to do what? What exactly did he mean by that?

Waylon, you are dead.

"How can they write this? How did they even know?" Maddie said, folding the paper nervously into quarters, eighths, six-teenths, and then just a package of what it was—rubbish and bad news.

Henry stepped forward and bowed with deliberate politeness, his gaze landing on Charlene. "Lady Charlene," he murmured, "an honor to make your acquaintance."

Oh the voice!

Charlene recognized it from the masquerade ball.

"I reckon you don't pay much heed to gossip. For neither do I." Mr. Grafton bowed and Charlene did as custom demanded—held out her hand and let him place a kiss on her knuckles.

It was respect. Formality.

Nothing like when she touched Adam and her veins heated with longing.

Charlene rose, her movements faltering as her brother's friend's attention shifted to the book she carried. His gaze, unpressed but curious, lingered on the faded brown leather cover. Maddie, seemingly unfazed, cleared her throat, retrieved the book, and extended the volume toward the table, but Mr. Grafton tilted his head slightly and read aloud the embossed title as if it were merely an afterthought.

"*Handbook on Matters of Seduction and the Heart*," he said, his voice even, polished, yet far from mocking. A faint smile played at his mouth. "Odd title for a reference book. And yet," he paused meaningfully, glancing at Charlene, "full of promise, I should think."

Charlene flushed when her brother turned his sharp eyes to her, before he said to his friend, clapping him on the shoulder, "Henry, make yourself at home as my guest. I have an engagement I must attend to. I'll return before dinner."

Hah!

"Of course," Mr. Grafton replied, inclining his head. "Your hospitality is already most evident." His eyes flicked back to Charlene, the corner of his mouth curving into something that felt both kind and, dare she say, teasing? "I can see that tea with the ladies will be exceedingly entertaining. Particularly if they're inclined to share such interesting reference materials." He nodded slightly toward the book still clutched in Maddie's hands, who promptly shuffled the book beneath her bottom with an air of forced nonchalance. Despite her outward composure, her cheeks flushed a terrible shade of scarlet, nearly as brilliant as Charlene's own.

"No such materials will be shared, I assure you, Mr. Grafton," Maddie declared, her voice unshakable despite the ludicrous picture she made perched above the incriminating book.

Charlene could barely breathe, her mortification swelling to unbearable heights. Could there possibly be a more laughable moment? Her brother's arms folded across his chest, looking just slightly amused now that he seemed to catch the tail-end of whatever chaos Mr. Grafton's comment had stirred.

"Well, Charlene," Waylon said lightly, "as the lady of the house, I trust you'll continue to extend our hospitality. See that Henry has everything he needs, won't you?" Without waiting for confirmation, he gave a slight bow to the group and left the room.

Waylon!

Heat surged across her face, reaching her temples, and surely it made her appear as crimson as the poppies embroidered on her tea towel. Could anything be worse than this? Not only were her feelings already in a hopeless mess, but now she was to entertain Mr. Grafton, of all people.

Her hands darted to her empty teacup, fingers fumbling at the saucer's edge. She wished desperately for access to a magician's trickery, to dissolve into thin air and retreat unnoticed. Yet here she was, clumsy and exposed in a way she never seemed to be around Adam.

Why was that?

With Adam, somehow, her guard lowered. For some reason, she never felt scrutinized around him, never felt less than herself.

The thought of Adam made her cheeks flush.

While Henry held charm in spades and everyone else in the room seemed enraptured by him, her heart still turned, unbidden, toward the man who truly left her breathless for reasons beyond mere appearances. Adam made her feel steady when all else wavered. How maddening, how utterly maddening…

"Ah, Charlene," Ashley's voice broke in, laced with teasing amusement. "I'm afraid I must depart." She flattened an imaginary wrinkle of her gown. "Maddie, come and I shall escort you home in my carriage." Then she nodded in Charlene's direction with an arched brow. "I suppose it only makes sense. You've a particular flair for hospitality?"

"The book is completely irrelevant," Charlene blurted out, but her words did nothing to abate the laughter that rippled through her small audience. "I'll show you to the dining room; lunch should be served by now."

Maddie, for her part, remained planted firmly on the scandalous tome, her posture so stiff one might mistake her for an immovable statue.

Charlene glanced toward the door, deciding whether to run away or not.

"Shall we go, Mr. Grafton?" she asked, her tone clipped and brisk in hopes of ending this agony swiftly. Ashley and Maddie rose to follow them.

"The honor is mine, Lady Charlene," he said with such unassailable politeness.

And as Charlene led him to the dining room, her face aflame, her thoughts betrayed her once again, circling back to Adam. How was it possible to miss someone so acutely? How was it possible that a simple memory of him could outshine all else? Whatever charm Mr. Grafton held, Adam had already captured her attention in his quiet, unassuming way. There was no uncapturing it. For the moment, at least.

But then Ashley tugged Maddie's arm and they stayed back.

"Charlene, we must take the carriage." Ashley gave a meaningful nod. "Maddie just reminded me that we need to purchase more ribbon for the invitations."

Maddie nodded vigorously.

Oh, please!

"You really ought to stay," Maddie added primly, though her lips twitched as if fighting a smile. "It's only proper that you do as hostess. We, however, must take our leave."

"I hardly think he requires more than my hospitality," Charlene muttered weakly, wishing with every fiber of her being for the earth to simply swallow her whole. Yet the others, evidently delighted by the notion, paid her protests no mind.

"Nonsense," Ashley chimed in. "You must stay." Her laughter, light and musical, draped easily across the room, only deepening Charlene's humiliation.

"I would be honored to have luncheon with just you," Mr. Grafton interjected smoothly, his tone so perfectly genteel it only worsened Charlene's plight. His gaze, steady and warm, met hers briefly. "Lady Charlene, if you'll be so kind." As expected of any well-mannered guest, he offered a slight bow, though the twinkle in his eye suggested he hadn't missed the chaos of implication surrounding them.

But all she could think of was how she wished she could see Adam again.

FOR BETTER OR worse, Charlene Fielding had claimed his thoughts. No amount of duty, however pressing, could distract him from that truth.

Adam swung open the broad, iron-bound door of the family estate, his every step echoing with restraint as he sought to keep his balance—not physically, but emotionally. The memory of Charlene, warm and vivid, tangled with the calm that had momentarily settled over him after kissing her. Her startled eyes, the soft press of her lips... Such thoughts could undo a man. He was certain it already had.

"¡Adam! Por fin!"

His musings were jolted by his mother's voice. She moved toward him, her jewel-toned skirts swishing unhurriedly but purposefully. Her arms opened wide, as if he were still a small boy returning from a romp in the fields instead of a grown man wishing to escape further chaos.

"Mother," he greeted evenly, stepping forward to drop a kiss on her offered cheek, braced for the way she would firmly grasp his shoulders and beam up at him with both pride and impatience. Carmen Cross, formidable in stature despite her shorter height, held him in place for a beat too long, her dark eyes narrowing as though seeking something unspoken.

"Hijo," she said dramatically, as was her way, "you look too thin. You've been working yourself to stone. No one will marry a statue, Adam! Have you even eaten today? You must sit and take chocolate with us."

Before he could muster a reply, she turned and clapped her hands sharply, startling a footman who had frozen mid-bow. "You! Go and see that our excellent cook prepares something for Adam. Now." She turned to a lady in a burgundy gown and gave an indulgent smile. "We've had the same cook for over twenty years, and she truly knows our ways."

"I assure you, Mother, I'm well," Adam managed, even as a kitchen maid rushed past with a tray clearly pilfered from the tea table.

"Well?" she repeated, tossing her hands in exasperation. "This is British modesty nonsense. Bah! Look at him." She gestured to no one in particular, as though seeking confirmation from the walls themselves. "Fine. Fine! He doesn't see what a sorry sight he is. Good thing Miss Martin has arrived to visit you. She will see to your entertainment, I'm sure."

"Miss Martin?" Adam repeated with a frown, just as an un-mistakable whirlwind of lilac and lace stepped into view.

"Oh, Adam!" a girl chirped after she rounded the corner, clearly summoned on cue. Her blonde hair was impossibly coiffed, bouncing as though even her curls sought attention. She made her approach as if on a carefully choreographed stage, hands clutching skirts that barely needed adjustment.

Adam stiffened, his patience fraying even before she spoke. Oh. Lorena Martínez was Miss Martin in England. How very flexible her name was, Adam thought. Judging by her looks, she was flexible in other ways, too. And in the ways David would enjoy but the ways Adam would fear—flexible morals usually meant trouble. And when it was his brother... that was particular-ly disastrous.

A distant, supremely distant cousin of his. He'd almost forgot-ten about this branch of the family. His late father certainly had tried to forget them, and Adam began to understand why.

"How you've changed since I last saw you. We were what... fourteen? Your mother has been so gracious to invite me to stay," Miss Martin said, sweeping toward him with a kind of feigned demureness that grated on every nerve he owned. "But, Adam, don't you think it's about time you considered settling down?"

He flinched at her continued use of his name. "Excuse me?" he muttered, caught between confusion and outright annoyance.

"You really ought to, you know," she said brightly, stepping closer. "You're quite the eligible duke, and, well, I do believe a man should marry someone acquainted with his ways. Someone who understands his family."

Behind her, his mother clasped her hands in agreement and said something under her breath in Spanish that Adam couldn't hear but knew would not help matters.

"I see you've all been very busy in my absence," Adam said slowly, keeping his tone polite. "I find myself in need of some fresh air before this enlightening conversation continues. If you'll excuse me."

"Nonsense!" Miss Martin piped up, but his mother cut her off with a roll of her wrist and a sharp "*Déjalo*. Leave him. He is being impossible."

Adam bowed stiffly and stepped away as Miss Martin made an exaggerated little sigh behind him. Once outside, the cool air braced him, though it did little to untangle the slow burn of frustration that had begun in his chest. He couldn't stomach the spectacle of orchestrated family interference any longer and needed the clarity that only town business might provide.

Charlene's laughter echoed faintly in his mind, offering a momentary respite, but even her memory couldn't fully soothe him.

He wanted to see her. Feel her. Kiss her.

Work. Duties. Yes, he decided a distraction pertaining to his legacy was the best way to handle the chaotic women at home and the chaos the one he couldn't bring home caused inside him.

Once Adam managed to extricate himself as politely as he could from the fangs Miss Martin had on his home, he walked to his barrister's office. Time to be duke again. For at home, with his mother and her new guest, he was little more than marriage material.

But it made no sense. His heart belonged to Charlene, and he'd never marry anyone else.

It was a long walk, but after nearly an hour had passed, the brisk walk through the cool autumn air had cooled his nerves slightly.

When he arrived, the Inner Temple with all its old legal traditions exuded a centuries-old solemnity similar to the quad at Oxford—a weight of tradition that pressed down on Adam as he crossed the cobbled pathway leading to the office. His gaze swept over the view. In the background, the River Thames murmured faintly, its current steady and deliberate, contrasting with the bustling voices of merchants and hawkers from the strand. The late afternoon sun broke lazily through a patchwork of gray clouds, casting long, slanted shadows across the courtyard's tidy gravel paths. A few stately trees stood at its center, their edges tinged with the fiery hues of autumn. Leaves stirred in the crisp air, drifting lazily down to settle at the roots.

Distinguished.

Calming.

Inside the barrister's building, a creak from the heavy oak door announced his arrival, joined almost immediately by the soft groan of the wooden planks beneath his heels. The space was narrow, the low beams overhead making one feel uncomfortably large, though Adam had been in enough offices like this to know it bore no ill intention.

The smell of parchment mixed with faint traces of damp stone and old coffee seemed to linger perpetually here, as though the very walls held their breath around the ebb and flow of all sorts of life and death matters. It reminded him of the day after his father's death.

His barrister himself matched this flow.

The man was somber, his desk swathed in papers that looked to have grown roots in the dark wood surface. Behind him, row after row of ledgers lined the shelves, their spines varying in shades of brown and gray, embossed titles faded almost to obscurity. A single window at the far end of the room barely allowed a threadbare shaft of light to filter through. Adam noticed how it landed softly, almost tenderly, on the edge of the desk, illuminating a small inkpot and the sharp, gleaming nib of a quill. A small bit of life in an otherwise dreary place. Much like Charlene.

He was reminded of her even here.

He said little to the clerk who guided him in, his thoughts already wheeling toward business. After all, routine formalities offered their comfort. Distance was useful when his every nerve felt exposed, and repetition steadied him as no human connection could at that moment.

"Your Grace, what brings you here at this hour? Did I not address all of your questions satisfactorily?"

"Good afternoon to you, too. How unusual the tone even for you, Hartford." Adam sat in the chair across the barrister where he hadn't sat since the week his father had died. "Mr. Hartford, I must entrust you with a matter concerning the estate's tenants," Adam said, his tone measured but authoritative. "Have you collected the rents owed for this quarter? I would have managed the task myself, yet pressing business has called me elsewhere as I am only beginning to learn how to manage the estate."

The barrister inclined his head respectfully, his hands resting atop the neatly ordered ledgers on his desk. "Of course, I have seen to the matter personally. And as I already told you, it's all been carefully accounted for."

"Told me?" Adam felt a familiar tension in his stomach but didn't dare think the thought to end.

"Yes, and I ensured each payment is accounted for precisely and recorded against the tenants' leases. The ledger must be immaculate, as inaccuracies would serve neither tenant nor landlord." The barrister narrowed his eyes.

"Agreed," Adam said.

"Indeed, sir," the barrister assured him. "I shall carry out the task with the utmost diligence."

"As you always have, Hartford."

"Correct."

Silence stretched for what felt like eternity but was probably less than a minute. "So why have you come back today?"

"Back? When was I—"

Oh no! Please no!

Adam nodded curtly, adjusting the cuff of his coat as though the movement steadied his thoughts. "I am relying upon your discretion in this matter, Mr. Hartford. It would reflect poorly on all parties, were the matter to invite unnecessary speculation but are you unwell?"

"You have my word," the barrister said solemnly, "I'm healthy and well. Sober too."

With that, Adam inclined his head slightly, the faintest hint of trust bestowed. "Very well. Then why are you asking why I was back?" Adam had to ask even though he already knew the answer. Sometimes, one's worst nightmare seemed a little less true if it was spoken by another person.

"The collection was already sorted this morning," the barrister said, his voice meticulous as he set a ledger to one side. The man spoke as though every syllable were balanced carefully over an abyss, unwilling to tip too far toward error.

Adam halted mid-motion, his fingers still tugging lightly on one glove. The air seemed to shift, a subtle squeezing sensation around the chest that sharpened his focus. His words, low and deliberate, carried the faintest edge of disbelief. "The collection?"

"Yes," the barrister replied, seemingly oblivious to Adam's stillness. "You came earlier. The receipt is signed, and the tenant rents noted as received. Most efficient."

Behind Adam, the soft chime of a distant church bell drifted through the room, blending seamlessly with the muffled cadence of cartwheels rattling over cobblestones. He barely noticed. His attention had narrowed to the ledgers stacked on the desk, the barrister's ink-stained fingers flipping to a precise page with smooth precision. Every creak of the building seemed louder in that moment, as though the wooden skeleton of the office itself waited for his response.

Adam leaned closer to examine the record, but his chest

tightened at the sight. There it was, his name sketched in ink—but he recognized the exaggerated flourish to the 'A' as vividly as if it had been seared into his mind. His brother had signed the receipt, his hand unmistakable despite the pretended impersonation. The room, so small, so crowded with papers, now seemed impossibly large and hollow, the burden of realizing the betrayal filling every inch of space. Even the radiance of the small courtyard, visible just beyond the window, seemed dimmed by the sudden weight pressing on Adam's shoulders.

Adam's jaw clenched. "There's been a mistake," he said, barely containing his ire. "This receipt was not signed by me."

The barrister blinked, then leaned forward. "Would you like me to alert the authorities?"

"No," Adam said firmly, his voice sharp. "This is… a family matter. Leave it with me."

By the time he arrived home again, his head was a storm of thoughts colliding against one another. The betrayal amplified with each step. What was his brother playing at? And worse, as Charlene's image surfaced once more, a sinking guilt clawed at him. Should he warn her? She deserved to know. But what came of pointing out her vulnerability when Adam had failed to protect her regard for him by tolerating this scandal within his own family?

Over the uproar of Lorena's arrival and his mother's sharp directives to the household staff, Adam resolved to keep this to himself, at least for now. Life was complicated enough without adding another thread of chaos. For better or worse, Charlene deserved that much. But even as he made peace with his silence, the weight of it pressed on his chest, burying itself deeper with every unspoken truth.

Chapter Thirteen

CHARLENE HAD SPENT the better part of an hour debating whether she ought to attend the St. James's ball or not. She'd come. Then, after arriving, she spent the better half of the next hour debating whether she had made the right choice and whether she should leave. She stayed. It was rather vexing how on the one hand she didn't want to come, on the other hand she couldn't stay away.

She should have stayed home and pruned a plant.

But she had to admit, the Bennetts have outdone themselves. Candles were placed everywhere. It all looked so romantic when she first glimpsed it, her heart couldn't help but skip a beat. As for the rest, the music, the dancing, the laughter, while it all brought the scene to a pretty picture, Charlene couldn't muster up the energy to enjoy the beauty.

"Is he here?" Charlene asked and glanced at Maddie tapping her foot to the beat of the music. She, at least, was enjoying herself. Charlene wasn't even certain Adam would attend. However, she had hoped that if she attended, he would, too.

"I can't see him yet," Maddie said with an air as if she didn't have a care in the world. Well, typical Maddie, wasn't it? There was hardly a problem she couldn't cure with one of her potions, tinctures, or salves.

Maddie suddenly leaned in. "You look like you've swallowed an entire tray of lemon tarts. Try to smile."

Charlene let out a breathy laugh and flashed a short smile. "Is that good or bad?" She loved lemon tarts. However, too much could give a girl a rush, like a certain duke.

"I cannot say. It's a rather uncomfortable expression."

Charlene schooled her features. "How about now?"

"Not better."

She glared at her friend. "You are not helping, you know."

Maddie chuckled. "I didn't mean to help; I meant to point out. You have to appear where you might if he's not calling on you. You read it in the handbook, didn't you?"

Yes. Charlene exhaled and slumped her shoulders. "Well, this is all because of Rotheworth, isn't it?" Maddie stretched her spine to remind Charlene to mind her posture.

"You've set your cap on him. So the next step is to rein him in."

Charlene sighed. "I don't know how to face him, honestly."

"Then don't. Dance, drink punch, and pretend you don't see him and feel him approaching you."

Charlene suppressed the urge to put her hand on her forehead in despair, but the sentiment was no less heartfelt. "Does the handbook teach you everything in life?"

"Much of it, not everything. I have a few other books on alchemy, botany—"

Charlene groaned and stopped listening.

"Patience, however, is not something I can administer, dear. You've got to practice the skill yourself." Maddie nodded in the direction of some other guests she seemed to know. "You have no other choice as a lady."

Patience. A good suggestion, but a futile one. She was afraid she wouldn't be able to help herself, just as he couldn't seem to help himself. Was it all hopeless? She followed the movement of the dancers with her eyes, recalling their first dance all those weeks ago.

How had they looked to the people watching them dance? The society papers had certainly noticed. Probably like the most awkward pair. Certainly not all smiles with the orchestra playing the kind of song that made one believe in second chances. But everything had started with that dance.

Would everything end with dance, too?

Maddie sighed dramatically. "You are making this far more complicated than it needs to be."

Charlene arched her brow. "Am I?" She didn't think so. It was all rather complicated from the start, wasn't it? With that man being his brother. It was a memory she had buried deep, and so far, with Adam returning, the memory had still remained neatly tucked away. But for how long?

"Yes. He is a man, not a mythological hero."

Charlene scoffed. "You say that, but you have never tried to have a sensible conversation with him."

Maddie tapped her chin. "That is true. I imagine it must be terribly difficult when one is too busy gazing longingly at him instead."

"I do not gaze longingly at him."

Maddie shot her a look.

Charlene crossed her arms. "Fine. Perhaps I have gazed. Once or twice. By accident." Liar, liar.

Maddie grinned. "Of course. Just as I once ate an entire plate of biscuits by accident. Those things do happen."

Charlene gave her a flat look. "Yes, they do happen."

"I am sure." Maddie twirled her fan idly. "So what exactly is your plan? Lurk in the corner all night, hoping he does not see you? Hoping he does?"

"The former is an excellent plan." Honestly, Charlene didn't know what to do. She didn't know how to act. But most vexingly, she didn't know what she wanted. *You do,* a little voice whispered.

You want him in all those ways the handbook forbids.

Did she?

Perhaps.

Maybe.

Yes.

No.

All right, she might as well admit she did want him. The realization of that didn't particularly shock her, but what that meant for her future did.

What did one do with a man like Adam Cross, Duke of Rotheworth?

His dark eyes swam in her mind. He wasn't a man who could be forgotten once he burrowed into your head. He was stubborn and sharp and maddeningly confident. And those eyes—she swore he saw through her every single time. And let's not forget that smile. It had the power to rob her of her name, let alone her common sense.

And worse—he knew it.

She wouldn't believe otherwise.

She wanted him, yes, but she also wanted her peace, dignity, and the ability to hold on to the self she had so carefully stitched together these past few years.

And yet...

How did one reconcile desire with defense? How did one fall and still hope to land on her feet? She didn't rightly know. And perhaps she didn't need to know. Not right now.

"It is a terrible plan."

Charlene sighed. "Then what do you propose?"

"Simple. You march right up to him, smile sweetly, and say something cutting enough to remind him that you are an intelligent, formidable woman who absolutely does not care that he is here."

Charlene pursed her lips. "That is remarkably specific."

"I have given this much thought."

"I can see as much."

Maddie tilted her head. "Or you could simply admit you are hopelessly in love with him and throw yourself into his arms."

Charlene nearly choked. She looked at her friend incredulously. "Have you been drinking too much ratafia?"

Maddie grinned. "Not yet. But there's still time." Nothing else was happening at this ball.

Charlene shook her head, but despite herself, she was smiling.

And then she felt it. The shift in the air, the awareness prickling along her skin.

And then—there he was.

Adam stood across the room, tall and devastating, with a… with a… Charlene's blood ran cold. He stood with a woman on his arm. A woman who was smiling up at him as though he were her world.

Ah, arrogance. It had felt good earlier. It didn't feel so good now.

As if sensing her gaze, he turned. Their eyes met.

Charlene's breath caught.

And he didn't look away.

ADAM ENTERED THE ballroom with all the enthusiasm of a man marching to the Tower of London. It certainly felt like his execution. And the person leading him had the grip of a hangman as Miss Martin clung on his arm with the familiarity of a woman who had clearly decided she was already his betrothed, while his mother followed a step behind, smug with victory.

I need to get away from them.

They might as well have announced their intentions to the whole world.

Needless to say, annoyance was the mood of the evening.

He had tried everything to escape this insufferable arrangement, short of being immensely rude, and considering fleeing the bloody country on his ship. His mother, however, was nothing if not persistent, as always.

I just hope Charlene won't be here to see this.

Now he'd almost been blinded by the sheer light of the ball-room. Why did they have to use a thousand candles? The air was thick with candle wax. And perfume. The combination assaulted his senses as much as the crowd, and he truly wanted to be anywhere else. Even a mathematics exam at Oxford would be more enjoyable than this ball.

"Will you dance?" Miss Martin asked him with a bright smile.

"No." *Certainly not with you.*

Only with Charlene.

The thought formed before he could stop it, as natural as breathing. He had no interest in dancing with anyone but his Charlene. Just the idea of other women—Miss Martin—their smiles, their hopeful expressions, none of it touched him. In fact, it bothered him for he already felt as though he belonged to Charlene.

"Oh, but I already put your name on my dance card."

Also, Adam realized as she held it up to him, his name was there more than three times. A wedding announcement in the *Times* couldn't be any more conspicuous. "Miss Martin, I'm not playing your games. Neither am I in the mood to dance."

"Oh, stop it, Rotheworth," his mother said with a touch of exasperation. "Dance with her. The girl, Adam. You practically grew up dancing together, did you not?"

Yes, and no. Those childhood days felt like a distant echo of no significance. They were both adults now. Things were decidedly… different. And then there was Charlene. But he did not tell his mother that. It would only stir memories that were best left undisturbed, memories tied irrevocably to his brother that he didn't wish to burden his mother with. She'd only just come out of mourning and the one good thing about Miss Martin was that she'd led Mother to the first ball since Father's passing. And he did not want to think about that scoundrel twin brother of his, not tonight. What he had unearthed at the barrister's office lingered like a dark cloud over him, but until it solidified into a storm, there was no point in troubling anyone. It was his problem to handle as duke.

Yet, should he warn Charlene?

The thought darted through his mind before he quickly banished it. No. Not yet, not until he had something concrete. To broach it prematurely would only send her guard up, and he needed her guard down. He was uncomfortably aware of how selfish that seemed, but he had only one chance to set things right.

Adam's thoughts trailed to the paper. He'd carried the apology with him all year and still hadn't delivered it. Unless he did, he didn't dare woo her. He didn't dare ask for her father's permission. And if that brother of hers found out that he'd already kissed her, he'd probably demand to duel him.

Thus, if he misstepped, if he erred in this delicate matter, the chance to win her family's trust, to truly gain her favor, might vanish forever. And the newly found trust between them was fragile. The specter of his brother's misdeeds whispered at the edges of his thoughts, an intrusion both unwelcome and inescapable for they threatened to shatter it all.

Miss Martin's laugh cut through his reverie, light but brittle, an attempt at charm that only grated against his nerves. Charlene's laugh was different, softer and more sincere, with a lilt that lingered. Without meaning to, his gaze raked idly over the gathering when, suddenly, he saw her.

She was half-turned, the pearls at her throat catching the candlelight as she tipped her head in response to some jest he could not hear.

Charlene.

The sight of her, so composed yet achingly vibrant, hit like a blow he should have braced for but hadn't. Everything stilled inside him. For an instant, the room fell away, the clamor of the crowd dissolving until there was only her. She wore an emerald-green gown that would have paled on anyone else, but on her, it glowed, a perfect match for the hue of her sharp, perceptive eyes.

His pulse lurched against his will.

Even from across the room, it was clear she knew precisely how many sets of eyes were wandering too long in her direction. She did not so much as blink under the attention. Present, yet always apart. This was Charlene.

"You're so dreadfully serious this evening, Adam," Miss Martin said with another feeble attempt at flirtation.

"Call me Rotheworth," he replied absently, still watching Charlene.

"Why?" she pouted. "That's so formal."

"It is proper," he returned coolly, finally dragging his eyes away. "Which I prefer." With you.

"Honestly, Adam," his mother snapped with impatience. "A dance is not a proposal. One would think you were being dragged to the gallows, not the ballroom."

She put my name down without my permission. Four times! How is that fair warning?

He resisted the urge to agree, as it wasn't far from the truth. Their plans thrummed like alarm bells in his head, and the way Miss Martin's gloved fingers tightened on his arm as though fearing escape only solidified his decision.

Smart woman. He just might run away from her.

But always toward Charlene.

No, he most certainly would.

"You are not at the gallows," he muttered when his mother arched a brow. "Is dragging me around like a prize bull with Miss Martin truly the method you think best?"

"I want what is best for this family," she said off-handedly. "And it certainly isn't spending the evening glowering in corners while everyone whispers about your brooding. It wouldn't kill you to enjoy yourself."

"It might," he muttered. Not if the reason for his enjoyment wasn't here. But she should be, so he had to get rid of his mother and Miss Martins.

Miss Martin gave another laugh. "If you don't wish to dance, shall we at least take a turn about the room then?"

And then the back of his neck prickled, and his eyes crossed the ballroom, locking with hers. His breath hitched.

Charlene.

She stood near the farthest edges, her chin lifted in that defiant little tilt he knew too well. He couldn't tell what, if anything, flashed in her gaze, but she was still the most beautiful woman in the room. Her gown wasn't the flashiest in the room—but the way the candlelight clung to her curves, the swell of her breasts, her pale neckline… he couldn't breathe.

He couldn't look away.

She didn't smile.

Did she even see him?

She didn't frown either.

Her gaze moved to Miss Martin beside him.

Adam stiffened. He had forgotten about her.

The fingers on his arm suddenly felt like shackles, and he nearly wrenched his arm free. Fortunately, he kept his composure, but Miss Martin's hand still felt like a tentacle that refused to unwrap from him.

Charlene saw them. Of course she did.

And she was still looking.

What was going through her mind?

Did she think that he had chosen this? That he wanted this? That he was willingly paraded like a bull for auction?

Panic flared in his chest. He was going to be sick. Or punch someone. Maybe both. Yes, she must. What else? He didn't know. But his limbs couldn't work. His brain wouldn't work. He tried to step forward, to call her name, to do something—but Miss Martin tugged him closer with that hideous grip, and he inwardly cursed. A foul one.

Charlene's brows lifted—just a fraction—but it was enough.

She turned away.

No.

Not again.

He would not lose her to a misunderstanding. Not after everything. Not now.

He didn't care if he pulled his arm from Miss Martin's with enough force to startle a gasp from her. He didn't care if the whole damn room watched. He didn't care if the whole world burned.

But it didn't come to that.

Because Charlene suddenly turned back to him, and with chin held high, marched straight toward him.

Chapter Fourteen

CHARLENE WANTED TO walk away. It was certainly what the handbook would urge.

So she didn't.

She didn't know how she felt about what she saw, but—No. She did know. She just didn't know how to explain it. It didn't feel good seeing another woman on Adam's arm. Terrible actually.

And the most baffling part, it was confusing after what he'd said and done. Why this now? Even though they had kissed. None of that changed anything when it came to the root of the problem. In fact, she ought to feel vindicated, if nothing else. It proved her right about him. That roguish blood ran through his veins. The same as with his brother.

But the sight of that woman leaning in, smiling up at him as if she belonged there, felt like a splinter beneath Charlene's skin. It festered with something she didn't want to name. Not jealousy—surely not—but it carried teeth, that feeling. Sharp, unexpected teeth that scraped at her insides and made her throat feel tight.

It was only now that she realized she didn't want to be right. When it came to him, she wanted her mind to be oh, so, very wrong. If only she could follow her heart. Because she didn't want someone else hanging on his arm. She didn't want him to allow such a thing. And perhaps most frightening of all, she didn't want him to ever look away from her.

Because the man she'd glimpsed—the one with both protectiveness and shadows in his eyes—that was the man she wanted to believe in.

So, she did something she never thought she'd do. She turned on her heel and marched up to him. It was the craziest, most brazen, and boldest thing she'd ever done, but she couldn't stop herself. Not even the wide-eyed glance she glimpsed from Maddie was enough to stop her.

Even his eyes widened fractionally.

Good!

She smiled at him. "Rotheworth, what a delightful surprise."

"Lady Charlene."

"Ah, Charlene," his mother stepped up. "It's been ages since we've had a chance to meet."

Yes, my family didn't come to the late duke's funeral because of what David did.

Charlene inclined her head. "I am sorry about my silence all year."

A furrow appeared between the duchess's brows, but that was nothing to the scowl on the woman sticking much too close to his side.

Charlene glanced back at Adam. "My apologies for the intrusion, but I promised you a dance." Just a tiny, big bluff.

"The duke is not dancing tonight," the woman at his side said.

"Oh," the duchess motioned to the woman. "This is Miss Martin. She's a distant relation but a close friend. Miss Martin, this is Lady Charlene Fielding, daughter to the current Earl of Beveridge."

Ah.

So they have history. A faint memory itched in the back of her mind. She believed the brothers had talked about a cousin they grew up with when they were young. So, this was the woman.

"It's a pleasure to meet you, Miss Martin," Charlene greeted, even though she felt the chill of the woman's gaze.

"A pleasure to meet you, too, Lady Charlene."

She doubted that, but Charlene kept her smile in place as she returned her attention to Adam. "Well, since you are not dancing, how about accompanying me for a glass of punch? We can dance another time. I have something to discuss with you anyway."

His lips pinched as though he tried very hard not to grin. Extracting himself from Miss Martin, he nodded at his mother. "Please excuse me. I shall come find you later. Have some fun, Miss Martin. Dance. You, too, Mother."

Charlene didn't miss the two women's looks, but she almost laughed. She placed her hand on Rotheworth's offered arm. When they were out of earshot, she murmured, "So, Miss Martin seems highly interested in you."

"Are you jealous?"

She scoffed. "Hardly. Why would I be jealous?"

He let it go, instead, asking, "Do you truly wish for punch?"

No, that had been the first thing that popped into her head. If she were honest, she wanted to withdraw from this crush, and quite frankly, Miss Martin's blazing gaze which she felt stabbed between her shoulder blades. "I actually thought we might take a stroll in the garden."

"The garden?"

"Well," she said drily. "You do know how I enjoy vegetation."

He laughed. "I believe your preferences are more refined than that."

"I'm not so sure," she tossed back. "Here I am walking with you."

He laughed again, and Charlene couldn't help but be mesmerized. She must have heard this laugh a thousand times before, and quite a few times recently, and yet had it ever sounded like this? So... what would be the word to describe it?

Carefree?

Delighted?

Dazzling?

Perhaps all three?

He shifted their course, steering her with ease toward the tall French doors at the end of the ballroom.

"Everyone will notice," she murmured.

He motioned to Lord Thomson stumbling through the card room, shouting a string of words she couldn't make out. "No one will notice us. Besides, I've learned to be rather stealthy."

"Is that so?" However, now that she thought about it, he wasn't wrong.

The moment they stepped past the threshold and into the night, Charlene released a breath she hadn't realized she'd been holding. Or rather, she had noticed it; she kept it deep within her lungs until the cool air kissed her skin. It was something she'd noticed lately. Her inner denial had become less and less. Oh, there was still plenty of churning about that she didn't care to poke, but with some things, with Adam things, they were shrinking by the moment.

"Shall we?" He motioned to the stone steps leading from the small balcony to the garden.

She inhaled a deep breath before nodding. If there ever was a moment to turn around, this would be it. "Let's."

They descended the stairs slowly, yet a bit faster than normal. Then he said, softly, "Thank you."

She glanced up at him. "For what?"

"For coming to save me. I was one comment away from dancing myself into an early grave."

"I thought you weren't dancing tonight?"

"That was the exception. And you. You are the exception, too."

"You were hardly in distress," she replied, but her lips quirked. "Though I admit, her grip on your arm looked... possessive."

He glanced down at his sleeve, now thankfully free of Miss Martin's talons. "I feared she might leave bruises."

Charlene smothered a laugh. "You poor thing."

"Pity me," he agreed solemnly.

"I wouldn't pity you even if the world came to an end."

"So harsh."

She smiled and looked ahead, toward a stone bench half-hidden in the darkness. "Shall we sit?"

He didn't answer, but the next thing she knew, his hand was at her lower back, guiding her gently toward it.

"Do you think someone will see us?"

He glanced back at the house and then at the bench. "If they can, I doubt they'll be able to make out who we are."

How disappointing.

The thought brought her up short.

Disappointing?

Dear saints, Charlene! You have lost your mind.

And perhaps she had.

She glanced at Adam as they took a seat. And she'd lose it all over again if it meant she could share this bench with him.

ADAM'S HEART HADN'T stopped pounding against his chest since the moment their gazes locked back in the ballroom. Well, it had stopped briefly when she turned away from him but started to race again the moment she turned back and strode right up to him. It hadn't settled since then.

In fact, he thought it couldn't beat louder.

But he was wrong.

Now she was beside him on a bench, so damn beautiful, each beat of his heart an explosion, and he couldn't breathe properly.

Not with her scent in the air. Not with her skirts brushing his legs. Not with the knowledge that no one could see them here.

Not clearly.

This was a mistake.

A big one.

Especially since their kiss. Especially since all he wanted to do was kiss her again. And especially since his heart beat faster and faster, he wasn't sure he'd survive it. He'd traveled to many countries before. But traveling from the ballroom to this bench might have been the most thrilling travel of them all.

It should have terrified him.

Instead, with that one tiny thing of peace in his chest, he felt steady. The most steady he'd felt in weeks.

Charlene Fielding had that effect on him. Always had. Even when they were growing up together. Even now, when she made him feel as though he still had something worth fighting for that didn't have anything to do with duty and estates.

He glanced at her from the corner of his eye, careful not to move too quickly. To act too obviously.

Too late for that, friend.

"You still," he began, trying to steady his voice, "enjoy raising orchids?"

"Raising?" She chuckled, turning her head slowly to him, a soft smile playing at her lips. "I suppose that's right. We do raise plants, do we not?"

He nodded, adjusting his posture on the bench. "I've heard they're finicky little things."

"Orchids certainly," she replied, her voice light. "Some orchids require the utmost attention. You can't water them too much, nor too little. They must be placed in just the right amount of light, and at the perfect temperature, or they won't bloom."

"Much like relationships."

She blinked but then nodded. "Also, true."

Damn it, he shouldn't have said that. Had he ruined the moment? But before he could try to mend it, she spoke again.

"Do you know that some flowers only bloom at night?" she asked.

There were such things? "I didn't."

"They are quite marvelous, being capable of doing that, to only reveal their beauty after dark. It's almost as if they don't want to be seen during the day."

"Indeed," Adam said, leaning a little closer. Just a little, so that their shoulders almost touched. "Perhaps they prefer a little mystery."

"Mystery, eh?" she mused, smiling. "And here I thought flowers had no need for secrets."

A rush of heat filled his chest at the note in her voice, and for a moment, he forgot to breathe.

Both a good rush and a bad one. One that loved her smile and the other wilting because he had a secret.

Tell her.

If there ever was a time, now would be it.

No. He didn't want to ruin the mood of tonight. He'd tell her next time.

"Some of those flowers," he said softly, "must feel quite solitary, blooming only in the dark." Much like them. Except for that first morning before everyone rose, they only ever got together at night, didn't they?

A chuckle joined his thoughts. "I don't think they mind."

Yes, he was reading too much into this flower talk, wasn't he? But there were some things they just couldn't talk about. Some things they didn't dare broach. Perhaps someday they would be able to. Or perhaps they would forever remain locked in the dark, like those secretive flowers.

Adam decided then and there, he wouldn't let it.

"Quite the maudlin conversation we're having," he said with a wry smile, straightening up a bit. "I never knew talk about flowers could go this deep."

Charlene laughed. "I mean, in the world of courtship, every flower has a meaning, so it can go deep."

"Wonderful."

"So, remember that if you ever give Miss Martin a flower."

"Are you cursing me now? Why would you ever bring up that chit in a moment like this?"

She shrugged. "A cautionary note, if you will. One that might prevent misunderstandings."

"Good point." A horrible thought, though, creating a misunderstanding with Miss Martin. Though, there seemed to be one already. Perhaps he should gift her a flower that meant "no."

"I would rather not be reminded of her and my mother's meddling."

"Ah, so your mother is pushing Miss Martin on you?"

"Why else do you think I arrived with her on my arm?" Adam said almost sourly.

"It seems that perhaps you do need a touch of pity."

He flashed her a grin. "Has the world ended, then?"

She stared at him a moment. There was no judgment, no teasing—just a note of contemplation as if she were deciding something. Then, she leaned in. The shift of her body was slow, deliberate, her lips coming toward his, whispering, "Not pity."

"Then what?" he whispered back.

"Comfort."

Comfort? And then her lips pressed up against his. Soft. Pure. Comforting. Every part of Adam's body went hard as a rock. The sensation was so simple, yet so powerful, all he could do was respond in kind, his hand reaching for the back of her neck to pull her closer, to keep her in place, and let his tongue trail over the seam of her lips, begging them to open.

She opened.

Dear heavens, she opened.

He pushed them to the farther, darkened end of the bench as he swept his tongue into her mouth. And he didn't hold back. She had kissed him. Charlene Fielding had kissed him. Kissed him first. Something he had dreamed only about in his deepest dreams but had hoped for beyond hope. And who would have known a comfort kiss could make a man lose his damn mind?

＊

Chapter Fifteen

CHARLENE HAD NEVER felt so alive as in this moment. Oh, there were certainly moments that were breathtakingly thrilling, and most of them with Adam, and she'd also felt alive in those, but in this moment, with this kiss, she felt alive.

In. Every. Sense. Of. The. Word.

A sense she had lost on that fateful night so long ago. Not even when David Cross had pushed himself on her, but afterward, in her bedroom when the shock of it all had died off. And while those senses had returned bit by bit over the years, and with each encounter with Adam, they were rushing back now. Practically exploding. Like the fireworks.

Her hands curled around his lapels.

She dragged him closer, needing—no, craving—more. He tasted like danger, and she found she loved it even more than their first time. A hundred emotions flooded her, but she pushed them all back, allowing only the moment's excitement to exist.

Adam groaned softly, the sound so profoundly deep and masculine it found a home in her bones. The same bones covered by flesh and his hands, which didn't seem content to stay in one place.

Each second that passed, she reclaimed a bit of something back that had been stolen. Her fingers slid from his jacket and into his hair, tugging just enough to make him respond with a growl that only made her bolder.

She gripped tighter.

Another groan.

Lord, she could get addicted to these sounds of him.

He broke the kiss, eyes lifting to lock onto hers. "You are determined to drive me mad, aren't you?"

"What is mad if not mad about a kiss?"

His gaze darkened. "Then I must be raving," he said, his voice a gruff murmur against her lips, "because I haven't thought clearly since the moment I saw you again."

"Do you mean tonight?"

"I mean since I returned to London."

Charlene's breath hitched. "That was weeks ago."

"Yes, but even that doesn't bring any justice to my madness. Try years," he said, the soft stubble of his cheek against hers. "You think I ever forgot you for a second? That I didn't wonder how you were, or if you were keeping safe, or if you ever spared a thought for me."

Charlene didn't know what to say to that or feel about that. "I did spare a thought to you, though," her lips curled slightly, "they were never good thoughts."

"Well, that's a relief."

"I said they were bad thoughts."

"A thought is still a thought."

She laughed. "That desperate?"

"You have no idea, love."

"Desperation has never been a good look on a man, you know."

He shrugged. "Don't I look good now?"

Charlene arched a brow. "You're still desperate?"

"Even more so at this moment." He leaned closer, brushing his lips against hers. "Help me rid me of it, love."

"I don't know how I feel about this sudden endearment."

A rough chuckle. "Just love it, I say."

She huffed. "So incorrigible." She glanced back to the house spilling with light, music, and laughter before glancing back at Adam, saying softly, "I don't trust myself, to be honest. I don't trust this."

"You don't trust me," he whispered back.

"It's not about trusting you or not." This much she knew for a fact. "It's about opening a door that I won't be able to shut."

"And trusting that everything will be fine."

Charlene nodded. "I don't know if everything will be fine." Not while his brother was the very reason for the most hurt she'd experienced in her life. She certainly didn't want to experience it again, and while Adam would never hurt her in that way, it didn't mean she wouldn't get hurt.

He leaned in, his forehead resting against hers. "I don't want you to kiss me like that and pretend it means nothing. That's my biggest fear."

"Oh, it's the biggest?"

His eyes bored into hers. "At the moment, yes."

"Well, I'm not pretending at the moment," Charlene said softly. Tomorrow might be another story.

His thumb brushed her bottom lip. "Then kiss me again. No ghosts, no regrets. Just us."

She thought she'd been doing just that, but in hindsight, being so lost in the sensation of him, there was no way to think about anything else, so Charlene did just that. She pressed a soft, chaste kiss on his lips.

A peck.

But a true peck.

Not one of thrill, desire, or longing.

Just a soft press of lips against lips.

She pulled away. "How was that?"

"Bloody soul-shattering."

Charlene laughed. She couldn't help it. When the man said things like that with such a straight face, how else was she to respond but with true delight. The truth was, she felt the very same. There was no way to get lost in such a simple kiss. It exposed everything. Which might seem impossible, and yet here she sat with her heart pounding even harder than any other time they had touched.

This man had a way to wrap himself around her and make her believe in dreams again. He made her believe.

And she didn't know what to do about that. Did she fight it? Did she surrender? What were the consequences of both?

"You are doing it again."

She blinked at the man, the roughness of his voice sending a delightful shiver skittering down her spine. "Doing what again?"

"Thinking."

Charlene snorted. "What nonsense is this? No person can go without thoughts."

"True, but depending on the thoughts, some people are better left not thinking at all."

Her eyes narrowed on the man. "I'm sure that's an insult."

"To some maybe, but not to you."

"So you're saying I shouldn't think about anything but—"

"Me." He grinned at her. "If you are not thinking about me, it's best not to think at all."

Oh, but she was thinking about him. Always. However, she wasn't about to tell him that, lest she wanted his grin to turn all sorts of wicked.

Resistance would be futile, then.

And she wasn't done resisting yet.

CONTROL.

It had always been one of those things he had been good at. He had to be as the heir to the dukedom. He certainly couldn't allow it to slip when his brother almost, so very almost got engaged to the woman he had always been drawn to. But he had never grasped the depth of that pull until she'd been lost to him.

But that was before David had wrecked everything.

Something Adam both despised and rejoiced in at the same time. Despised, because he never wanted Charlene to hurt, ever. Rejoiced, because he had been given a chance. One he didn't even think—dare think about—until the moment he had spotted her in that ballroom at the first event he attended upon his return. Attended because he'd spotted her name. Attended because the moment he did, his control had already started slipping.

It had slipped with every encounter.

Every glare.

Every touch.

And now that she had kissed him? But not just any kiss, such a pure, simple kiss that if he'd not been sitting, he'd have been brought to his knees. Saints, threadbare couldn't describe the amount he had left. The only thing keeping him from pouncing on her and claiming her here and now was her ever-present hesitancy. It lingered. Always a reminder.

Patience, however, had always been a strength. On the other hand, patience and control were stout companions, and if the one disintegrated, he didn't know where that would leave the other.

And the way she was looking at him…

"We should head inside," he found himself saying before he defeated the moment with any of his urges.

"We probably should. Miss Martin should be green with envy by now."

Adam groaned. "Must you bring her up in this moment?" While he was rock hard and wanting. He certainly wilted at the mention of Miss Martin.

She shrugged and grinned.

Wench.

A spill of laughter reached them, and Adam's head whipped to the house, followed by a curse. In one smooth movement, he gathered Charlene into his arms and leaped to his feet, retreating deeper into the shadows of the garden.

"We've been here too long."

"Seems so," she murmured back.

He glanced down at her, slowly setting her to her feet. "Not afraid?"

She snorted. "I don't know why you would say that since this is not the first time we've been alone like this."

Yes, but it's the first time it felt different.

More raw.

More… bloody everything.

Before he could speak, she leaned in to get a better view of the crowd of six people, if he weren't mistaken.

"It looks like Miss Martin is part of the group."

"Of course she is," he muttered. In a few short hours, that woman had become the bane of his damn existence.

"Perhaps I should be flattered," Charlene whispered, tilting her head toward him, "that she sees me as such fierce competition."

Adam growled low in his throat. "She wouldn't, if I'd done a better job of discouraging her." And his mother for that matter. "I've been too preoccupied."

"Well, if it makes you feel any better, I doubt that would have deterred your admirer."

"It doesn't make me feel better, no."

A soft chuckle, very soft.

He glanced at her, a slow smile curving his lips. He loved that sound. He could listen to it every second of every minute of every day.

"Should we just stay here?" she asked, breaking the spell.

He glanced back at the group. "I don't know how long they'll be strolling."

"I think they might be heading this way."

The bench. "You might be right. Should we retreat farther?"

She nodded. "There should be another entrance for us somewhere."

Neither of them moved.

After a beat, she added softly, "But I find I'm a bit reluctant."

And damn it all, so was he.

The murmur of the group grew nearer.

"Quick," he murmured, reaching for her hand. "This way."

With this, she didn't hesitate, placing her hand in his, allowing him to lead her away from possible disaster. That didn't mean they couldn't, or wouldn't, encounter disaster anywhere else.

Which was exactly what they did encounter.

The distinct, very distinct, sound of moaning brought them to an abrupt halt. It was clear as day. At least to him. A couple was fornicating close by! He inwardly cursed and dragged her in the opposite direction, before breaking out in a run, with no clear idea where he was leading her to, only to get her away as far as possible from that.

He stopped near the edge of the garden on the exact opposite side of the house, and very close to the street running along the property.

"That was..." she trailed off, breathless from the dash.

"Don't even say it," Adam said, out of breath himself. "In fact, just put it out of your head."

She laughed. "If you insist."

"I do. I very well do insist." Else he might replace those sounds playing in his head with theirs. And then he'd be doomed.

"Do you think we're safe?" she asked, thankfully changing the subject.

"Define safe," he muttered, his gaze darting over the property. Who knew what they might find here?

"Safe from being seen."

"Oh. That." He leaned against a tree. "Then yes. Probably."

She tilted her head. "You don't sound convinced."

"Are you?"

Her lips twitched. "Not even a little."

He huffed a quiet laugh. The situation had certainly spiraled out of control. Control... Adam inwardly shook his head. He needed to get them back into that ballroom. She was too close.

Too tempting. Too much.

He had two choices—step away or give in.

And stepping away felt impossible.

He forced his gaze upward, away from temptation. "If we follow the street line, we should reach the house without any more encounters." They'd also probably reach a different side of the house, which brought along more sets of troubles, but he couldn't think about that now. The biggest trouble was staying here.

Because he realized with heart thrumming clarity. Control? It wasn't slipping. It had already shattered.

Chapter Sixteen

CHARLENE NARROWED HER eyes on Maddie, who in return narrowed her eyes on her.

"Don't think I don't know you disappeared with the Duke of Rotheworth last night," her friend said. "And for ages at that."

Charlene scoffed and broke eye contact first, turning her attention back to her orchid. Last night had been... well, she couldn't quite explain. It had been magical in the sort of way that had been freeing. Like at long last, shackles had unclasped and fallen from her ankles. But she didn't know how to explain that to her friends. It's not that they wouldn't understand if she tried; it's just that she didn't understand what it meant either.

At least for the future.

She was attracted to Adam. No secret there.

She fell deeper with every encounter. No secret there either.

But he was a Cross. Most certainly not a secret.

And while he kissed her at the fireworks and kissed her back yesterday, it still wasn't clear what he wanted.

Wasn't it?

Urgh. That little voice! But she'd almost been engaged to his brother. Yes, there, she finally allowed the thought to surface. Engaged. While that didn't mean they couldn't kiss and whatnot, his brother was still the one who hurt her.

How to navigate that tempest?

She didn't know. The only thing she did know was that his brother left England and stayed away. For which she was thankful. She didn't know what she would do if he ever returned. She would never have reconnected with Adam if he had. And speaking of that, Adam had left, too.

What if he left again?

And while some part of her rational mind knew he wouldn't just leave again, it was time to admit there was a small fear in her heart that he would. Perhaps not leave England, but what about leaving her for Miss Martin? Or someone else? Leaving, after all, didn't have to be physical.

On the other hand, since his return, he'd seen her. Listened. Touched her like she wasn't some broken-hearted person but someone worth holding onto. Worth kissing under fireworks, worth holding a conversation with under the stars, worth dashing through a garden.

It made her want things. Things, things. Adam things.

Like another moment with him.

And then another.

And then another.

And never stop another's. Did that even make sense? Her heart certainly thought so. As did her head. Her brother would certainly not, however. He had no time for a Cross, which was why she'd been thankful he hadn't trailed after her to events. Also, then there was Mr. Henry Grafton staying with them. He hadn't escorted her either. It seemed those two were neck deep in business transactions. That suited her just fine.

Charlene loved her brother, but she didn't need him breathing down her collar and fighting her on her choices. She needed to discover her heart on her own, even if it broke again.

"What are you thinking about?" Maddie asked, breaking through her musings.

Charlene blinked. "Orchids."

Maddie snorted. "Right, and I'm an orchid. Or should I say

Rotheworth is an orchid. Just admit it, you enjoy his company, so enjoy it. Lord knows, rare poisonous plants are easier to come by than love."

"Maddie!"

Her friend raised her hands. "What? It's true."

"Ashley and Sera found love. It's not that hard." She didn't mention herself. There was nothing easy between her and Adam. Except kissing, maybe. And talking. And laughing. Nothing else.

"Given they are the minority, I don't quite agree."

Charlene shook her head, a reluctant smile tugging at her lips. She couldn't argue against that logic. "You aren't wrong."

"Naturally." Maddie picked at a leaf.

"Don't you have anything better to do than pick my life apart?"

"Sad to say, your life is the most thrilling thing in mine."

"That is sad."

"Well, you know what is sadder, the Earl of Carry proposing to a pillar."

Charlene's eyes widened. "When was this?"

"When you were out and about with your duke."

Oh.

"You missed quite the spectacle," her friend added. "The man was so in his cups, but he looked at that pillar... well," she waved her hand, "like your duke looks at you."

"And how is that?"

"Like he's already halfway in love."

Charlene stilled, the words lodging somewhere between her heart and her throat. Halfway in love. It sounded impossible. Dangerous. Exhilarating. Still, she couldn't stop herself from asking, "Only halfway?"

Maddie shrugged. "Well, I haven't seen you together all that much. You keep disappearing with him."

True enough.

"I might be a bit halfway, too."

That earned her another snort. "I might not have seen you

with him much, but I have seen you. You are smitten. More than halfway. In fact, any more, and the way might lead you to Bedlam."

"Don't be ridiculous!"

Maddie laughed. "Whatever way it is, half-way or full-way, hold onto it. Before some Miss Marteen throws herself more fully in his path."

"Miss Martin," Charlene muttered.

"Exactly."

Charlene couldn't help but chuckle at that. "I don't think I have to worry about her." However, that did play straight into her worry. It might not be this Miss Martin, but there might come another. But then, something inside her scoffed harder than her little fears. Way louder. Because Adam wasn't like that.

He would never do that.

Not unless she pushed him away. She let him go. And so far, she hadn't been able to. She didn't think she would ever be capable of pushing him away.

"Do you think I'm foolish?" she asked her friend. "To want something more with him even though, you know, he's a Cross?"

Maddie looked her squarely in the eye. "I think you'd be foolish not to, even though he's a Cross."

Charlene stared down at the orchid, brushing a petal with her fingertip.

Then perhaps… just perhaps… she could be brave enough to find out what more might look like.

ADAM ROLLED HIS eyes. Inwardly, of course, but for what must be the hundredth time. Can a man not enjoy his luncheon without being badgered, for saint's sake? Neither his mother nor Miss Martin had given him any space to breathe since he returned from the ball last night. In fact, there were only two places in this whole damn house safe, and that was his study and bedchamber. The former being questionable and the latter being the safest. But he couldn't stay in his chamber every minute of every day, could he?

And his mother refused to send Miss Martin away.

The woman had a nest of bees in her bonnet when it came to this matter.

What made matters even more flinch-worthy was that he couldn't get Charlene and her kiss from his mind, which wasn't the flinch-worthy part. That was Miss Martin popping into view whenever he stepped from his study or chamber, ruining his thoughts with her coy smile and seemingly innocent gaze. There was nothing innocent about it. The woman was as calculating as his mother.

And they were most certainly in cahoots.

"You seem to be good friends with the lady of last night," Miss Martin said. "Lady Charlene, was it?"

More than good. "Yes."

"Still, Adam," his mother said. "That was rather rude to leave Miss Martin to fend for herself at her first ball in London."

"But I didn't leave her alone, now did I, Mother? I left her with you."

Both women huffed but said nothing further on the matter. But he wasn't fool enough to think this was the end of it.

"Adam," his mother began.

He was right.

He set his fork down, losing his appetite, and bracing himself for what was to come next.

"I do love Lady Charlene, you know this, but she was engaged to your brother. You must know how inappropriate it is to spend time with her."

He knew nothing of the sort. "They didn't marry."

"It's still not the point. She's your brother's ex-fiancée. How do you think he would feel if he returned to find you cavorting with her?"

Adam leveled a steely gaze at the duchess. "Take care with your choice of words, Mother."

And to hell with David.

His mother didn't know the damn truth. A decision he'd made not to tell her that might not have been the wisest, but he couldn't do anything about it now. She might not believe him, or she might, but she'd be hurt, and he didn't want to hurt his mother, no matter her antics with Miss Martin.

"Well," the chit piped up. "Let us not speak of that which will sour the mood, shall we?"

Adam cursed. Inwardly. His relationship with Charlene was not souring, and he wanted to point it out, but one look at the two women and he decided against it. Defending their relationship might only move them to more drastic calculations.

He'd rather avoid that.

At all cost.

But that didn't help with the matter of them now shadowing his every damn step.

"I hear there is a balloon ascension in a few days," Miss Martin added. "It's said to be a promising event."

Balloon ascension? Adam said nothing.

They would have to outright—

"Shall we go to the balloon festival?" Miss Martin's question came.

"That's a great idea," his mother chimed. "Right, Adam?"

"I can think of nothing worse." Unless Charlene was there, then he could think of nothing better.

Miss Martin pouted. He pretended not to notice. Then she gave a small sigh, the sort of sigh that carried too much meaning and not enough moderation. "I do love balloons," she murmured. "So very… much."

The emphasis on the last word alone made his eye twitch. *Don't lose your cool, Adam.* Patience always wins. What he would like very much was the image of Miss Martin being whisked into the sky on one of those balloons and carried over the ocean.

He swallowed and reached for his coffee, only to find the cup empty.

Bloody perfect.

His mother leaned forward with a smile that raised the hairs on the back of his neck. "A little air and company would do you and Miss Martin good."

"I have air," he bit out. "Plenty of it. What I lack is silence."

Miss Martin tittered. "Oh, you are funny, Adam. Please escort, please?"

Two pleases?

"And besides," his mother added, clearly undeterred by his darkening expression, "it would be an excellent opportunity for Miss Martin to enjoy more of London Society. Connections are crucial."

So was a man's sanity.

"I can't," he said. "I have a business meeting that evening."

His mother arched a brow. "A business meeting?"

His mind raced. "A business dinner, to be exact." With Charlene. Perhaps a balloon view? Talking about the business of... them.

Yes.

That sounded like just what he needed.

"Surely you can postpone that?"

Not in this life. In fact, he now needed to plan. A romantic night with Charlene. When was this balloon festival again? Where would be the best spot to watch the balloons from? He needed to get a man on that.

"I believe I cannot. This is too much of an important appointment." In the making.

He pushed back from the table, the chair scraping against the wooden floor. "If you'll excuse me, I still have matters to attend to."

Without waiting for a response, he turned on his heel and strode from the room. He had barely reached the staircase when the pitter patter of slippers behind him alerted him to a little unshakable pest. He picked up the pace knowing she wouldn't be able to catch up with his strides, and since she would never enter his chamber, he made straight for it.

If he could, he'd scale the walls.

How had it become that he couldn't even relax in his own home?

He needed Charlene. Or a drink. Preferably both.

* * *

Chapter Seventeen

T HE WANING SUNLIGHT stretched long, golden streaks across the rooftop of the Crescent Pavilion Hotel. Adam stood rooted at the wrought iron railing, the cold of the metal biting through his gloves, though he barely noticed. His gaze swept over Vauxhall Gardens, alive with murmurs of expectation. The faint strains of music, the noise of the crowd gathering on the ground, the occasional trill of laughter—it all reached him, distant and diffuse, as if filtered through the fog of his thoughts.

Charlene should be here by now. She should be here.

Yet, he couldn't be one hundred percent sure.

He had sent a note.

He hadn't seen her since they had escaped the garden of their last event. Not for trying, however. Every time he left his damn study or his bedchamber in the mornings, Miss Martin would pop up like a rat. Very well, he probably shouldn't call the woman a rat, but rats also had a way of scurrying from the shadows and scaring the soul out of people, didn't they?

But let's not think about her.

Charlene.

She hadn't responded to his note, but she never did so that couldn't be used as an indication. He did, however, trust that she would show. She wouldn't have trouble getting to the room, would she?

But her absence stung.

Where was she? Had something detained her? Had she changed her mind?

Behind him, the table was laid out just as he'd imagined. He now regretted the prematurely poured white wine—it would be all right for red, but this was ruined by now. Yet, two glasses gleamed with the amber tones of a heady liquid that had lost its sparkle; the chill of the bottle had left a delicate ring of condensation on the pristine linen. Everything had been perfect. Ready for her.

Adam's chest tightened. He wished he could see her weaving through the knots of couples and courting glances below. His jaw ached from gritting his teeth, a dying effort to keep composed, but the ticking of his pocket watch felt louder than both the scraping of his jaw and his heartbeat combined.

Adam closed his eyes for a moment. *Steady, man.* Patience was the best companion when it came to a woman. And courtship. And whatever this thing growing between them could be called.

His fingers eased off the railing, only to press into his palm. He wanted nothing else tonight but to hold her gaze, hold *her*, and tell her that she meant everything. Always had. Always would. He'd planned this carefully, as carefully as the running of an estate. He'd gambled on the vision of the balloons soaring into the sky with her at his side, the colors reflected in her beautiful eyes.

He glanced up at the balloons before drifting down again. There was still time—or so he told himself.

And then a figure emerged amidst the crowd below.

Adam's blood chilled.

Several foul curses lapped in his head.

The dip of the shoulders, the cocked head, the saunter far too self-assured—everything about that gait was familiar enough to burn. His fists clenched as his gaze zeroed in on the ridiculous green feather swaying in time with the strut. Rage flushed hot beneath his skin, surging, sharp and immediate, and he gripped the railing again barely keeping himself from hoisting himself over and causing a scene. And probably dying in the attempt.

His brother.

David Cross—a name like a bad omen...

If nothing else, that odd feather confirmed it, cheap as it was. It mocked him in its absurd falsity, just as its wearer always had—parading a painted pheasant plume as some grand relic carried back from distant lands. It was fitting, though. His brother had always pretended to be more than he was, fooling half the women in London in the process. Women who would fall into his orbit and leave with their hearts in tatters. So it was true, then. He was back.

The roar of his pulse filled Adam's ears, drowning out the soft music and laughter. He took a step back from the railing, the polished toes of his boots scraping against the stone.

Charlene.

He wasn't ready for his brother.

Adam didn't even tell her yet how he felt.

Or about the possibility that his brother was rumored to have returned.

Adam swallowed hard. He should have told her that night in the garden. It had been the perfect chance. But he hadn't.

What if she forgave David?

He couldn't fathom it, but the thought flared in his mind nonetheless, unwelcome, driving against the furious pulse throbbing in his throat. He'd waited ages for her in every sense of the word. He would've done anything to make tonight, no, every day of her life perfect. And yet this—this affront to his goodwill, his dwindling patience, to his careful plans, to his family's name—demanded something else entirely. All his plans for romance were momentarily eclipsed by the desire to throttle his brother for real this time. David was here to play his games, ruin lives, and spread his vile influence in the serpent's pit that was London's social set.

No one could tell him otherwise.

No one could tell him otherwise.

And Adam could not allow it.

He spun on his heel and marched toward the stairs that led directly from the rooftop to the ground. His boots struck marble in hard steps. He refused the greetings of the staff in clipped waves, his mind fixed and his hands trembling with more than exertion. Emerging onto the cobbled front courtyard of the hotel, the evening air rushed at him, thick with the smell of damp stone, roasting chestnuts, and the faint sharpness of coal ash from the passing carriages. His eyes cut through the milling servants and the finely dressed guests descending their steps. No sign. "No," he muttered under his breath. His brother had a knack for creating the worst surprises. Did he know he was meeting Charlene here?

Or was this but a mere coincidence?

Across the street, a crowd surged toward the gates of Vauxhall Gardens, the gates lit with elaborate lights spilling warmth onto the froth of activity. For a moment, Adam's heart sank into the churn of figures, hats, and parasols jostling against one another. And then he saw it—the cursed hat, green feather bobbing jauntily over the messy, rakish lower brim, his brother moving into the press of evening revelers with his head tilted high.

Adam clenched his teeth so tightly his jaw ached. His hands balled into fists at his sides as he stalked forward, his boots catching briefly on the uneven cobblestones before finding momentum through the street. He barely registered the exclamations of those he nudged aside. The lanterns of Vauxhall, the sounds of a string quartet beginning their prelude—the world you might have called magical only minutes ago seemed to twist into something else entirely. He pushed through the crowd, intent on catching that nasty rat of a brother and—

He cut off whatever thought threatened to follow.

This wasn't just about a man. It was about what he represented—the shadow, the stain, the awful pull of hostility when

Adam wanted nothing more than freedom from this… from him. Freedom for her.

THE SMELL OF lantern oil and crushed grass hung heavy in the air as Charlene stepped hesitantly from the packed thoroughfare onto the loose gravel near the hotel. Her skirts drew close around her legs with every rushed step, and her gloves clung uncomfortably as she dodged another stranger pushing past. She despised the way people pressed too near, their voices rising into one cacophonous roar that made her temples throb.

Tonight, though, she had no choice.

The carriage could only get her so far before the throng became unbearable even for the horses. Running late to meet Adam—again, no less—she had hurried on foot through the swelling tide of revelers gathering for the balloon ascension.

By the time she caught sight of the Crescent Pavilion Hotel, her breath came in quick pulls, her chest too tight with worry. It wasn't like her to be tardy, though these delays seemed cruelly ironic given how much this evening mattered. Adam had been such a gentleman to send a carriage. However presumptuous it might have been. And yet, here she was, scrabbling to reach him because she was late.

Her heart leapt when she saw him—or, at least, she thought it was him. He stood across the street, sharp even in profile, the set of his jaw unmistakable. The faint tilt to his head was familiar, though the slightly crooked top hat gave her pause, odd in its imperfection. Adam rarely looked unkempt. And she didn't quite know why her breath hitched as his tall frame began moving purposefully through the shifting crowd. His broad shoulders cut a clear path, his coat emphasizing the rigid determination in his gait.

But… why was he leaving the hotel?

She frowned. They were supposed to meet there, right? Had something gone wrong? Was there something urgent that needed his attention? Her fingers clutched at the folds of her cloak as a flicker of worry pricked her thoughts. She stole another glance at the rooftop, but she couldn't glimpse anything. Whatever had drawn him away, she couldn't just let him be swept into the festival without a word.

Charlene squared her shoulders and pushed forward, weaving through the crowd. Her boots scuffed against the dirt path, and twice she stumbled as someone stepped into her way. She pushed past the person.

"Adam," she called, lifting her gloved hand to wave. If he heard, he gave no sign. Her voice might as well have been a grain of sand against the noise—laughter, chatter, the sharp clinking of bells swung by children darting between adults. Her throat tightened as she called again. Still nothing.

Her determination steeled. His form hadn't vanished yet. Adam's locks caught the lantern light in fleeting glimpses; it had grown longer, she noticed, the soft waves unrulier than memory served. She hadn't realized how much the sight of him stirred in her—the reminder of his presence, solid and near, always without hesitation. But now, he seemed elusive, slipping just beyond her reach.

Charlene shoved through another cluster of chattering women, whispered apologies tumbling from her lips as she nudged past. At last, she saw him in clearer view. He had stopped near a circle of onlookers. His figure seemed to draw glances as naturally as bees to blooms. She exhaled a shaky breath, lifting her hand again. Relief started to loosen her anxiety... until she froze, her smile faltering on her lips.

He wasn't alone.

Then there was a woman. Dressed in a carmine velvet, she appeared first, her dress clinging to impossibly slim curves. Dark hair tumbled over her shoulders, and red-painted lips parted in a smile distinctly designed to draw attention. Charlene barely noticed the crowd's murmurs or the faint trill of a street violin nearby—the world stilled in that awful, frozen moment.

Adam—her Adam—reached for the woman, his strong arms wrapping around her slim frame with staggering familiarity. And then, as if the very pit of her stomach dropped away, he kissed her. Openly. Unapologetically.

The breath caught in Charlene's chest, sharp and painful. Her pulse roared loud enough to drown the voices around her, though tears blurred her vision before long. A numbness spread through her limbs as the scene burned itself into her mind. Her Adam—her duke, the man who had seen her, knew her, wanted her—held another so easily.

Her knees trembled, threatening to give way.

A man bumped her from behind, muttering a distracted "Pardon," but Charlene barely noticed. She wanted to turn away, to flee, but her legs betrayed her. She stared, unable to move, unable to catch her breath as he—no, this man—finally angled his head and turned back toward the sea of faces.

Her heart ceased entirely for one impossible beat.

The grin was wrong. Crooked, overconfident, and far too sly. The chipped tooth peeking at his smile's corner stood as undeniable proof.

This wasn't Adam.

It was him.

His brother.

David.

Charlene stepped back, waves of confusion and anger colliding in her stomach. The crush of the crowd, the heavy scent of lantern smoke, the heat of nearly a dozen bodies pressing too close—everything clamored at once. She understood his twin had long been a shadow haunting Adam, just as he haunted her, but to see this, to feel both heartbreak and fury in the same breath—she wasn't sure how she would stand.

How could he be back?

When had he returned?

Had Adam known?

She couldn't deal with this now. The world was a blur of motion and sound as Charlene turned, her skirts catching awkwardly on her hurried steps. The air seemed thicker now, heavier, as if even her breath fought to escape her chest. Tears spilled from her eyes, their heat blinding her further to the chaos of bodies pressing in around her. She pushed forward, arms brushing against coarse wool coats and silken shawls alike, murmuring breaths of "Excuse me" that no one seemed to hear. The hum of laughter and conversations buzzed uncomfortably in her ears, louder than before, though she could barely make out the words.

She needed to get away.

Away from the suffocating crowd. Away from the sight that replayed in her mind, over and over. Her steps faltered as the image stabbed at her once more—Adam's arms around that woman. And then, cruelly, her realization corrected the thought. It wasn't Adam, but his twin. His awful brother. Her chest tightened, anger pushing at the edges of her heartbreak, but there was no comfort in the distinction.

The crowd seemed endless, faces passing too quickly for her to focus, their features swimming as her tears blurred everything around her. One shoulder clipped hers, spinning her slightly off balance, but she stumbled forward, unwilling to stop. She ducked her head and pressed her palm at her cheek, wiping futilely at the wet streams. The smell of lantern smoke mingled with sweat and cheap cologne, stinging her nose as she tried to weave through the endlessly shifting mass of people.

Her foot caught on something—a raised cobble, perhaps—and she stumbled forward again, breathless, only to crash into the ground before scrambling up again.

How had the day come to this?

※

Chapter Eighteen

THE CROWD SURGED around Adam like a living tide, every movement shifting him farther from her. He craned his neck, his dark eyes darting over the sea of faces, hats, and bonnets. "Charlene!" he called, his voice cutting through the laughter and chatter, desperation lacing every syllable. But she was gone. Swallowed by the chaos of Vauxhall Gardens.

The gasp of a lady startled nearby, followed by the loud crack of a gentleman's cane hitting stone. Somewhere in the distance, a gunshot rang out, sharp and final. Adam jerked his head toward the noise, but his heart couldn't settle. The sound of it clashed with the rising cheers as hot air balloons lifted, the firelight beneath them flickering like colorful paper lanterns against the sky. He'd imagined this moment so differently. He'd imagined Charlene beside him, standing on the rooftop, her hand in his. He would've told her then. How much he loved her. How much he needed her.

Instead, this. A mad crush of strangers and a gnawing emptiness where she should have been.

His hands curled into fists at his sides as he spun to search again, but his movement faltered mid-turn. A face emerged, unmistakable even in the dim light cast by gold-hued lanterns strung throughout the gardens. His stomach churned as hatred surged to the surface, unbidden but impossible to contain. David.

His twin stood tall amid the milling crowd, his lips curved into a smug, lopsided grin that could rot even the brightest mood. Adam's heart kicked painfully in his chest. The resemblance between them was unavoidable, yet where Adam prided himself on honor, David wore his misdeeds as comfortably as his tailored coat.

"What are you doing here?" Adam growled, his voice low and rough as he closed the distance between them. His gaze darted past David again, sweeping the crowd for Charlene's familiar figure. She wasn't there. Of course she wasn't. She was out of reach now, thanks to his do-no-good brother.

"Good day to you too, Adam." David's grin widened, the liquor on his breath thick enough to make Adam's stomach turn. "Aren't you happy to see me after all this time?" His twin tilted his head as though amused, as though all of this were nothing more than a game.

"You have some nerve returning to England!"

"Why? Haven't I been punished enough?"

"A lifetime wouldn't be enough to punish you, brother." Not for what he did to Charlene. He would be rotting in a prison cell if it wasn't for the fact that if his deeds ever became known then Charlene would be completely ruined.

He would never allow that.

Which was why he wanted David gone.

"You need to leave."

"You mean go home?" David said. "I must say, I have missed our mother. I should call on her, don't you think?"

"I'm warning you, David. Stay away from my family."

"You mean our family."

"We stopped being your family the day you tried to force yourself on an innocent."

"You mean my fiancée, and is it forced if you are betrothed?"

"You weren't betrothed yet, and even if you were, that wouldn't make what you did right."

David waved his comment aside. "Can we not let bygones be bygones?"

"No."

"Well, I say yes."

"Don't toy with me." Adam's jaw tightened, his voice trembling under the force of his anger. "Return the tenants' money, David. Tomorrow morning. No excuses. And get out of sight."

"Or else?" David stepped closer, his body language all provocation. The crowd parted unconsciously around them, sensing the tension like a wolf scenting its prey.

Adam tensed as his brother's hand clamped over his forearm in a bruising grip, squeezing with just enough force to be a threat. "Or else I'll collect what you owe myself," Adam growled, resisting the sharp urge to retaliate. A public altercation would only solidify the scandal David seemed so determined to stoke. And Charlene… Charlene would never forgive him.

"Feisty tonight, aren't we?" David chuckled darkly, his other hand brushing down the lapel of his double-breasted coat. He leaned in, his smile venomous. "I see I've touched a nerve, brother. Could it be the lady herself? Have you grown fond of her?" His brow quirked, false sympathy painting his face. "Is she as good as I imagined she might be?"

Adam's self-restraint frayed dangerously at the edges. He sucked in a sharp breath, his nostrils flaring, but David continued his taunts, relishing every moment.

"Tell me, Adam," David drawled, leaning closer still. "When she screamed, was it your name or mine?"

Adam's temper erupted. He struck David's wrist, forcing his brother to release him, and stepped forward so quickly that his chest nearly collided with David's. His voice dropped low, sharp as a blade. "If you so much as speak Charlene's name again, I swear I will forget every last fiber of decency Father taught me. And I will disregard the fact that Mother wishes you well."

David smirked, unfazed, even as Adam loomed above him. "Protecting her virtue, are we? How noble. How dull."

Fury rolled through Adam, his hand tightening at his side. But when he spoke again, his voice was steadier, colder. "You will not drag her down into your mud. You will not sully her name. Not now, not ever."

"She doesn't belong with you," David sneered. "She'll come to her senses soon enough."

Adam's hand twitched, the urge to strike him nearly unbearable. But scandal would not make him a savior in Charlene's eyes. No. He would fight him another day. Quietly. Efficiently. He stepped back with deliberate control.

"She belongs nowhere near you," Adam said. His voice was hard, but he tipped his chin higher, staring down at his twin with an unflinching gaze. "Mark my words, David. You'll return what's owed. Stay out of my affairs and stay away from Charlene."

David smirked again, but Adam had already turned, his eyes darting once more through the crowd. Had she seen David? Was that why she didn't show up? His heart raced as he imagined Charlene lost out there alone.

CHARLENE PRESSED HER gloved hand over her mouth, stifling the sob that clawed its way up her throat. Her vision blurred as tears spilled, warm and unwelcome, tracing cold paths down her cheeks in the late afternoon chill. The houses along the street cast uneven pools of light on the slick cobblestones as the sun went down and more and more lights came on, but her eyes darted past them, unfocused. She stumbled as her satin slippers slipped on a loose stone, catching herself against the wrought-iron railing of a townhouse. For a moment, she clung to it, the cool metal biting against her palm, and gasped for breath.

Her chest heaved, every inhale tight and shallow, but the weight pressing on her ribs wasn't the fabric; it was the betrayal, the lie. Her heart ached with the sheer force of it. She had trusted Adam. She had dared to believe in him, in his character, in those solemn words that had promised her nothing but honesty.

But he had lied, hadn't he?

He would have known, wouldn't he have?

And she had once again fallen for a blazing Cross.

The city seemed an endless maze of noise and movement, but Charlene felt completely alone. The clip-clop of horses, the rumble of carriage wheels, and the raised voices of passersby blurred into an indistinct hum as her surroundings grew distant and meaningless. A child's laughter rang out somewhere nearby, shrill and carefree, and it only made her throat tighten further. She pulled the edges of her cloak tighter around her, feeling as though the chill in the air had seeped straight into her bones. Her fingers curled into the fabric, trembling with the effort to hold herself together when all she wanted to do was collapse onto the street like a castaway left behind.

Her steps quickened as she turned onto quieter streets, the cracks in the cobblestones snagging the hem of her gown. But she didn't stop to free it, didn't care. She needed the sanctuary of her home, the walls that would shield her from the world. Where she wouldn't have to see Adam or the confusion that lingered in his eyes. That pain... Anger flickered in her again, reigniting where grief had softened her. How dare he! He had kept the truth from her, stood there with those sincere eyes, and withheld the one thing she had asked of him.

To not be his brother.

Not like David.

Never David again.

She wiped at her tears, but they welled again, hot and unrelenting, spilling over faster than she could wipe them away. She couldn't help but remember that night... when David had lured her into the alcove.

He'd slipped his hands into her bodice, pressed his mouth against hers and more... cold dread washed over her at the embarrassment, humiliation, and disgust alone.

And what was worse, she couldn't tell if it was David's or Adam's face just now. It was David, she knew that, and the hit she'd managed to deliver with a vase from the side table had broken his tooth. But that moment of uncertainty had been awful.

Fortunately, he'd been marked as the dirty man he was and... Charlene heaved for air... it was a way to keep him apart from Adam after all. Thanks to that vase. David was not like Adam—at least not on the outside.

But Adam had kept the truth from her.

But then again, Adam had also been the one to help her that night. It hadn't come cheap for him to ensure the hosts of the evening did not learn of the matter.

And he had never told a soul about the humiliation.

Being compromised for nothing—no sparks, no love, not even the slightest bit of affection. David Cross was a man who only loved himself.

And he hurt people.

Hurt *her*.

One hand pressed hard against her mouth as a shuddering sob escaped, stolen into the cold air. She felt foolish, utterly undone. This was why she kept herself guarded, why she had promised herself never to invest in tender words and trusting smiles again. And yet Adam had cracked through her wall, his steady kindness leaving her exposed to shattering heartbreak.

Somewhere deep within her, she knew he wasn't truly to blame, that David was the source of it all. However, that man's shadow hung over her life like a dark omen, filling every quiet moment and every new glance from a gentleman with the fear of the past repeating itself—it had been so for a year until that night at the masquerade ball.

David had left wreckage in his wake, as relentless and cruel as a storm. And now he had returned, dragging that chaos into Adam's life, and by consequence, hers.

How was she to distinguish between the chaos in Adam's life versus David's? And where would she fall into all of that?

She didn't.

She wouldn't.

But that didn't lessen the sting of Adam's actions tonight. Whether David's reappearance was beyond Adam's control or not, it didn't change the fact that he seemed to have hidden things from her while knowing how much his brother had already stolen from her.

Another sob broke free, her lips trembling as she hurried faster down the street, her reflection flickering in the dim shop windows she passed. Her cloak flew behind her, catching the wet evening breeze, but she barely noticed. She turned another corner, her footsteps echoing in the narrowing lane. The familiar sight of her townhouse came into view, but the relief she expected didn't come. It only dragged down the lump in her throat, making her feel more isolated than before. Adam's words replayed in her mind, treacherous and warm, as if she could still feel the deep timbre of his voice.

She gritted her teeth, her eyes finally dry from tears. He had lied. He had lied to protect her, perhaps, but a lie was a lie, and she was left to face the consequences of his silence. All over again.

You don't know that.

Didn't she?

At last, Charlene stepped onto the marble tiles of the entryway of her home, her breathless sobs replaced by shallow, uneven breaths. The footman, alerted by the sound of the door, swung it open for her, his brow furrowed in polite concern. "Milady," he murmured, but she only acknowledged him with a nod. Her mind screamed for solitude, for her bed, for the safety of her own locked door. She clutched her cloak tighter, intending to rush past him and up the staircase without looking back.

She stopped short, her slippers scuffing against the floor as her gaze darted toward the hall bench. A dark figure stood, his shadow stretching long beneath the low chandelier. When he turned, stepping fully into view, Charlene blinked at the sight.

"Mr. Grafton," she gasped, surprised. She dropped her damp gloves into her cloak pocket hastily and wiped at her cheeks, hoping he couldn't notice the red-rimmed state of her eyes.

Probably a hopeless wish.

Just like she had wished David Cross would never step foot in England again.

Mr. Grafton inclined his head, his expression gentle, but his eyes sharp and watchful. A gentleman through and through, he wasted no time acknowledging her distress but did not remark on it directly. "Lady Charlene," he said gently, his tone well-practiced and steady. "I beg your pardon for intruding, but I wished to speak with your brother this evening. It seems he has yet to return."

Charlene's hands trembled as she stepped farther into the hall, the soft click of the door closing behind her causing her to flinch. "You might find him at White's," she replied, her voice lower than usual and unsteady despite her attempts at composure.

"Forgive me," Henry said softly, stepping forward in measured movements, keeping a distance that felt respectful rather than intrusive. "But I sense you've had a rather trying encounter."

Charlene swallowed hard, her throat raw. She tilted her chin, digging desperately for a shred of pride. "It is of no importance," she murmured, blinking back the tears threatening once again to spill. The lie felt hollow even to her.

Henry studied her for a long moment, his aristocratic features drawn in quiet understanding. He gestured toward the bench he had occupied, as if offering her a place to sit, but made no moves to coax her into it. "If you'll allow me to venture an observation… sometimes the importance of a thing isn't always apparent in the moment. And yet, if left unspoken, it festers."

She bit down on her lip, hard, a few wayward tears slipping down her cheeks, no matter how turned away her gaze. There was no use pretending here, not beneath his discerning, deeply kind eyes. "It is…" she began, the words faltering before she cleared her throat and tried again. "It is…" She didn't dare tell him about David. Couldn't even if she tried. "A man…" The words trailed off, and Charlene wanted to kick herself for sounding so utterly wretched.

Henry's expression remained calm, though one eyebrow rose. "Of course it is."

The simplicity of his response caught her off guard. It was neither condescension nor surprise, but rather the surety of someone who already knew the chaos that a gentleman could leave in his wake.

"Well… I'd rather not bore you with my troubles."

"Woman troubles would never bore me."

A sliver of amusement pierced through the pressure in her chest. "Spoken like a true gossip."

"I daresay we all enjoy a bit of gossip."

She couldn't actually refute that.

"I just heard another one the other day."

Charlene arched a brow, but something in the way he looked at her gave her pause. "Oh?"

"Your brother—"

Ah.

"—mentioned he would very much like to see you wed before the season is out."

A chill ran down her spine. She wasn't ready. Not for anyone her brother might have in mind just like she wasn't to face David. "Has my brother told you what he intends to do?" she asked cautiously, her voice breaking just slightly on the last word.

The thought that another meeting with David—even one brokered by the rigid code of honor among men of their station— might result in more destruction filled her lungs with dread. "Because if he intends…" she trailed off, unable to finish.

Henry sat forward slightly, resting his hands on the silver head of his walking stick. "Your brother wants you happy." He paused, reading her face before finishing. "That is the want of all brothers, I believe."

"If he wants me happy, he shouldn't meddle," Charlene muttered. "I don't want it," she said suddenly, her voice firmer than before. "Any of it. It's madness." Her brother meddling. David back. Being lied to by Adam.

Henry's brows lifted slightly. "You have every right to want peace, Lady Charlene. And I assure you, whatever measures your brother sees fit to take, please remember he loves you very much."

Her chest ached at his words, at the caring tone that carried both reassurance and understanding. For the first time that night, the oppressive weight on her shoulders felt lighter, the noise in her head quieting enough for her thoughts to find a measure of clarity.

"Thank you."

"I'm here if you ever need an ear to listen." He gave a meaningful nod. "It would be my honor to be at your service. Personally." He smiled. "In every way."

His words were reassuring, but they didn't give her the true reassurance she needed. How different the two brothers truly were. And had she been fooled again?

$$\mathcal{C}hapter\ \mathcal{N}ineteen$$

THE NASTY SUSPICION that filled his gut brought Adam to knock on Charlene's door, consequences be damned. If there was the slightest chance she had run into his brother, glimpsed his brother, he had to know.

This is what you get for holding off on telling her your suspicions.

The butler had informed him to wait, but his feet were as restless as his heart. He followed and almost wished he hadn't.

He heard voices, Charlene's and another man's. Her brother?

Then the butler announced, "The Duke of Rotheworth is here to see you, my lady."

A short silence before, "Tell him I'm not available for callers at the moment—"

Adam stepped up behind the servant before he could think better of it. He needed to see her, and the fact that she didn't want to see him, confirmed his suspicions.

She knew.

She knew about David.

His eyes fell on her before moving to her companion. He had expected many things when he decided to call on Charlene, but this was the very last. Her alone in a room with Mr. Grafton. Not a stranger to the Ton. Not a stranger to him. The man's reputation preceded himself. In a good way. Despite his lack of title, Mr.

Grafton wasn't a bad man. In fact, he was one of the more respectable ones of the Ton.

And he was here.

Alone.

With Charlene.

He didn't miss how her gaze swung between him and Mr. Grafton.

The nasty suspicion that filled his gut brought Adam to knock on Charlene's door, consequences be damned. If there was the slightest chance she had run into his brother, glimpsed his brother, he had to know.

This is what you get for holding off on telling her your suspicions.

The butler had informed him to wait, but his feet were as restless as his heart. He followed and almost wished he hadn't.

Adam cleared his throat. "Lady Charlene. I'll only take a moment of your time if you can spare it."

Mr. Grafton crossed his arms over his chest. "She cannot spare it."

Adam bit down on his jaw. "And who are you to speak for her?" He cocked his head. "Who are you, anyway?"

"I am family." He cleared his throat. "A family friend."

Did being Lord Waylon's friend make him a family friend? Adam thought not. "That's quite the coincidence; I am a family friend as well." The true family friend. Minus some obstacles along the way.

"I've never heard of you before," Mr. Grafton said, and Adam wanted to swat the man trying to provoke him with that statement.

"I haven't heard about your family relations yet. They must not have been terribly noteworthy."

"I'm Henry—"

"Names and titles all blend together for me. No need for formal introductions." *I hate any men who come close to Charlene.* He didn't want to lose her to another man again.

Charlene sighed, and Adam's pulse leaped at that small

sound. He wanted to look at her, stare at her, search for any sign that she was furious or resentful, but he couldn't with this pompous dandy in the room. He didn't want to do anything that would make life even the tiniest bit harder, although he couldn't seem to stop that from happening either.

"Gentlemen," she said. "Please, if you cannot be civil, leave."

"Civil is my first name," Mr. Grafton said.

"Of course it is," Adam muttered, but inclined his head. "Civil is the marrow in my bones."

Charlene pressed her fingers to her temple, as if staving off a headache. "Enough. Both of you."

Adam clenched his jaw before inhaling a deep breath. "Lady Charlene, please. I came only to speak with you, and a few minutes is all I ask."

Mr. Grafton, the stubborn fool, did not budge. "I'm afraid that would be improper."

Improper? "Then by that token, I walked into something improper, didn't I?"

"Mr. Grafton is waiting for my brother," Charlene spoke up before she met his gaze. "What could be so pressing that you needed to call on me this very moment?"

He flinched at the note of accusation in her gaze. He couldn't very well tell her about his brother and that she didn't show up for their appointment. Not with the barnacle in the room. "There is a matter that came up. It's imperative—"

"If it was so imperative," she interrupted, "why only bring it to my attention now?"

"I only confirmed it today."

"So you had suspicions you couldn't inform me of? Or didn't want to inform me of?"

What could he say to that? He could have informed her several times, but he hadn't wanted to ruin the moment. Ruin her happiness.

And that had left her vulnerable for unwelcome surprises.

"I didn't mean to keep this from you."

"But you did."

He did, yes. And that was perhaps the cruelest part—he always did. Always holding too much back and never finding the perfect timing. What would it cost him this time?

CHARLENE'S HEART LEAPED at the same time her breath seemed to be swallowed into her lungs. She still couldn't believe Adam had come to her house. He should know how her brother felt about him, and still he came.

But the reason he came…

He was a man caught!

She couldn't deal with this right now. Her mind was in a shambles. She needed to regroup. To settle this unsettlement inside her as well as gather her wits before she spoke to Adam.

The last thing she wanted to do was to fall apart.

In front of him.

Again.

Once in her lifetime was enough.

It was enough that she was ready to march straight out the door, manners be damned. Yet her feet remained rooted on the spot. Fortunately, the tears had dried, but she found herself battling to keep her eyes from attaching themselves to Adam's face. Searching. For any sign that he had betrayed her. Lied to her. Kept the horrible truth that his brother had returned from her.

But with Mr. Grafton here, she couldn't. Lest their conversation make its way back to her brother. It wasn't that she didn't trust him, but men would always be men. If they thought it was for a woman's good, her wishes rarely counted.

She'd rather not take the chance.

But she didn't want to send him away either. He was her shield. At least, for this moment. But Adam's cryptic, her cryptic conversation…

Mr. Grafton, bless his soul, cleared his throat. "Perhaps this is a conversation for another time?"

Adam dragged a hand through his hair, and all Charlene wanted to do was ease the lines forming between his brows. But she refrained from softening. If she softened now… No, she had to be strong. She had to clear her head.

"I agree. I'm rather tired and think I should get some rest."

Adam nodded, but he didn't move an inch. His eyes, dark and broody, stayed locked on hers, and something passed between them. Something that burned hotter than her confusion, than her fear.

Something her addled brain simply couldn't explain at the moment, but she had to grip her skirts, bunching the fabric in her fists to keep herself from reaching for him. To keep from scattering caution to the wind.

His words from earlier sprang to mind. The comment about properness, and Charlene knew, she just knew, he wouldn't leave her alone with Mr. Grafton. She honestly didn't know what to feel or what to make of this short interaction, but the throbbing that started in her temples didn't seem like it would go away if she stayed.

So, she said, "Then if you will excuse me, gentlemen, I believe I shall retire to my room."

Silence stretched.

Then Adam asked in a low, hoarse, tone, "Can I call on you tomorrow?"

She didn't know how to respond to that. Didn't know if she could. All she wanted was to fall back on the bed and forget this day ever happened. If she could, she would like to return to the moment before she'd spotted David Cross in the crowd. Any moment before. No, the moment she was in the garden, and she kissed Adam. But then, that moment was tainted now, wasn't it? Because he should have already had his suspicions then, shouldn't he?

"I just—" he went on, but she shook her head, and he fell silent at once.

"Later," was all she managed. They could speak later.

When her heart wasn't so dangerously close to betraying her all over again.

Chapter Twenty

RAGE OVERSHADOWED ANY defeat Adam warred with when he stepped into their family drawing room to the sight of his brother and his mother arguing.

"Life abroad was ever so difficult," David complained.

"Then why did you leave? If it was so difficult, why didn't you return?"

"There were circumstances…"

Circumstances?

Adam wanted to laugh.

His mother had always been blind to David's sins. Did she really think David would just leave because he wanted to leave?

Miss Martin, who Adam just noticed, scooted closer to his brother. "You are much handsomer than I remember, David."

Adam rolled his eyes. Hard.

"Thank you, Miss Martin."

"How accomplished you are, traveling abroad and seeing to your own needs."

Adam crossed his arms. "Oh, and what exactly did you pay for?" That didn't come from the family coffers you stole? But he would never voice that out loud in front of his mother, no matter how much he wanted to.

David arched his brow. "Why, for the whole house, of

course."

"What house?" Adam pressed.

"I purchased a small chateau in Provence. It's an investment for the family, of course. Mother ought to come and visit to see how much I've put into it."

For the family? Oh please! So that was why he was swindling money from them. Again. He might have bought a house in Provence, but it would not have been for this family. David was much too selfish, much too greedy for that.

"How accomplished!" Miss Martin exclaimed, and his mother nodded along.

"Accomplished? There are hundreds of people depending on me. Over three hundred families directly connected to my estate and countless more in the region whose livelihoods depend on how I manage their affairs." His eyes bored into his brother. *And you are stealing from them.*

"How overly dramatic, Adam," David said. "As always."

"Is stealing money from the family dramatic?" Adam demanded before he could rein in his tongue.

"What are you talking about?" his mother said with a frown marring her brows.

"I'm saying I would never steal money for the family to build an immoral love nest in France of all places! Why not send money to Napoleon directly? David is the worst kind of traitor for the family name, and I am ashamed to look like him."

"Adam!" his mother exclaimed, leaping to her feet. "I forbid you to speak about your brother that way!"

Forbid? Such an interesting little word.

But Adam couldn't help himself. David had returned to London, ruined all the trust he had rebuilt with Charlene, and now he was worming his way back into his life, his house, like nothing ever happened.

Charlene's red-rimmed eyes flashed in his mind.

The pompous Henry Grafton.

The words David had spewed to him before the hotel.

He would never forgive his brother.

Never.

"Why? Why would I want to resemble a man who tried to force his attentions on an innocent woman? Why should I want to be the brother of a man who steals from the farmers who have supported the lavish lifestyles of this do-no-good for almost three decades?"

More importantly, how could the world be so blind to who David truly was?

Adam, for one, would never want to be near the man who disrespected a wonderful woman like Charlene Fielding. Never. Ever.

He didn't say the last part.

Not with Miss Martin in the room. She was a way to send David away without causing Mother too much heartache.

Not with his mother taking David's side. He didn't want any unwelcome and dangerous attention on her. She had suffered enough.

"David Cross is no brother of mine." His eyes narrowed on David. "You are not welcome in my house. Get out."

He turned on his heel and slammed the door in his wake.

CHARLENE SETTLED ON her bed, pressing a cool cloth to her forehead and shutting her eyes, willing the ache behind her temples to retreat. It had been a wretched afternoon with David's return, Adam's deceit, and Mr. Grafton's being placed in the middle of it all. The events all clawed at her nerves until she fled to her chambers.

Sanctuary, at last.

Or it had been—until her door crashed open. Her eyes snapped open as Maddie and Ashley hurtled in like twin cannon-balls.

Charlene mumbled to herself, the ache in her temples flaring.

"Char!" Maddie cried, nearly tripping over the hem of her gown in her haste. "We are so glad you are here!"

"Yes, and unharmed," Ashley said, flinging herself onto the foot of Charlene's bed.

Unharmed?

Why wouldn't she be unharmed?

"What are you talking about?" She lowered the cloth and glared at them. "And can you please mind your voices. My brain is trying to split my head in half."

"Apologies," they both chirped, softer this time.

"But this is important," Maddie said, rather urgently. "There are whispers going about."

"Whispers?" Was this about David's return? Was that what they meant? But Charlene had never told them about her shameful past. Not because she didn't trust them, but she truly did feel ashamed forever believing David had a good bone in his body. She was also supremely ashamed she'd allowed that deception to happen to her. That she trusted the wrong man. If she hadn't been so trusting, none of it would have happened... and yet, the fact that it did shed light on who the better man was.

Somewhere in her heart, Charlene had always known.

But she'd needed confirmation of Adam's attention to her.

Which seemed to be the theme of her life.

Trusting the wrong men.

"Were you near a hotel today?" Ashley asked.

Charlene stilled, dread forming in the pit of her stomach. "Why?"

"So that's a yes," Maddie said, nodding.

Charlene sat up slowly, the pounding in her temples intensifying. "Yes. I was. Now tell me." Before her heart climbed from her throat!

Ashley sighed. "Someone saw you. In Vauxhall. With David Cross."

Maddie nodded, her curls bouncing with each one.

Very well. They saw her. That didn't mean anything. "So, they saw me."

"It's also being said you fled from a man like a—what was it?" Maddie asked.

"A hare being pursued by a wolf," Ashley supplied.

Charlene's mouth twisted. "How poetic." David certainly was a wolf. And not the romantic, good kind. The evil, sadistic kind, more like.

"It's most likely going to be in the papers tomorrow," Maddie said, voice dropping to a whisper as though the walls might be listening.

So it had come to this.

Charlene dropped her face into her hands with a groan. She could already picture it: her name smeared across every scandal sheet, whispered in drawing rooms and behind fluttering fans. She would be labeled reckless. Perhaps even compromised. Tainted.

Tainted.

Adam could never pursue a woman who had even the faintest hint of scandal clinging to her. And she—Charlene squeezed her eyes shut—she would never be anything but a stain on his spotless lineage.

Well, not so spotless. But most men could weather storms of scandal. Women could not.

Even if he had wanted her—which, she thought he did—he could not have her now. Not a duke. Not a man with big duties to be fulfilled.

And truth be told, part of her still seethed with his betrayal. Adam had suspected David's return, had hidden it from her. Perhaps he had been trying to protect her, but it had left her unprepared, exposed all the same.

Better to lose him now, before the dream grew any sweeter.

Better not to hope.

Charlene drew a shuddering breath. "Very well," she said coolly. "I shall simply have to endure exile with as much grace as

I can muster."

Ashley stared at her. "You cannot possibly intend to simply accept this. You were going to meet Adam, were you not? He needs to step up and take responsibility. And why on earth would you run from him? Did he do something to you?"

"I didn't run from him," Charlene admitted. "I ran from his brother. David Cross."

"David Cross?" Maddie murmured. "Why would you run from him?"

"Because he hurt me." And then Charlene explained what happened to her that fateful, nightmarish night. From the almost engagement, his sweet smiles, to the moment he had tried to take what he wanted, and she refused. What happened after. And now he was back.

Tears had sprung to both her friends' eyes, and their faces had turned rather pale. Charlene didn't want that. She didn't want them to pity her. "I am here, and I got through it. So, I shall have none of your pity."

"We don't pity you," Ashley said, her face resuming color before turning to bright red. "I shall kill him for you. No, Linsey shall kill him for you. I cannot believe scum like him returned to London! How dare he!"

"I agree. I know where to find hemlock if you ever need a dose," Maddie said darkly.

Charlene suddenly laughed. Her world was seemingly crumbling around her, but she still had her friends. In the grand scheme of things, that was all she needed.

And yet still, her heart throbbed with the same intensity as her temples. No good would come of her being seen today. But it was hard to tell how things would spiral. At the moment, with all the aches in her body, it was also hard to care.

But one thing she did know.

She didn't want to live in a city where that horrible creature prowled.

"Pox on all Crosses anyway," Ashley announced. "Who needs

them when there is a pool of good, fine gentlemen in the world?"

Maddie chuckled, joining them on the bed.

Charlene found herself laughing, too. Short, sharp bursts that teetered on the edge of tears. Oh, it hurt, loving and losing all at once. But at least, among her friends, it didn't feel quite so heavy.

She tossed the cloth aside and pushed to her feet, squaring her shoulders.

"If I must be a scandal," she said grandly, "then by Jove, I shall face it with my head held high."

Ashley grinned and clapped her hands.

Maddie wiped her eyes. "There's our Charlene."

Yet deep inside, where no laughter could reach, Charlene felt something shatter. Quietly. Irreparably. Forever.

Chapter Twenty-One

STEAM ROSE GENTLY from the teacup cradled in Charlene's hands, the faint aroma of bergamot mingling with the sweetness of the sugar she stirred into the amber liquid. Across from her, Maddie sat perfectly composed, her sharp green gaze settling on Charlene with an expression equal parts curiosity and suspicion.

"What if I wanted to do something terribly stupid, romantic, and final?" Charlene's voice was soft, almost as if she feared the weight of her thoughts might shatter the delicate porcelain teacup she held.

Maddie paused, her silver teaspoon hovering mid-air before she set it neatly onto her saucer. "I would always advise against stupid," she replied, arching a brow. "Particularly if you're aware of it beforehand. Romantic can be excused, provided it doesn't teeter into scandal. But final? I must caution against it entirely."

Charlene hesitated, the teaspoon slipping from her hand with a muted clink against the edge of her cup. "But what if I can't stop myself?" she asked, her voice quieter now, almost a whisper meant more for herself than Maddie.

Maddie tilted her head, studying her friend as one might a complicated puzzle. "Do you want it to happen?"

"Yes," Charlene admitted after a long pause, though her

confession tightened something low in her chest, a tension between desire and dread. But *I shouldn't*, she thought firmly, though the words rang hollow even in the privacy of her mind.

"Then perhaps," Maddie said with the patience of someone untangling a knotted ribbon, "you ought to provide me with the details. I can hardly be expected to offer sound advice otherwise."

Charlene found herself fiddling with the edge of her linen napkin and avoiding Maddie's steady gaze. "It's about Adam," she said finally. The name felt heavier than it should. "And a certain flower I've been thinking of giving him. One that doesn't grow in my greenhouse."

There was a sharp, familiar tsk from Maddie, her disapproval clear before she even spoke. "Don't," she said plainly, her lips tightening slightly over the single syllable.

"Why not?" Charlene's words had an edge now, though whether it was defiance or desperation, she wasn't sure. "I want to."

Maddie leaned back in her chair, her expression thoughtful beneath the faint rigidity of propriety. "You can't possibly know what it is you want to do, having never done it," she said matter-of-factly. "Therefore, you mustn't."

"When you put it that way, it sounds dreadfully reasonable," Charlene muttered, though it didn't soothe the quiet ache of longing she had tried, and failed, to push away. "But... what if I long to know what it is I'm missing?"

Maddie sighed, the exasperated sound only tempered by the concern etched into her features. "Do you recall your fourteenth birthday?" she asked suddenly, her voice gentler this time.

"No," Charlene said quickly, too quickly. She knew where this was going, and she hated the way her pulse skipped at the memory.

Maddie's smile was faint but knowing. "Of course you don't. But I do," she said. "You cried all night, and I stayed with you until you finally fell asleep."

"You're a very good friend," Charlene murmured, her eyes

fixed on the rim of her cup, unwilling to meet Maddie's gaze.

"There's more to it, isn't there?" Maddie prompted softly. "You don't need me to remind you why. You did something then. Something romantic, stupid, and terribly final. Does that not sound familiar?"

Charlene exhaled slowly, the resistance draining from her shoulders. "I remember," she admitted at last, though her voice was low, as if speaking the words might summon the humiliation anew. "I gave Adam my first dance."

"And how did that go?" Maddie asked, though her tone suggested she didn't truly need to hear the answer.

Charlene swallowed hard, her throat suddenly tight. "My father played the pianoforte, and I... thanked Adam afterward. I... I thought it was a lovely dance," she said carefully, though the memory of the moment still stung. "Then he told me I wasn't girlish at all, and that I danced poorly."

Her voice faltered as she tugged at the lace edging of her sleeve, refusing to look up. "I told him that 'girlish' isn't even a proper word, then ran to my room before the cake was served."

Maddie reached for her teacup but waited a moment before lifting it. "Exactly," she said, her tone calm but firm. "And this one, whatever it is you're scheming about now... it could be so much worse."

Charlene's fingers tightened around her cup, her shoulders stiff under the weight of Maddie's warning. Somewhere between reason and desire, between Maddie's logic and her own burning want, sat the truth she wasn't ready to face.

ADAM FOUND HIMSELF once again before Charlene's house the next morning. He'd left the house after he'd tossed his brother out and spent the night at White's, hoping some miracle answer might descend upon him on how to manage a situation he was not equipped for.

He brought a hand over the breast pocket where his very old apology still lay.

Apologies didn't help much, verbal or non-verbal.

His brother was a perfect example.

But he still needed to apologize and explain, even if she didn't expect either. However, he suspected he would have to get past Waylon Fielding first.

He strode up to the door and knocked.

Of all the things he didn't expect, which was becoming rather a theme of his life, it was to enter Fielding's office to find him and Mr. Grafton.

"Fielding." He nodded at Charlene's brother. "Grafton," he muttered as an afterthought, refusing to look at the man.

"Rotheworth," Fielding said. "What brings you to my doorstep this early in the morning?"

Adam's jaw ticked. "The same thing I suspect brings your current guest."

"He is a friend, not a guest. Soon to be family if fate allows."

Adam barely refrained from balling his fists, a gesture that these men wouldn't miss. So, Grafton asked for Charlene's hand, and Adam would just have to do the same. Though, admittedly, he loathed doing so in these circumstances.

The choice was still up to Charlene.

"So, she has a suitor who asked for her hand. Now she has two."

"I'm not inclined to accept your proposal," came the flat reply.

"Since I didn't ask for your hand, I don't see how that matters."

"My father isn't here."

"That didn't stop your friend. Why should it stop me?" Adam shot back. "And you seem to forget, while you are your sister's guardian, you cannot force her to marry a man against her will."

"But I can stop you from ever setting foot in my house or

near my sister again."

"And how would she feel about all this dictation?"

"Dictation? This isn't dictation."

"I don't know. What would you call it if you ordered or did things she didn't want you to do?"

"Protection."

Grafton cleared his throat. "Quite right."

Adam ignored him. He wouldn't win against both of them. Short of spelling it out, he had made his intentions clear. Besides, while he'd known he might have to contend with Fielding, the man was not his goal this morning.

"I'm here to call on your sister."

Fielding crossed his arms. "That is not happening."

"Shouldn't she be the one to decide whether that is happening or not?"

"Henry told me you upset her yesterday."

"A miscommunication."

The man snorted, "There seems to be a lot of that in your family. I heard your brother is back."

"He is," Adam bit out.

"I might not know everything that transpired between him and my sister since she didn't tell us, but I do know he hurt her, and I don't want you or him near her."

"He won't be a problem."

"Just like he wasn't a problem a year ago?"

"He won't be staying long."

"You see, I don't believe you."

"Not even if I give my word?" An absurd question, but he had to ask.

Fielding looked him over with no small amount of disdain. "You expect me to take you at your word, Rotheworth? After everything?"

Adam met his gaze, unwavering. "No. I expect you to let your sister make her own choices." It would always come back to this.

"And if she chooses wrong? I won't let that happen. Again."

"Her choice is her right," Adam replied quietly. Just as it had been when she chose his brother back then. "You don't get to guard her heart by locking it away."

Grafton shifted uncomfortably beside Fielding but said nothing. Good. Adam had no desire to hear more nonsense from the man.

Fielding exhaled sharply through his nose, eyes narrowing. "I don't know what you did last time, but even if I did allow you to see her, she wouldn't see you. She's not in a forgiving mood. I'm wagering it has something to do with your brother."

It did. "I don't expect her to be," Adam said. "I only ask for a moment. She may still turn me out, and I will accept it. But I need to face her. Not you. Not him. Her."

There was a long pause. Fielding's jaw worked as if caught between two impulses—overprotective brother and not-so-overprotective brother. The last just meaning he'd allow her to boot him from the house.

"It's best if you give her some time," he said. "Come back tomorrow. It's up to her if she will see you then. If she doesn't, leave, or I will make you leave."

With that promise thick in the air, Adam inclined his head, turning on his heel and marching from the room. He'd just stepped from the study when a voice stopped him.

"May the best man win."

Adam looked over his shoulder and finally looked at Mr. Grafton in the eyes. "That will never be you."

MAY THE BEST man win.

That will never be you.

What had they been discussing?

Charlene blinked. She stood on top of the staircase staring at the door of her brother's study. Adam had stayed all of five minutes and seven seconds before the door opened and he stepped out, followed by those ominous words of Mr. Grafton. She'd only glimpsed him fleetingly when he entered, but it was him. She would know him from anywhere.

Except when it's David.

Which, she had come to the conclusion, was one of the biggest reasons her emotions had erupted the afternoon before. She'd confused the brothers.

You didn't know David was back.

That still wasn't an excuse.

Their very essence was different.

But that wasn't what she should focus on at the moment. It seemed something important happened in the study, and for the life of her, she couldn't even begin to think what except one thing.

A duel.

Which was ridiculous.

But also, not?

Not given how Mr. Grafton had found her, tear-stained, yesterday and Adam turning up. But wouldn't he have defended her supposed honor then? No, not without her brother, he wouldn't. He didn't have that right. But did these things matter? She didn't know. What she did know was she couldn't allow them to duel!

Her brother was a crack shot.

And Mr. Grafton? Well, that she didn't know, but he would probably be her brother's second.

"And by the by," Adam's voice echoed. "You can find me at the Duchy Hotel, where I'll be staying until my brother leaves London."

He didn't wait for an answer, and she watched as Adam strode from her home, wanting to call out but her voice stuck in her throat.

What had just happened?

Her legs moved of their own accord, one step forward, then

stillness.

I have to go after him.

But what would she even say?

Another step. Then pause.

Charlene gripped the railing, fingers curling tight around it to keep from rushing over to him. She could demand he return and explain, ease her mind. She could shout at him for all the wrongs she felt in her heart. She could slap him. Or kiss him.

Urgh! Charlene!

She drew a breath, her fingers uncurling, and took another step. Her slipper hovered over the stairwell, and she froze again.

What was she doing?

She turned halfway, facing the corridor behind her. She should go back to her room. Pretend none of this happened. Let her brother and Mr. Grafton decide her future. That would be easier. Neater. Safe.

And entirely unbearable.

She turned back toward the stairs. Her heart thudded a traitorous beat. He'd said he was staying at the Duchy. Where they had kissed. Where fireworks exploded around them. Was it because of David?

That would mean his brother had returned home.

A lump formed in her throat.

She turned back to the staircase, her foot hovering once more.

Then she set it down.

And lifted it up again.

Drat it all, Charlene, move! Decide!

But her feet wouldn't obey. Her hands twitched uselessly at her sides. She didn't even know what she wanted—an apology? A declaration? A future with him?

She pressed a hand to her temple. None of this made sense.

And yet, her heart whispered go.

She took the flight of stairs with a rush, hoping her brother and Mr. Grafton remained in the study long enough that she could escape without their notice. She might not know what she wanted to hear from him, what she wanted to do after all the revelations of the past twenty-four hours, but she knew if she didn't follow him right now, she might just regret it all her life.

Which was mad.

But then, perhaps she was a little crazy.

A lot of madness.

Crazy for him. Adam.

If only her pride didn't weigh quite so much. Whether that was good or bad, she didn't know, but she couldn't hide behind the past pain and future fear anymore. She had to claim.

And she wanted to claim him.

Even if that meant he'd break her heart.

"Charlene Fielding! Where do you think you're going!" Her brother's voice boomed.

Her heart sank to her toes.

Chapter Twenty-Two

CHARLENE PACED THE wide stone path of her greenhouse, her boots tapping against the damp floor. Sunlight filtered through the paneled glass above, casting muted green and gold light onto the riot of plants surrounding her, but she could not enjoy it. Normally, the dense foliage brought her serenity. Normally, the delicate orchids lining the far table would command her attention. But now her gaze skimmed over the blooms as though they were no more remarkable than field daisies.

Her brother had stopped her before she could slip out from the house and chase after Adam. He also refused to tell her what had been discussed. Mr. Grafton hadn't been any help either.

However, a letter arrived.

Her hands shook as she unfolded the letter again that had been delivered by special courier only minutes before, Adam's bold script cutting across the page. She didn't need to reread it, but she did anyway, the words imprinting themselves deeper into her mind.

If you need me, find me at The Duchy Hotel, for I shall not return to my home.

Her throat tightened. Not return? Find me?

Did he mean forever? Her stomach twisted. The words couldn't mean anything else. Adam wasn't the sort to flee from something he deemed his duty. He was the sort to face the barrel of a pistol at dawn without flinching. He was going to duel. For her. The thought hit her like a hard slap, setting her pacing anew.

He could be hurt.

Or worse…

She read on, her pulse quickening.

Before tomorrow morning, I must give you something I have so long owed you.

The meaning eluded her, leaving her in a tangle of uncertainty. What did he owe her? Her mind raced, but it latched onto nothing. Even her orchids provided no foothold for her thoughts. That was the strangest thing of all. Normally, she would find solace in the soft pearly hues of her slipper orchids or the speckled gold of her smoothed blooms. But now, they sat like silent spectators to her failing composure.

"Dash it all!" she muttered, startling the gardener's boy sweeping near the door. He scurried out without a word, leaving her alone with her turmoil.

The sound of footsteps snapped her upright, and her father appeared beneath the greenhouse archway, his frame silhouetted by the bright light beyond. "Has a villain attacked your precious plants? Or do you aim to frighten the poor boy into tending them better?" Lord Fielding crossed the threshold with his usual air of unshakable calm, his spectacles slipping slightly down his nose.

"Father," Charlene said breathlessly, clutching the letter. "When have you returned from your tours of the estates?"

"Just now." He peered at her closely, taking her in, and arched a brow. "My darling Charlene, you look ready to swoon."

"No."

"Then perhaps Henry? You seem to get along well?"

She glanced away, her thoughts tangling. "This isn't about Henry. This is…" She gestured vaguely, then thrust the letter toward him. He made no move to take it, only raised a brow.

"This is…"

"No riddles, if you please," he said lightly. "Waylon's notes have been riddled with the Cross brothers, but I know he thinks little of them these days. Speak plainly for once, my dear. What is vexing you? Is it because I didn't tell you about my meeting with Rotheworth earlier?"

Charlene bit her lip, heat rising in her cheeks. "Waylon. And Adam. Rotheworth. He's written to me. I think… he's going to fight a duel." She flung the letter onto the planting table, its corner brushing the soil dusting the surface.

Her father adjusted his glasses. "A duel? Over you? Hmm." His mouth curved slightly, but to her astonishment, it wasn't with amusement. "I gather the poor man's intentions toward you are not entirely dishonorable, then. So, his father was right then?"

"Whatever do you mean?"

"It was shortly before he died, Charlene. When Adam was taking his final exams and bound to return. His father must have known that he was dying because he told me he'd hoped for a love match of our families."

"Oh dear, Papa!" Charlene exclaimed, though her rebuttal came with little conviction. "This is not the time for teasing!"

"On the contrary, it seems an excellent time to determine why you look more inclined toward leaping into your carriage than arranging a vase of orchids." His gaze sharpened slightly. "You've made up your mind about Henry then? There's no love match with any of the Cross brothers?"

Charlene hesitated. The sunshine warming the greenhouse did little to ease the chill building in her chest. "I can't marry Henry. I won't." She clasped her hands tightly to stop them from trembling.

Her father nodded, as though this was no more surprising than an afternoon rain shower. "And Adam?"

Her throat worked as she swallowed hard. "I must see him."

For a moment, her father said nothing. Then he inclined his head in a rare show of approval. "Well, I shan't keep you plotting here where even your orchids seem of little comfort. But take the carriage. Your reputation is not entirely worthless yet."

With one last glance at her father, Charlene gathered her bonnet and gloves, tying the ribbons with shaky fingers as she hurried outside. The light breeze caught the edge of her skirts as she climbed into the waiting carriage, her heart thudding wildly.

"The Duchy Hotel," she instructed, gripping her gloved fingers together tightly.

The driver urged the horses onward, and the carriage pulled away with a creak of its wheels. Charlene allowed herself a single breath. Reputation, sensibility, and consequences faded behind her as the greenhouse disappeared. Only Adam's cryptic words lingered. *I must give you something I have so long owed you.*

And she would get her answers even if it meant sacrificing everything.

ADAM SCOWLED AT the papers he was busy drawing up for the solicitor. The only way to stop David from destroying the family fortune and controlling the situation was by getting him out of England.

For good.

Forever.

So, he would create a stipend that could only be redeemed in Provence and lapsed the moment David returned to England. It was the only way to keep that scoundrel from returning.

And he would return. Again and again.

His twin knew exactly how to needle him. How to push.

Which is why exile had to be absolute.

For Charlene.

And for him.

His mother.

But mostly for Charlene. Their future. If they still had one.

A knock startled him. Sharp, firm. He stilled, the quill in his hand dripping ink onto the desk. It was late. Too late for the solicitor's man. And no one else knew he was here besides his friend and…

But no.

She would never come here, would she?

Another knock—firmer this time.

Adam pushed back his chair, rising. He crossed the room in sure strides, only hesitating a slight moment at the door before yanking it open.

He inhaled sharply.

Could it be? She was here.

Was she? Or had his mind finally splintered and he was imagining things?

"Charlene?"

A brow arched. "Expecting someone else?"

It was her.

She stood in the doorway like an angel—breathless and beautiful—and utterly stealing his rational thought. Pure instinct had him step aside quickly so that she could enter before anyone saw her.

"What are you doing here?" What was he even saying? He'd sent her word of his whereabouts. "Do you need me?"

"You said you had something to show me?"

Yes, but he hadn't thought she'd actually come. He'd hoped… but never dared believe. "Yes, I—"

"You mustn't do it," she interrupted in a burst of air, her voice low but urgent. Something was wrong. Off.

"What are you talking about? Did something happen?"

"I just…" she shook her head. "I can't let you do it."

Adam stared at her, blood thundering in his ears. What? She wasn't making any sense. His mind raced, scrambling for meaning. What did she think he was doing?

Wait.

Was this about David?

About exiling him?

His gut twisted. How could she possibly know? Had David gone to her? Pleaded with her? Begged for mercy with those same pitiful eyes he'd used a hundred times before?

Adam's jaw clenched. He wouldn't put it past his brother.

But if that was the case, how could Charlene forgive the man who had hurt her easily?

"It has to happen," he bit out. He couldn't imagine it any other way.

Her eyes widened. "You'd go that far? Over a matter of pride?"

His chest burned. "Pride? No—Charlene, this isn't about honor."

"Honor! What if he dies! That will be on you! You will have to carry that for the rest of your life!"

David die? No, weeds don't die that easily. Besides, he survived this past year just fine, did he not? What the devil had David told her?

"So, you mean to forgive him and allow him to stay here in London like nothing happened?"

She blinked at him. "What? What are you talking about?"

"My brother. What are you talking about?"

"The duel!"

"What bloody duel? I don't know of this! Who told you there would be a duel? Wait, who am I dueling with?"

Her eyes went wide before a small furrow appeared between her brow. "Mr. Grafton… You're not dueling with him?"

There had been one terrible misunderstanding. "No."

"Wait, then you thought I was talking about your brother?"

Adam nodded. "He won't be in London much longer once I set things in motion. I'm sorry I didn't tell you that he was back, or that there were rumors he might be returning."

She let out a shaky breath. "I wish you had."

"I know. I didn't want to ruin things by talking about him, but not talking ruins things, too, it seems."

Her shoulders sagged, the fight in her deflating. "Oh." A breath. Then another, sharper. "I should challenge you to a duel for that, you know."

He chuckled. "If I'd known a duel would have you hunting me down, I'd have pretended a challenge much sooner."

"Rogue!" But then she smiled.

"No one saw you, right? You were careful?"

She nodded. "In any event, my reputation is a mask." A snort. "Just like your face."

He took her hand in his, squeezing. "Don't even jest about that, Charlene."

She squeezed back. "I'm sorry I didn't see it sooner," she said, stepping up to him. "That I didn't listen when you wanted to explain. You're not David. Not even close. You never were."

He couldn't speak. Could barely breathe. Those words alone could be the fuel his heart beat from for the rest of his life. He wore the same face as his brother. He couldn't change that. And while he hadn't thought about it much, couldn't for his sanity's sake, a part, a deeply buried part, had always feared she'd only see his brother, his brother's sins, when she looked at him.

But she didn't.

And that was the most precious thing in existence.

She came closer. "I see you. Not the mask. Not the name. You."

He grinned at her. "And you don't want me to die in a duel. That means you care."

"I care. More than I ever let on."

It was all so unexpected, Adam didn't know how to feel. Didn't know how to suddenly express himself. "Come with me somewhere. Please."

Chapter Twenty-Three

THE ROOFTOP OF the Duchy Hotel was cast in a golden haze, the last rays of sunlight brushing against the silver trim of Charlene's gown. The soft hum of the gathering crowd below was distant now, like the murmur of ocean waves too far away to reach her. Vauxhall Gardens stretched out in a lush, glowing expanse, lanterns glittering among the trees. She could smell the faint sweetness of honeysuckle carried up on the evening breeze, but her focus was entirely elsewhere. All the trees had turned in their glorious hues of oranges, reds, and yellows. A painter's palette couldn't have captured the beauty of the colors at this time of the day.

She couldn't believe what had happened. The misunderstanding... it was almost laughable. Try as she might, no matter how she recalled the previous conversation she'd overheard, it still sounded as if there would be a duel!

But there would be no duel.

David would be leaving London again.

And now she was alone with Adam. On a roof.

He stood close, had kept close since she entered his room, his gaze fixed on her with an intensity that made her throat tighten. She couldn't look away, even as her cheeks warmed under the weight of it. His hand, steady but unassuming, reached for hers, his leather gloves brushing against the fine embroidered silk covering her fingers. That simple touch sent a thrumming ache through her, unexpected yet undeniable.

"I thought I'd lost you after yesterday," he admitted, his voice low and rippling with emotion. "You disappeared in the crowd, and I…" He trailed off, his dark lashes shadowing his eyes for a moment before they lifted to meet hers again. "I can't bear it, the idea of you being lost from me."

Charlene swallowed, her voice caught somewhere in the pit of her chest. No one had ever spoken to her like that. No one had looked at her like she was the center of their universe, their every thought. Her hand, still dwarfed by his larger one, trembled slightly. "I'd have come to my senses eventually. I did, in fact."

He chuckled. Then, weaving his fingers through hers, Adam lifted her hand to his lips.

The kiss was soft against the back of her glove, but the feeling of his warmth seeped through as if the fabric weren't there at all. Her pulse fluttered, uneven, and her other hand instinctively reached out to balance herself—falling naturally against the smooth velvet lapel of his tailored jacket.

"Adam," she said finally, though it was barely a whisper. The word carried so much more than his name—questions, trust, longing. He tilted his head slightly, his expression softer now, less restrained, as though whatever storm had churned within him had begun to settle.

"Yes?" A simple response, but it vibrated through her too deeply. One word, spoken as if it carried every secret she'd yet to utter. The connection between them tightened. She could feel it, as real as the breeze teasing the tendrils of hair loose from her carefully pinned curls that had already started to come loose.

Before she could say anything more, Adam stepped closer. The space between them closed until it was nearly nothing, and still, there was so much tethering them together. The wind curled around them, but Charlene didn't feel the cold, not with the warmth radiating from where he lightly cradled her gloved hand.

Adam slowly, deliberately reached up and brushed his fingers against her cheek. His gloves had been removed; his hand was bare, and she could feel the roughness of his palm as it cupped her skin. The motion was unhurried, almost reverent, and yet it left her breathless. She tilted her head toward his touch, a small sigh escaping her lips.

"I've waited so long to tell you something," he murmured, his voice softer now, but it wrapped around her like the richest silk.

Charlene's heart skipped, her pulse roaring in response. "Then tell me," she said, the words almost a plea.

Adam stepped even closer, his other hand coming to rest lightly at her waist. Her bodice felt too tight suddenly, as if it couldn't contain the rush of emotions surging within her. His presence was overwhelming in the best way, each point of contact sending a fresh wave of sensation through her.

"I love you," he said, his voice raw, almost breaking on the words. "More than I've had the courage to admit until now."

Her breath caught. For an instant, time felt suspended, as if the universe itself had stilled to listen.

"I love you, too," she managed, every syllable trembling with vulnerability but underscored by absolute certainty. The words left her lips, and with them, all the hesitations she hadn't realized she carried.

Before she could say anything else, Adam leaned in, bending his head toward hers. The pause before their lips met was infinite, heavy with anticipation, and then the moment broke as he kissed her.

His lips were soft yet firm, deliberate yet tender. Charlene felt herself dissolve into the moment, her hand sliding up from his lapel to rest against his shoulder. The sheer intimacy of the kiss, the depth of emotion behind it, unraveled her defenses completely. Her entire world narrowed to the feeling of him—his warmth, his strength, the gentle but insistent way his lips moved against hers.

When they broke apart, just enough to breathe, Adam pressed his forehead to hers. Both of them were slightly unsteady, as if the weight of what had passed between them had physically shifted something within.

But the moment didn't end. Instead, his hands moved—without urgency but with unmistakable intent. He brushed his palm lightly down her arm, tracing the contour of her elbow before resting just above her hip. The slight pressure sent shivers cascading down her spine, and when he pulled her gently toward him, she didn't resist.

"Is this all right?" he asked, his gaze searching hers, open and vulnerable despite the strength that came so naturally to him.

"Yes," she whispered, her cheeks flushing as she nodded. Her voice cracked slightly, but she didn't care. There was no uncertainty, no hesitation now.

Encouraged, Adam's hands brushed over the curve of her waist, the layers of her gown a faint barrier against his touch. At the same time, his lips found hers again, more insistent this time. The kiss deepened, igniting something that Charlene hadn't allowed herself to feel before.

A warmth unfurled within her, spreading outward, filling her chest and making her knees feel unsteady.

His hands roamed further, skimming to the small of her back. Each movement felt deliberate, carefully testing her boundaries, but she had no intention of stopping him. Her fingers intertwined with the soft hairs at the nape of his neck as she tilted her head for better access to his kiss. The sensation of his steady strength, guiding but not forcing, left her completely undone.

When they broke apart a second time, his breathing was uneven, matching her own. Adam looked at her, his thumb brushing her cheek as his hand cradled her face again. His tenderness, in contrast to the hunger she had begun to feel in his touch, left her dazed.

"Charlene," he said softly, her name a promise, a plea, and a declaration all at once.

"I'm here," she murmured, her voice trembling but steadying under his gaze.

His lips curled into a gentle smile, rare but devastating, a side of him few had seen. "I'll never let you forget how much you mean to me. Not tonight. Not ever."

Charlene couldn't speak. Instead, she closed the remaining small gap between them, pressing her lips to his once more. Every spark she felt was new but familiar, as if she'd been waiting her whole life for this moment without even realizing it.

The sounds of the crowd below dimmed, the rooftop became their universe, and for the first time in what felt like forever, Charlene allowed herself to truly believe that this was where she was meant to be.

Perfection.

The warmth of her lips against his—soft, yet insistent—sent a shiver rippling down Adam's spine. He felt it deep in his chest, an ache so sweet it tethered him entirely to the moment. Charlene. Every thought, every feeling narrowed to her, as if the rest of the world had simply fallen away. How had he waited this long to kiss her, to hold her like this? How had he survived without knowing what it felt like to have her trust him so completely?

Her hands, delicate but firm, clung to the back of his neck, her fingers threading through the unruly strands of his hair. He swore he could feel her pulse in the faint, trembling pressure of her movements, a steady rhythm that matched his own. Adam moved one hand upward, his thumb grazing the curve of her jaw as he cupped her face, anchoring her to him. He wanted her to feel safe, wanted her to know she was cherished—all while every nerve in his body burned with the need to be closer.

He pulled back slightly, just enough to rest his forehead against hers, their breaths mingling in the cool night air. She was flushed, her cheeks warm beneath his palm, and her lips parted as though she couldn't quite catch her breath. Adam couldn't help but smile at the sight, though his heart thundered in his chest.

"Are you all right?" he asked again softly, his voice rougher than he intended. The words were simple enough, but they carried the weight of everything he wanted to give her—comfort, reassurance, choice. He needed to know she was here with him as completely as he was with her.

Charlene nodded, her gaze locking with his. Her eyes, bright even in the fading twilight, held a depth that undid him entirely. When she placed her hands lightly against his chest, letting her palms rest over his heart, he felt the unsteady drum of her heartbeat beneath his skin, mirroring his own.

"I'm more than all right," she whispered, her voice trembling but steadying as the words filled the air between them.

Her answer shot straight through him, lighting a fire deep within his core. Adam's lips curved into a rare, unguarded smile that he knew only she could bring out of him. He was a man so often controlled, measured, and deliberate. But here, with Charlene, he felt utterly free.

Sliding his hand from her jaw to her neck, he marveled at the soft skin just below her ear, so delicate that he could feel the faint flutter of her pulse against his fingertips. The intimacy of the moment left him breathless, but it was more than that. It wasn't merely the touch or the taste of her. It was her—the woman who had consumed his thoughts for months, the only person who had unraveled the tightly knotted threads of his soul. And now… she was here, truly his.

Slowly, he leaned down again, brushing his lips over hers. This time, the kiss was gentler, deeper, as if he could pour every unspoken word into it. He held her carefully, afraid of overwhelming her even as his need to be closer threatened to break his composure. His free hand settled on the small of her back, pulling her closer, steadying her as her balance shifted toward him.

The feel of her was intoxicating—her warmth, the faint rose-water perfume that lingered on her skin, the way her breath hitched softly as his hand roamed to the curve of her waist. Adam tried to pace himself, to keep his focus on the woman in his arms rather than the heat pooling low in his stomach. He wanted this moment to last forever, unmarred by haste.

"You're trembling," he murmured, his lips brushing hers as he spoke.

Charlene pulled back just enough to glance up at him, her cheeks colored with the faintest blush.

"I—" She hesitated, her voice small but steady as she added, "It's not the wind."

The honesty in her words left him undone. He cradled her face in both hands now, stroking his thumbs over the line of her cheekbones. "It's the same for me," he admitted. "You make me a disaster, Charlene. And I hardly know how to feel about that."

Her quiet laugh, soft and breathless, brushed over him like a warm breeze. She didn't pull away—in fact, she leaned into him, her hands tightening their hold on his coat lapels as if grounding them both. That small gesture was so entirely her—tentative yet bold, seeking balance even as she placed her trust in him.

Adam couldn't help himself; he pressed a kiss to her forehead, letting the tip of his nose graze the crown of her hair. His heart felt too large for his chest, and he took a steadying breath to remind himself not to lose control. He moved his hand along her arm, brushing over the satin fabric of her puffed sleeve, before resting it at the curve of her shoulder.

"Charlene," he said, his voice low and earnest. "I need you to understand something."

She tilted her head slightly, her curls brushing his wrist, her wide eyes fixed on him with unguarded curiosity. "What?" she asked, her voice so quiet it was almost lost to the sound of the wind raking through the trees below.

Adam hesitated for a split second, his thumb brushing slow circles along her shoulder as he gathered the courage to speak.

He'd faced so many moments of risk and uncertainty in his life, but none felt as monumental as this.

"I've never been more certain of anything than I am of you." His voice hitched slightly, his throat tightening under the weight of the truth. "Being with you feels like the only kind of freedom I've ever wanted."

Charlene's breath caught in her throat, her fingers curling reflexively into the front of his coat. For a moment, there were no words, only the soft rustle of the breeze and the faint hum of violin music from the gathering below. But when she finally spoke, her voice was full of emotion, rich and trembling.

"Adam," she said, her tone a mix of disbelief and wonder.

He wanted to tell her that he did know. That he understood, because standing here with her under the glow of the setting sun, among the sea of forgettable faces down below, he felt for the first time what it was to belong entirely to another person. But instead, he kissed her again, pouring his heart into the way his lips ghosted over hers, slow and deliberate.

The rooftop was their sanctuary, separate from everything else, and Adam knew as he held her that this moment would linger with him long after the night was gone. All he wanted now was to stay here, with Charlene pressed against him, their breaths syncing as the world beyond faded into insignificance.

He steadied Charlene in his arms. Her breath was shallow against his shoulder, her form delicate beneath his hands. Every fiber of his being was tuned to her, to the way she rested against him, to the way her nerves gave way to trust.

Slowly, he slipped his hands down her arms, the fine silk of her gown cool beneath his touch. Pausing for a moment, he searched her gaze, his thumb brushing lightly over the edge of her shoulder. He needed her to know this was her choice—that whatever boundaries she set, he would honor them without hesitation.

When Charlene nodded, her lips curving into the faintest, trembling smile, his throat tightened. The weight of what was unfolding between them left him breathless, but he steadied himself, letting his fingers move to the first line of tiny pearl buttons along her back. His movements were deliberate, careful, as though even the smallest misstep could shatter the fragile intimacy between them.

The buttons came loose one by one, a quiet rhythm punctuating the stillness of the rooftop. With each release, the fabric loosened, slipping away from her form to reveal more of the smooth, pale skin beneath. Adam's eyes lifted to her face as he worked, catching the soft rise of color blooming across her cheeks. Charlene didn't look away. Her trust, her openness, left him raw in the best way. He felt as though his entire heart had been placed in her hands.

Finally, the last button slid free, and the gown loosened completely. For a brief moment, it clung to her shoulders, suspended, before slipping down in a soft whisper of fabric. The breeze tugged at the edges of the silk as it floated to the tiled floor, pooling in a shimmering ring around her feet. Adam couldn't look away. She stood before him, vulnerable but unafraid, and the sight of her—for all her quiet strength and beauty—left him shaken.

"You're..." He paused, his voice catching as a flood of words fought to escape his lips. But none seemed to do her justice. "You're exquisite," he murmured finally, the words barely louder than the hum of the wind around them.

Charlene's smile wavered, her lips parting slightly as she released a breath she'd been holding. Her nervousness was apparent, but so was her resolve. She trusted him. She had given herself to this moment fully—just as he had.

Carefully, Adam bent down, his fingers brushing against the soft fabric now resting on the floor. His free hand reached for her waist, anchoring her as his other arm moved beneath her knees. With a deliberate motion, he lifted her into his arms, the movement slow and sure. She gasped softly in surprise, her arms instinctively circling his neck.

"Adam…" she murmured, her voice trailing off as her cheek rested gently against his lapel.

"I'm here." He repeated her words from earlier, his voice roughened with emotion. His grip adjusted slightly, pulling her closer so their bodies fit seamlessly together. The feel of her warmth against him—the weight of her trust in his arms—was something he never wanted to forget.

Charlene shook her head faintly, her hair brushing against his jaw, but she didn't speak again. Instead, Adam felt the soft press of her lips against the edge of his collar, a quiet affirmation that sent a new surge of heat coursing through him.

Without a word, he turned, carrying her toward the settee tucked beneath the rooftop's trellised covering. Each step felt measured, his focus entirely on the woman he held and the wild rhythm of his heartbeat that seemed to echo hers.

When they reached the settee, Adam eased her down carefully, the carved wooden frame creaking faintly beneath their weight. The moment of separation—a brief pause as he stood back—was almost unbearable, but he needed it. He needed to see her, to take in the quiet vulnerability she wore like armor.

Charlene's arms rested against the edge of the settee, her gaze searching his. The soft lantern light brushed against her bare shoulders, highlighting the curve of her collarbone and the slight rise and fall of her breathing. And yet, it wasn't just her beauty that held him captive. It was the quiet strength in her expression, the way she didn't flinch or shrink under the weight of his attention. She was here—not just physically, but utterly present in the space they shared.

Slowly, Adam lowered himself beside her, his fingers brushing lightly against her arm as he leaned closer. His free hand reached for hers, gently lacing their fingers together.

"Charlene," he whispered, his voice breaking slightly. "There's no part of me that isn't yours."

She exhaled a laugh, one that seemed more like relief than anything else. And then, as if to answer, she leaned forward, pressing her lips to his. The kiss was softer this time, less fevered but no less consuming. It wasn't just passion—it was a promise, an unspoken understanding that neither of them was holding back anymore.

Adam's hand slipped to the curve of her back, steadying her as she leaned into him. Slowly, he trailed his fingers upward again, feeling every shiver that coursed through her beneath his touch. She was all warmth and softness, and he was so utterly lost in her that he felt he might never find his way back—nor did he want to.

Time seemed suspended as they sat together, their breaths intertwining, the rooftop retreating farther into shadow. Adam held her closer still, his hand pressing against the small of her back as his lips found hers again. He couldn't bring himself to pause. Not when every touch of her fingers, every tentative press of her lips against his, was a revelation. And as the night unfolded, Adam knew he would never forget the weight of this moment—the undeniable clarity that she had, and always would, hold every piece of him in her hands.

The air felt heavier now, thick with sensation and possibility, as Charlene leaned into him, her leg curled around his hip. Each shift of his touch sent waves of fire coursing through her, unraveling every bit of composure she had left. Adam's hands were firm and warm, one pressing against the small of her back, the other steadying her hip. There was nothing rushed in his movements, only a deliberate tenderness that somehow made it all the more maddening.

SHE KNEW SHE should stop—knew that by every measure of propriety, this was entirely inappropriate. The heat of his lips, the deep pull of his gaze, the way her body betrayed her with every arch and tilt—it was as though all her years of carefully guarded manners had been stripped away, leaving her vulnerable, exposed. And yet, she couldn't bring herself to push him away. She didn't want to. The thought of stepping back, of separating her body from his, made the air catch painfully in her throat.

"Charlene," Adam murmured, his voice low and edged with a depth that sent a delicious shiver down her spine. His forehead rested against hers, their breaths mingling in the small space between them. "Tell me if you've had enough. Just say the word, and I'll stop."

She trembled at the tenderness in his tone, her fingers tightening in the fabric of his coat. Her guilt threaded through the haze of desire, whispering warnings of impropriety—the kind her upbringing had ingrained in her. But his touch… Oh, he was undoing her, piece by piece. Every slight shift of his hands, every heated brush of his lips, was unlike anything she'd known she could feel.

"I should stop," she whispered, though her voice lacked conviction. Her lips, traitorous and unsteady, brushed his as she breathed the words, heavy with her reluctance. "I should tell you to stop."

Adam tilted his head slightly, his lips finding her jaw as he whispered, "Then tell me." But he didn't pull away. His voice carried not a hint of pressure, only the promise to honor her choice. "Do you want me to stop?"

Her breath caught, his words filling her ears and igniting something intoxicating in her chest. Her teeth grazed her bottom lip as her hesitation wavered. The consequences—everything that could come from giving into this moment—flashed through her mind. And yet all she could focus on was the solidity of his body against hers, the intoxicating scent of cedar and spice lingering on his skin, the warmth of his hands that made her feel held, cherished, craved.

"No," she finally admitted, her voice a quiet thread of honesty, trembling but clear. Her hands slid up, tangling in the curls at the back of his neck as her resolve unraveled entirely. "I can't ask you to stop."

Adam groaned softly, a sound that reverberated through her, sending flames licking down her spine. "You have no idea what that does to me," he murmured against her skin, his lips brushing just beneath her ear. The combination of his words and his touch sent her heart into a frantic rhythm, a surrender she could neither resist nor deny.

His hands shifted, one settling along the curve of her waist as he pulled her closer, the other splayed firmly over her back. Her middle pressed flush against his, and the sensation made her gasp, a desperate sound that only further inflamed the tormenting hunger she felt building within her. She tilted her hips instinctively, seeking more of him, more of the delicious tension that was quickly overtaking her thoughts.

"Adam," she whispered, unsure whether it was a plea or a prayer. Every inch of her own body was betraying her good sense, moving of its own volition as her leg tightened around him. Heat pooled low in her stomach as she gave herself over fully to the pull of him. "I've never..."

He stilled just slightly, his brow furrowing as he pulled back to look at her. Her admission, vulnerable and naked, hovered between them. But his gaze didn't falter, his lips curving into a soft but teasing smile that set her nerves alight. "I know," he said softly, tracing his thumb along the curve of her cheek. "And I swear to you, Charlene, I'll take care. Of you. Of everything."

The words broke something in her—a boundary she'd been clinging to but no longer had the strength to hold. Adam leaned forward, his lips finding hers again in a kiss that was slower this time but no less consuming. She responded instinctively, her body arching into his as though he were the only thing tethering her to the earth. Her hands roamed across his shoulders, memorizing the breadth of him, the way his muscles moved under her touch.

"You're incredible," he whispered against her lips, his voice thick with reverence and want. His hands moved to cradle the back of her head, his fingers tangling gently in her loose hair as his breath came faster, heavier.

Her pride at his words warred with the lingering guilt that clung faintly to her thoughts, but she couldn't bring herself to pull away—not when he made her feel like this. Like she was beautiful, wanted, irreplaceable. She allowed herself to drown in it, in him, tilting her head back as his lips traveled down the length of her neck. A soft moan escaped her lips before she could catch it, and her cheeks flamed at the sound, though she didn't stop him.

"Adam," she managed, her voice wavering as her fingers tightened on his shoulders. "You make me... you make me lose all sense."

He chuckled softly, the deep, rumbling sound brushing against her skin. "Then we're even," he murmured, lifting his head just enough to meet her gaze. His dark eyes were burning with something she didn't quite have the words to name, but it left her breathless all the same. "You drive me mad, Charlene."

A faint, trembling laugh escaped her lips as the weight of his words sank into her, warming her from the inside out. She cupped his face in her hands, her thumbs brushing over the faint stubble that darkened his jaw. "This... this is madness," she said softly, her voice catching on emotion. "But I don't want it to stop."

He didn't answer with words. Instead, Adam's lips captured hers again with a tenderness that set every nerve in her body alight. His hands held her steady, supporting her as they moved together, their bodies fitting against each other in ways that felt as though they'd been designed for this moment. And for the first time, Charlene didn't feel shy about how much she wanted him, how much she needed to feel him close. Because in this moment, there was only him—Adam, with his intoxicating strength and quiet adoration—and the way he made her feel alive in a way she'd never known before.

Chapter Twenty-Four

T HE SOFT MORNING light spilled into the room at the Duchy Hotel, streaking across the polished wood floor and gilding the edges of carelessly discarded clothes. A crisp autumn breeze drifted in through the open window, carrying with it the faint scent of turning leaves. Adam leaned against the headboard, his dark hair still mussed from sleep, his shirt haphazardly buttoned, while his gaze rested solely on Charlene.

She stood by the window, a vision of effortless disarray. Her hair, the color of rich honey, caught the draft and danced about her shoulders with a kind of wild grace. She turned her head slightly, directing those sharp, steady eyes of hers out over the rooftops. The flush in her cheeks from the chilly air only made her seem more alive. Changed, yes—that was the word for it.

"You're different this morning," Adam murmured, his voice carrying an unmistakable warmth.

She looked back at him, one brow quirking as curiosity softened her features. "Am I? How so?"

He allowed himself a slow, lazy grin, the kind that always seemed to disarm her just slightly. "You're more feminine in ways I'd never imagined." His words were measured, but his tone carried the quiet gravity of a man thoroughly undone.

A laugh escaped her, light but wry. "Your mother would

disagree entirely. She once declared me a hoyden. Repeatedly, in fact." Her words carried no bitterness, only the faintest lilt of amusement.

Adam shook his head firmly, his expression softening even further. "She has no idea, Charlene. Not a single notion of who you truly are."

His voice held the conviction of every word he hadn't found the courage to say before. He got to his feet now, crossing the room in a few long strides. Standing before her, framed by the light streaming in from behind her, he reached out to lightly brush a lock of hair from her face. She didn't flinch, nor pull away. Her lips parted just slightly as if on the verge of some thought not yet formed.

"You are lovely," he said softly, his eyes taking her in as if he might never forgive himself for missing a single detail. "Utterly, completely."

Her gaze dropped for a moment, though a faint smile touched her lips. She gathered her composure and looked up at him again, softly exhaling. "This... This was my awakening."

Something shifted in his chest. He quirked a brow, though the corner of his mouth tilted upward in a teasing smile. "Awakening, was it? If you mean what we've just done... well, over and over all night, I'm happy to take credit for that." He reached to tuck one of her hands into his, brushing his lips over her knuckles in one smooth movement. "I assure you I'm feeling completely awake this morning, and ready for more enlighten-ment."

Charlene's laughter was warm, almost embarrassed, as she tugged lightly at her hand but didn't pull away. "Not that," she said softly, her tone taking on a richness that silenced even his playful amusement. "I don't mean..."

He furrowed his brow slightly, watching her face with careful attention as her expression shifted, revealing a quiet vulnerability he hadn't quite expected.

"It's my heart, Adam," she said simply. "I fell in love this autumn." She paused, gaze flicking to the narrow panes of the window and the kaleidoscope of tawny leaves flickering in the distance. "And it's the season for harvest, is it not? Reaping what we sow?" She looked back at him then, and her words softened to a murmur. "I think this... this is what we've been planting all our lives. We've been preparing for it without even realizing."

Adam's chest tightened, the weight of her words sinking straight into the fabric of his being. He didn't speak, not yet. He only brought her hand to his chest, pressing it lightly there, over the steady drum of his heartbeat.

"That," he said eventually, his voice roughened into something quieter, more intimate, "is the most beautiful thing I've ever heard."

Adam dipped his head, his forehead brushing hers as if he needed that closeness—that connection to her—to breathe. Her gaze remained steady on his, unwavering, yet there was a softness in her expression, something that captured the essence of her confession from moments before. He cupped her cheek, his thumb grazing her skin in slow, deliberate strokes, committing every inch of her to memory.

Then, gently, as though savoring the moment more than the act itself, he kissed her. Her lips were warm and pliant beneath his, her breath mingling with his in a way that sent heat coursing through his veins. The world beyond the room dissolved; there was only the faint rustle of the wind through the open window and the press of her against him. It wasn't the hunger of self-indulgence but the quiet, certain kiss of a man who knew, down to his marrow, that this woman was his everything.

When they parted, barely an inch between them, Adam rested his forehead against hers, his palm still cradling her face. He could feel her breath against his skin, the faint rise and fall of her chest as if she, too, was anchoring herself to him. His voice was low and rough, his words spilling out as if he couldn't stop them even if he tried.

"I want to marry you," he said, the weight of it settling between them like a vow already made. His thumb skimmed the curve of her jaw as he searched her face. "Not next month, not next season. Now. I don't want to waste a single moment more."

Charlene's eyes widened, soft green pools shining with something he couldn't quite name but that gripped his heart all the same. She reached up, her cool hands finding his face, and the unexpected tenderness of her touch left him utterly undone. Her fingers slid just along the edges of his jaw, steady and sure, as though she were grounding him with nothing but the press of her palms.

"You don't waste time, Adam," she said, her voice no more than a whisper, though it carried a conviction beyond its quietness. Her thumbs brushed against his cheekbones in a lingering stroke, her lips curving into the faintest echo of a smile. "You savor them. And that, I think, is why I shall love you for the rest of my days."

She kissed him then, a kiss that was its own promise, as sure and certain as the words she had spoken. Adam felt the heat build within him again, but this time it came intertwined with something far deeper, something he could only describe as the fullness of knowing who he was meant to be with. A life with Charlene, a lifetime of this, seemed to unfurl in his mind, as vivid and tangible as the press of her lips against his.

Adam's hand moved slowly, curving around the delicate line of her waist as he pulled her closer. His lips pressed more firmly against hers, a deliberate, unspoken plea for her to stay in this moment with him. Her fingers tightened against his shoulders, and she melted into him, her breath hitching softly as the kiss deepened, each passing second weaving an invisible tether between them.

But then, a sharp knock rang out, jolting its way through the air, shattering the cocoon of warmth they had built around themselves.

Charlene startled, her body tensing as her lips broke away from his, though she lingered impossibly close. Her breaths came quick and shallow, brushing against his mouth with each exhale.

Her eyes shifted to the door but flickered back to him almost instantly, a trace of hesitation glimmering in their depths. Adam's jaw tightened as he turned toward the source of the intrusion, the taut energy in the room pressing against him like a weight. Yet his thumb, unbidden, swept a gentle line along her jaw, his own breath measured and steadying as if to remind her that they were still here, still together. The silence between them brimmed with unspoken words, a pact neither needed to voice.

Whoever stood beyond that door could wait. What had just passed between them was immutable.

Chapter Twenty-Five

THE DOOR BURST open before Charlene had even taken a steadying breath, swinging wide with an air of authority that made her flinch, her knuckles tightening on the edge of the bedsheet. The scent of scrambled eggs and toast from the plates mingled incongruously with the clatter of the breakfast cart as it rolled forward, laden with polished silver cloches that gleamed in the morning light, the hotel's crest engraved across their domes.

"There you are!" The unmistakable voice of Adam's mother filled the room, her Spanish lilt lending the words an almost musical quality. She strode in with the kind of presence that could eclipse the sun itself, her gloved hands managing the cart expertly. "The waiter informed me I ought to keep my voice down because the Duke of Rotheworth is present. Can you believe such nonsense?"

At the doorway, the aforementioned waiter, a pale young man fidgeting with the tails of his jacket, froze awkwardly under her hawkish glare. Then, under no further instruction but the weight of her silent dismissal, he turned on his heel and disappeared down the hallway in a stiff, hurried shuffle. Adam's mother, satisfied, gave a faint sniff of approval before turning her demanding gaze back to the scene before her.

"So, look at you two," she tsked.

And then, she narrowed her eyes. Her sharp eyes latched onto Charlene first, clothed in nothing more than her chemise, the thin fabric clinging to her every contour. A crimson heat flushed Charlene's skin from her throat to the roots of her hair. Her hands hesitated between reaching to cover herself and retreating into the sheets entirely. She couldn't find the strength to move either way.

Next, Adam. He had pushed up on the mattress with a strangled, "Mother!" one hand clutching a pillow to his lap with hastily summoned decency. His shock was all too transparent—from his wide eyes to the way his usually self-assured voice scratched at the pitch of embarrassment. "What are you doing here?"

"I should be asking you that," his mother replied smoothly, her tone implacable as she slid her gloves off one finger at a time. She nudged the cart farther inside, as though she had no intention of leaving until she had her say. "You, the man of the house, lounging in your friend's luxury hotel instead of attending to your duties at your own residence. What is this, Adam? Are you a visitor in your own country?"

A low, awkward silence filled the room, and Charlene wanted to disappear beneath the floorboards. If mortification could kill, she was certain Adam's mother had just wielded it with expert precision. Instead, she remained frozen, caught between the escalating tension across the room and the humiliating weight of her own predicament. A visitor in her own life, she thought hollowly, her hands gripping the linens as though they might shield her from the judgment wrought by such a glaring scene.

"And now to you, Charlene." These simple words had an edge, its purpose as deliberate as a needle prick.

Charlene blinked, too stunned and far too warm now to respond. The heat in her cheeks threatened to overwhelm her, and her gaze dropped to the cloches as though they might offer some sort of safe haven.

"Mother, I beg of you, leave us," Adam cut in sharply, his bare chest rising as he exhaled, his free hand fumbling to pull on his breeches while still holding the pillow in place. "We can discuss this at home." His tone was pitched low, his usual commanding presence just beginning to reassert itself.

"No! You didn't come home, and David wants to leave," his mother said flatly, her hands now clasped primly at her waist. "I've been silent for too long. There are matters here that need addressing."

"Matters?" Adam echoed in a growl, his brows knitting together, but his mother barely spared him a glance.

"What is this, Charlene?" she pressed, her dark eyes pinning Charlene like a butterfly under glass. "One year it's David, and now it's Adam? Charlene, your parents raised you far better than this." She tsked and narrowed her gaze. "First you drive one son of mine away and this, this... Has it taken you a whole year to think of how to seduce a duke this autumn?"

"Mother!" Adam thundered.

But at the mention of David, a dagger-like stab of pain sharpened the nausea building in Charlene's stomach. Charlene's pulse hammered wildly, each beat a deafening echo in her ears. Her throat tightened, and she swallowed against the scorching heat spreading up her neck and into her face. Her fingers fumbled with the edge of the sheet, gripping it harder as if she could anchor herself in the chaos around her. Words hovered on the brink of her tongue, but her lips parted only to release a shallow, faltering breath that caught in her throat.

She barely registered the shift in the air until Adam moved. His bare shoulders rolled back as he stood, every inch of his tall frame unfolding with calm precision. The morning light caught the planes of his back, the defined muscles shifting with a quiet strength that stole her breath for reasons beyond mortification. His movements were unhurried but deliberate, an undeniable presence that drew all eyes to him, silencing the crackling unease in the room with nothing but his sheer command.

"Enough, Mother," he said, his voice cutting through the room like steel slicing velvet. He stood tall and imposing, his back to Charlene, and she couldn't help but notice the effortless strength in the way his muscles flexed as he reached to fasten his breeches, movements swift and restrained.

Despite the sheer enormity of the embarrassment, Charlene found her gaze drawn to him, a strange comfort blooming alongside her. Trapped in the wreckage of this morning's events, there was no denying the presence he carried. And for just a fleeting moment, she could believe he was a shield against it all.

But there was no escaping the reality of the shipwreck unfolding before her—not Adam's mother, standing her ground with a face like granite, nor the sound of Adam's measured, heated breathing as tension coiled tighter in the air. Against her better judgment, Charlene could only sit, stay silent, and brace herself for what was to come next.

The air in the room grew unbearably thick as Adam's mother's voice cut through the fragile moment like a rapier. "How long has this been going on?" she demanded, her sharp eyes flicking between Charlene and Adam with the precision of a dagger.

The words struck Charlene, dragging all the air from her lungs. Her lips opened, but only the faintest sound emerged, a pathetic wisp of a stammer that failed to form an answer. "I... we..." she tried, her voice barely more than a whisper as her mind scrambled for something, anything, that might diffuse the situation. But her thoughts fluttered chaotically, refusing to settle into coherence. Her cheeks burned so fiercely, she was certain they would scorch her skin.

Without a word, Adam moved in front of her, blocking her from his mother's penetrating gaze like a shield. "This is none of your concern, Mother," he said, his voice firm, but with an undercurrent tight enough to betray his rising irritation. Charlene's breath wavered behind him, her hand clutching the sheet tighter as shame and fear warred within her.

Adam's mother scoffed, unfazed by his attempt to assert control. "It is my concern," she snapped, her accent sharpening her vowels into arrows. With a deliberate motion, she pushed the breakfast cart aside, the clattering of its wheels echoing in the strained silence. Planting her hands on her hips, she leveled a glare at Adam, her gaze as unflinching as stone. "Especially if the reason is the woman who made my son leave the country."

Charlene froze, her pulse battering against her ribcage as the words crashed over her. It felt as though the room tilted beneath her, and she struggled to keep herself upright, though she hardly trusted her legs to support her, even when seated. The sheet beneath her now bore the deep imprints of her nails.

"Where would I go?" Adam growled, his irritation flaring. "I have so much work with the estate, it's going to take me a lifetime and a half to even begin to sort it all out." His tone was clipped, but Charlene could practically feel the heat radiating off him as he straightened.

"Not you. David!" His mother's voice rose an octave, reverberating off the walls as she gestured toward Charlene with a dramatic wave of her hand. "This hoyden broke his heart, Adam! She sent him scurrying off to France like a beaten dog. Isn't that right?" She pinned Charlene with a poisonous look, her expression curling with disdain. "And yet, here you are, spending your coin on these little trysts at the hotel while my David starves in France. Is that how you care for him?"

The words were a hammer blow, reducing Charlene's fragile composure to ruin. Her throat tightened painfully, making breathing impossible, much less speaking. She wanted to contradict the accusation, explain, and defend herself—but her tongue refused to obey. The shame was palpable, an oppressive weight bearing down on her chest until it hurt to sit still. Her ears rang, magnifying the silence that dragged on too long after Adam's mother's vicious declaration.

Adam's sharp exhale broke through the suffocating tension. His hands ripped through his hair, sending the black strands into wild disarray. Charlene's gaze betrayed her, drifting to trace the unruly locks as they fell against his forehead. Even now, drowning in her humiliation, the sight of him unguarded stirred something warm in the pit of her stomach.

Then his eyes found hers, and his expression had nothing but resolute calm. Beneath the embarrassing chaos unfolding around her, a flicker of gratitude bloomed as he met her gaze with a reassuring softness, the corners of his lips lifting faintly. It was impossibly brief, like a hidden lifeline tossed her way before he turned his attention back to his mother.

Adam rose to his full height, his broad shoulders squared in defiance. "It's not like that at all, Mother," he said firmly, his voice low and unyielding. Charlene felt the shift in the room like a crack of thunder, his authority palpable. He tilted his chin upward, meeting his mother's cutting glare head-on.

"And it's time you knew the truth."

The declaration dropped into the silence like a stone into a pond, sending ripples outward. The air practically thrummed with tension, the unspoken truths circling just out of reach, waiting to be uncovered. Charlene's stomach twisted as equal parts dread and curiosity coiled tighter within her, daring her to brace herself for what was to come. How could she ever hope for acceptance when she was both the casualty of one son's betrayal and the keeper of the other's heart?

Chapter Twenty-Six

THE STILLNESS IN the room made the tension almost unbearable, but Adam held his ground, refusing to yield to the chaos threatening to overwhelm them. His mother's eyes darted to him, her expression a storm of hurt and confusion, but he spoke as gently as he could manage. "First of all, David should go to France. Even farther away. But you ought to know that the duchy can't continue to pay for his lavish lifestyle."

Her head snapped back as though his words had been a physical blow. "Lavish?" she echoed, her voice trembling despite the incredulous note she tried to inject. She shook her head slowly, as if the weight of incomprehension had settled there. "He told me the house needs new staff and renovations before I could visit. He needs money to maintain a standard of living befitting the brother of a duke."

Adam exhaled deeply, a bitter edge coating his tone. "He lied, Mother. As usual." His eyes flicked briefly to Charlene, who had wrapped her arms around herself. The sight of her, so quietly retreating into herself, made something twist painfully in his chest.

His mother's trembling turned to a vibration of indignation. "How dare you call your brother a liar?" Her voice cracked though her attempt at authority surged on, but he could tell she lacked her earlier conviction. He understood. She didn't want to believe it. "And in front of our friends' daughter, no less! After what you've done with the girl!"

"Mother." Adam instinctively reached out for Charlene's hand, but she jerked back, the move subtle yet impactful, making his arm hang awkwardly between them. He didn't withdraw immediately, though her reaction stung far more than he could admit. "He is a liar," he pressed instead, his voice lower, firmer. "He lies whenever he opens his mouth."

Her next words erupted like cannon fire, shaking her index finger in the air. "Name one lie!"

For a heartbeat, Adam faltered, his gaze swiveling to Charlene before returning to his mother. The defensive set of Charlene's shoulders nearly unspooled his composure entirely, but he gathered himself again. His voice cut through the static. "What did he tell you about why the engagement with Charlene never came to be?"

The question struck its mark. His mother faltered, blinking rapidly as though clearing fog from her mind. But no response came.

"And why he broke his tooth?" Adam pressed, taking a cautious step forward.

Her hesitation unraveled into a pointed accusation as her gaze locked on Charlene. "She did it."

The air thickened. Adam didn't flinch. "Yes, that's true." His voice dropped, his tone a blade's edge. "And she should have done worse, if you ask me."

Charlene flinched visibly, her arms tightening around her body, her mouth pressing into a firm, pale line. Adam swallowed hard, his chest tightening at the sight of her retreating even further into herself.

His mother's voice lowered, quivering under the strain of what she didn't want to hear but felt pressed to understand. "What are you telling me?" Her voice cracked, fingers trembling as they clutched at her skirts. "Tell me, Charlene, what happened that you broke a vase on my son's face? Or was that a lie, too?"

Charlene's response came after a breathless pause, her words as fragile and quiet as paper. "It wasn't. I did that."

"To my son!" The words trembled out of his mother's lips, half incredulity, half anguish.

"Yes, Your Grace." Charlene shrank even further, her tone nearly swallowed by the weight of the moment.

His mother stepped back, the slightest wobble betraying her intent to keep control. "Why?" The demand held no heat now, only a note of raw disbelief.

Several seconds of excruciating silence passed. No one moved.

Finally, Adam stepped forward. The words were heavy in his mouth, and he steadied himself with a deep breath before letting them fall in Spanish. "He forced himself on her and he would have done worse if I hadn't caught them. She fought back, and that's when she broke his tooth."

The trembling returned to his mother's frame, violent enough now to make her waver on her feet. Her hand fluttered to her mouth, covering it as a soundless gasp escaped. Her eyes fixed on Adam, searching his face as though searching for any trace of exaggeration or deceit. Tears pooled at the corners of her determined gaze, and her lips moved wordlessly before she whispered, almost inaudibly, "Sins of the flesh."

Adam's jaw tightened, the words cutting deeper than they intended. He took another step forward, his voice gaining strength, but it carried no malice. "This is what David spends his money on, Mother. A castle in France. Lavish banquets. Entertainment far removed from decency. He lives above and beyond his means with no regard for the dukedom." His voice grew quieter, almost a solemn lament. "With no regard for anything but his own needs."

Only his own.

And Adam was finished with that. All of that.

THE DOWAGER DUCHESS'S eyes raked over Charlene with a mix of scrutiny and contempt, as though she were deciding whether Charlene was a victor or a villain. A warrior or a harlot. Charlene felt the weight of that gaze settle on her like armor too heavy to wear. Her stomach churned, and her cheeks burned like fire. The walls felt too close. She had to leave.

Her hands flew to her shawl draped over the nearby chair. She could hardly see what she was doing for the blur of emotion in her eyes. Her fingers stilled for a moment as Adam's voice broke through the rising roar in her ears.

"Don't go."

She didn't dare look at him. Her breaths came shallow and quick, her fingers fumbling with the fabric. "I'm ruined," she said, her voice tight and brittle. "Thoroughly so. I have to go."

"You bring shame to our family," the dowager duchess said, breaking the tense silence with words that lashed like a whip.

Charlene froze, shoulders flinching under the coolness of the words. The duchess's tone hadn't risen, but its sharpness was unmistakable. It cut deeper than any accusation could have.

The air shifted with the sound of Adam's steps. He moved in front of her, his imposing figure drawing the heat of her shame to him. His voice filled the room—not loud, but tempered steel.

"Don't ever speak of her like this again," he spat with measured intensity before stepping closer to his mother. His jaw tightened, his hands flexing at his sides. "Do you understand me?"

The dowager duchess, for the first time Charlene had seen, faltered. Her eyes went wide, and her head tilted back slightly, as though his words had struck her physically. "Are you," she stammered, her voice quivering as her gaze darted between them, "are you telling me, *mi hijo*, that you… she and you?"

Adam didn't relent. "I've asked her to marry me." His words filled the space, bold and unshakeable. He turned to Charlene, his tone softening but losing none of its resolve. "And if she accepts my hand, I will spend the rest of my life trying to live up to the honor, strength, brilliance, and beauty she brings to this world." His voice, steady as a vow, made Charlene's chest ache. "Once you decide," he continued, his eyes on hers, his gaze alight with something she had never dared imagine for herself, "I'd most humbly hope you'll tell me your decision."

Charlene could hear the dowager duchess sucking in a breath to protest, but Adam raised a hand halfway, palm out, a soundless command for silence that the duchess obeyed without a word.

Lowering his hand, his gaze stayed locked on Charlene. "There would be nothing I'd wish more in my life than... than you, Charlene. You make my life worth living. My service to the country has meaning when I know there are people like you in this world."

Her knees wobbled, and she felt hot tears gathering at the corners of her eyes. His words unraveled her, piece by tender piece, exposing the depths of a love she could have never hoped for.

And then Adam sank to one knee, tilting his head up to look at her. His hand found hers, careful, reverent. Her breath hitched.

"Please," he said, his voice cracking slightly, his vulnerability laid as bare as if he were unarmed in battle. "Please say yes to me despite the face I share with the devil."

Charlene drew a trembling breath, her eyes never leaving his as she stepped closer, her voice soft but brimming with emotion. "Adam," she began, her heart pounding louder than the words leaving her lips. "The face you think you share with the devil... it's my sanctuary. How could you not see that? Every time I look at you, I only see the man who has fought for me, defended me, and shown me what it means to be truly loved."

She paused, her hand lifting tentatively to touch his cheek, her fingers grazing the skin as if to commit it to memory. "I know every feature of your face, every line, every curve. Your smile..." She swallowed hard, feeling her voice shake. "It begins on the right, as though even the sun hesitates to rise all at once, afraid to outshine you." Her chest tightened as she tried to steady herself, her voice growing firmer, though tears shimmered in her eyes. "And your words, Adam. With just a sentence, you can set every part of me alight. No one else has that power. No one else could make me feel like this—with a single look, a single touch. There is no shame I've felt, no pain I've endured that your love hasn't been strong enough to banish." Her hands pressed to his, warm and steady now as her lips curled into a trembling smile. "Do you see now? You've given my life a meaning I never thought possible. You've made me believe in something I never thought I could have. And that's why I choose you," she whispered, tears slipping down her cheeks. "It will be the easiest choice of my life. I would choose you over and over again, in every moment, in every lifetime—for you are my light, Adam. You are my love."

Her voice cracked on the last word, but she didn't falter. She gazed into his eyes, her heart full and open, ready to claim the love she had never thought she could deserve. She swallowed back the lump in her throat, her voice trembling with her first word. "Yes." A smile broke through the tears cascading down her cheeks. Louder this time. "Yes!"

A laugh bubbled out of her, soft at first and then freer, unrestrained. Her hands flew to her mouth, and she shook her head in amazement. "Yes, Adam," she said again, her voice strong and sure now. "I would be honored. I would be proud."

Adam's face broke into that lopsided smile she loved so dearly. Without hesitation, he rose and pulled her close, his arms wrapping around her as if to shield her from every judgment, every cruel word. Her heart raced wildly, and in that moment, she felt undeniably, irrevocably his. And as for the dowager duchess, well, Charlene would deal with her another day. Today, she chose love.

I CHOOSE LOVE.

The hotel room felt oppressively quiet despite the ticking of the ormolu clock on the mantel. Charlene held herself upright, though her breath hadn't fully returned since the dowager duchess's cutting words. Passed from one brother to the next. The accusation echoed in her mind like the toll of iron bells, unraveling the fragments of her composure. Her fingers curled into the thin fabric of her gloves, nails biting through the silk where she clung to poise as though it were her last defense.

I choose love. From now on, she'd always choose love.

Adam's voice broke the silence, firm and steady, as though the weight of the moment didn't slice at him, too.

"Mother, Charlene is coming with me. And once we're wed, make no mistake, the world shall see her as the Duchess of Rotheworth."

Charlene's head lifted at his words, her heart giving an unsteady lurch as anger warred with disbelief in her chest. His mother's face hardened, flashing imperious disapproval. "Adam," she said tersely, "there is no need for dramatics. My carriage is just outside. Charlene can depart with some semblance of discretion. It's the least we can do for her."

Adam turned to face her, his brow heavy with the kind of unbending determination that could move mountains. "I will not hide her. I will not insult her dignity by suggesting she skulk away like some scandalous footnote. Charlene is under my protection, and by my honor, she will walk beside me—not behind me."

Every word landed like a whispered vow in Charlene's ears, and though her heart ached with gratitude, shame coiled deeper inside her. Adam's mother wasn't entirely wrong; hadn't she spent weeks doubting herself, questioning whether she had merely fallen into Adam's arms as nothing more than a remedy to his brother's rejection? Her gaze flickered to Adam, his eyes fierce and infinitely steady as he held his ground. He had never looked at her as though she were lesser. He had never made her feel unworthy.

Everyone else, however, had.

"I'm not certain this is wise," Charlene managed in a thick voice. "You've given me your heart, Adam. Must you stake your very reputation?" She tried to sound resolute, but the tremble broke through. "There are other ways."

His expression softened, though his determination did not. Stepping closer, he took her gloved hand in his, his thumb pressing reassuringly over her knuckles. "Yes, Charlene. I must. Because none of it matters without you. They can think what they wish, but I know what kind of man I am with you, and I will not yield to their judgment." His gaze searched hers, offering her a choice rather than demanding allegiance. "Come with me," he said simply, the plea and conviction entwined in every word.

"Wait," the duchess said to Charlene.

"David? Is this true? Did he try to hurt you?"

"He did hurt me," Charlene said softly. "But you'll have to ask your son that yourself. What type of person he is."

Her eyes suddenly widened. "If that is true, how have I not seen this before? I have always been able to tell when my sons lie."

"Perhaps," Charlene added, her whole body cold and drained. "You didn't want to see the lie."

"No, I—"

"Yes," Charlene interrupted, her throat tightened painfully. Adam chose her. He had always chosen her. And though the world's whispers might follow them, they would face them together. But now, she had to protect him. Stand up for him. Choose him. Again. "If you had looked closely, you would have seen your son, Adam, had been in pain."

"His father—"

"Passed, yes, but even so. Do not claim ignorance if you cannot stand firmly behind your reasoning. No one expected you to know the truth since Adam had done his best to protect you from it, but admit when you are wrong, when you have been duped, and have some more faith in your son."

They got dressed quickly and Charlene took Adam's hand then. "Lead the way."

He nodded. "Let's go home before my brother finds us here."

By the time they reached the townhouse, Charlene's anxiety had settled into a tenuous peace. Even the smallest distance between them had only seemed to heighten the ache of their mutual devotion. Adam guided her inside with a steadying touch, but the tableau waiting for them in the parlor dashed his calm entirely.

Charlene came up short.

David sat sprawled in a chair by the cold hearth, though his disheveled state undercut his lazy nonchalance. Beside him, or more accurately on his lap of all places, sat Miss Martin, her face flushed to a vivid scarlet. Her hair tumbled from its complicated coiffure, a sharp contrast to the rigid embarrassment she barely masked.

Charlene's steps faltered, but Adam didn't hesitate. "Well, David," he said coolly, his voice like a blade unsheathing, "what a completely vexing and yet expected sight. I expect you at least have the grace to explain yourself."

David merely smirked, quick as a fox, firing back, "Oh, you're one to talk of propriety, dear brother," he said, deliberately slow. "Dragging Charlene to a hotel to complete her ruination and then to parade her right under the family's nose? How gallant." He gestured dismissively to Charlene, his eyes glinting with malice. "A shame she had to settle for second-best before she caught a better prize."

Adam's chest burned. "You dare say that to me. I'm the duke."

"I could be the duke."

Charlene wanted to box the man's ears at that statement.

"Enough!" Adam's voice lashed like a whip as he took a step toward his twin.

Charlene sensed the raw protectiveness spilling into the cold space between them. Adam's presence loomed, commanding the room.

"You will not speak of Charlene in such a way again."

"Adam…" What was Miss Martin doing with David? Something didn't feel right.

Adam turned back, his face softening like the first light of dawn. "I won't have you doubt even for a second where I stand," he said gently before looking back to David, his ire rekindling.

He had misunderstood, but how to explain to him about the dread sprouting in the pit of her stomach?

"You are in my house," Adam ground out. "You've lived off the title long enough, and I won't have you disgrace it further. Have your scandal if you wish it, David. But you will not poison my name and title. Charlene will join our family as she deserves, with honor and dignity."

My heart.

For the second time that day, and the first time facing David since that nightmarish incident, despite her growing unease, Charlene found her voice steady, her touch light as her hand grazed Adam's arm. "Adam," she whispered, meeting his gaze. "It's enough. You've already given me everything I could ask for."

He shook his head, lowering his voice for her ears alone. "Not everything. Not yet." His eyes burned with quiet promise. "But I will."

And just like that, the weight of all her doubts began to lift.

And then Miss Martin shifted and cleared her throat. "There's something you ought to know."

THE AIR IN the room felt thick, suffocating even, as Adam faced the woman who had inserted herself into his family with sly smiles and toxic laughter. Miss Martin tilted her head, a curl slipping from its pins as she dragged the moment out, lips forming words meant to cut deeper than daggers.

"Oh, the morning papers will have quite the tale to tell," she said, her voice a syrupy imitation of the society columnists.

"'Shocking Scandal! Lady Charlene Fielding Caught in the Duke of Rotheworth's Chambers at the Duchy Hotel!' Just imagine the outrage, my dear duke. The whispers alone would slice through what's left of your reputation."

Adam's fists clenched at his sides, knuckles white beneath the tension. "It was you, wasn't it?"

Miss Martin feigned surprise, her eyes wide, though the smirk lurking just under the surface betrayed her. "Whatever do you mean?" she asked, her tone sickly sweet, before flashing teeth that gleamed like a serpent ready to strike. Only the truly vicious were proud of their blackmail.

"You have been leaking information to the scandal sheets," Adam thundered, taking a step closer. "That's why you've been fostering such familiarity with my mother!"

At that, his mother, seated and trembling, looked sharply at Miss Martin. "Lorena," she breathed, her voice brittle, "is this true?"

Miss Martin smoothed her skirts, calm as if she were the mistress of the house. Although, to Adam she looked more like a harpy on his brother's lap.

"Perhaps," she said with a dismissive shrug. "But how else was I to discern which brother could weather the storm?" A delicate hand reached up to adjust her hair, pinching her cheeks with practiced precision until they bloomed a rosy hue. She shot David a knowing glance, and to Adam's disgust, his twin grinned back like a devil relishing her work.

Charlene's steady voice, edged with disbelief, broke through the tension. "You mean which brother would end up with the fortune, don't you? That's what you were after all along."

Miss Martin turned to Charlene then, her gaze sharp as a blade. "And how would you know anything of it?" she sneered. "You're just a little pawn who stumbled into the Cross brothers' games and came out empty-handed."

"No," Charlene said, her voice quivering with emotion but strong in its certainty. "I never sought anything from David, and there was nothing between us that I mourn to have lost. But you, Miss Martin. You've been at his side all along, haven't you?"

Adam's brow furrowed as he turned his attention to Charlene, confusion flickering in his eyes. Her fingers twisted nervously at her side as she explained, her gaze trained on Miss Martin. "I didn't put it together before when your mother introduced us, but I recognize her from the masquerade. She was there. But more clearly, I remember her from that night. She brought David a handkerchief when his lip bled. I didn't realize it then, but now… it was a scheme, wasn't it?"

Miss Martin arched a brow, but it was David who replied, leaning lazily into his chair as though the room wasn't seconds from combustion. "A test, darling," he drawled. "No more, no less."

His mother's lips parted in confusion. "A test?" she echoed, her face reddening.

Adam wanted to throttle his brother. A test that tore a family apart.

Oh, Charlene finally realized it wasn't her fault.

"Loyalty," David said. "You see, not every woman in England has the stomach to siphon off funds from the dukedom and funnel them to France. And poor Charlene here? She failed." He grinned, smugness oozing from every word. "Didn't you, sweet little Char?"

Charlene's chin tilted upward, her eyes burning with indignation. "Don't call me that."

Adam stepped forward, his voice sharp. "You helped him steal from the solicitor," he said, accusing Miss Martin now. "That was when you came to visit my mother. You conniving, shameless—"

"Ah ah," Miss Martin interrupted, smirking as she held up a hand for a pause. "Not so fast, Your Grace. You mustn't be so quick to cut me down before hearing my terms."

"Terms?" Adam spat the word like venom.

"Of course." Miss Martin's tone dropped, her false humor

giving way to raw ambition. "What use is the annual income I've already acquired? I want it all."

Adam's posture straightened, every inch of him radiating fury. "Why would I give you anything?"

Her lips curled into a wicked smile as she stepped closer, her voice low and taunting. "Because, Your Grace, if you don't, the entire Ton, the House of Lords, and every bloody society dame in London will know of your scandal. Your intended, the darling Lady Charlene Fielding, shared a room with you at a hotel. It will be your ruin to take your brother's mistress while I have been paraded in society as the woman you intended to court."

"I never—" Adam shouted.

But the Ton would gobble up the gossip without question.

"Wait!" Charlene stiffened beside him, her face pale as her breath quickened. "You're the one who started the rumors?" she managed, her voice barely above a whisper.

Miss Martin didn't respond directly, but her predatory smile deepened.

The dowager, still seated, looked helplessly from Adam to Miss Martin. "What is she saying?" she asked, her voice trembling.

Charlene took a step back, her expression twisting with a mixture of hurt and realization. Her words came slowly, dread weighing on each one. "Why didn't I see it before? My friends. My brother. Everyone warned me." She stopped, her eyes fixed on Miss Martin as though looking at something monstrous. "It's you."

Miss Martin inclined her head, unabashed. "I am the empress," she said, sneering. "The *M-Press*, if you will. And you've made me rich with your gullible little dreams. But don't fret—I've plenty more to gain."

Adam felt his fury bursting to the surface, but as Charlene's hand brushed his arm, something inside him redirected that fire. It wasn't just anger now. It was for a purpose. Protecting her, defending their future, wasn't just a desire. It was his duty. He squared his shoulders and looked Miss Martin squarely in the eyes.

"You may think yourself untouchable," he said, his voice low but charged with resolve. "But make no mistake. The lies you've spun, the schemes you've crafted, end here. You will not harm Charlene or this family any further."

And with that, the balance of power in the room began to shift.

∗ ❧ ∗

Chapter Twenty-Seven

CHARLENE STOOD ALONE in her greenhouse, the gravel path beneath her slippers warm from the lingering heat of the afternoon sun. It was the hour before dusk, when the world softened into lavender shadow and time seemed to slow, just enough for hearts to do the same. But her gaze wasn't on the flowers. She was waiting. Not for Adam, though she always was, in one way or another. Today, she was waiting for his mother.

Lady Rotheworth had sent word through a footman. Not a summons, precisely, but not a suggestion, either. A quiet request that Charlene meet her.

Alone.

Charlene didn't know what to expect. She had not spoken privately with the dowager duchess since the night of the gathering—since the scandal with David and Miss Martin had finally, painfully, come to light.

She heard the soft hush of silk before she turned.

Lady Rotheworth approached, regal as ever, though the creases beside her eyes seemed deeper now. Her mourning weeds were gone—replaced by slate-gray silk trimmed in black velvet—but the weight of grief still hung about her like a veil. And something else, too. Resolve.

"Charlene," she said, her tone warmer than expected. "Thank

you for waiting."

Charlene curtsied, dipping low, though her heart pounded unevenly. "Of course, Your Grace."

The duchess's gaze rested on her face a moment too long. "Walk with me."

They moved in silence along the path between the raised beds, passing the marble bench where Adam had once… but this was not a thought to be had before her future mother-in-law.

"I owe you an apology," Lady Rotheworth said, not stopping. "Not only as a mother but as a woman."

Charlene blinked. "Your Grace?"

"I was blind to David," she continued, her voice steadier than Charlene expected. "To what he had become. And worse—I let him continue under my roof."

The words cut the silence with gentle brutality.

Charlene's throat tightened. She had not spoken of David since Adam had told her, quietly and without gloating, that his brother had left England. Disgraced and exiled to manage some faraway estate, David would no longer touch the lives of those he had wounded.

Miss Martin had not been so fortunate. Her whereabouts were unknown, though Adam suspected she had returned to her family in Spain. There had been no official scandal, but it had been enough. Enough that Charlene could breathe again.

Still, she had never heard a word from Lady Rotheworth on the matter. Until now.

"My son," the duchess said, and Charlene couldn't help but glance up. "Adam has always tried to protect everyone. Even David. Especially David. It blinded him, too."

They reached the end of the path, where a small sundial caught the last light. Lady Rotheworth turned and faced her fully.

"He nearly came to blows with your father," she said quietly. "Not because your father was angry, but because Adam insisted on making things right. He wouldn't let your name be tied to disgrace. He defended your honor when others—myself included—were slow to act."

Charlene felt her breath catch. She had not known that. Adam had told her very little of what happened after that night. She had been too lost in shame to ask. Too uncertain of whether she even deserved to know.

"I tried to protect David from consequences," the duchess said, softer now. "Adam chose to protect you instead."

Charlene swallowed past the knot in her throat. "He didn't have to."

"He did. I know now that he was right to because you, my dear, are our future and deserve our protection. And, because he loves you."

Silence stretched between them, but it was not heavy. It was full.

Lady Rotheworth reached into her reticule and withdrew something wrapped in fine linen. "This belonged to Adam's grandmother," she said, unwrapping a delicate pendant of deep green peridot set in gold. "It has been passed down to the women in our family since before Rotheworth was ever a dukedom."

She extended it to Charlene, whose fingers hesitated just above the chain.

"This is for you," the duchess said simply. "Not because you will be duchess one day, but because you have shown more courage, grace, and dignity than most women twice your age. And because you already are my daughter in my heart."

Charlene's eyes burned. She took the pendant in trembling hands, the warmth of the metal startling against her skin. The peridot glowed as if lit from within.

"I don't know what to say," she whispered.

Lady Rotheworth smiled. "Then don't say anything. Just wear it. And know that I see you."

Tears slid down Charlene's cheeks. The shame that had clung to her for so long, the burden of that night, lifted. Not erased—but acknowledged. And that, more than anything, set her free.

The duchess touched her shoulder, just briefly. "Adam chose

well. I am glad he did."

Charlene could only nod, too full to speak. They stood together in the fading light, two women bound now not just by circumstance—but by choice. And family.

Chapter Twenty-Eight

THE DRAWING ROOM at Charlene's house was quiet, save for the subtle crackle of the fire and the steady ticking of the longcase clock. Adam stood near the window, his gloves clutched tightly in his left hand, his right smoothing the lapel of his coat out of habit. He had waited too long for this conversation, and now that he stood in the Fieldings' home, preparing to ask for Charlene's hand, the silence pressed in like a verdict.

The door opened with a soft click.

"Rotheworth," came Fielding's voice, even and measured.

"Adam," Waylon added, nodding as he followed their father into the room. He looked both curious and cautious.

Adam turned and bowed. "Thank you for seeing me."

"You wrote requesting a private audience," Lord Fielding said as he gestured to the armchairs near the hearth. "I gather this is not to discuss the weather."

A flicker of humor in his tone, but not much. Charlene's father was a formidable man even in his gentler moods.

They took their seats, Waylon beside his father, Adam across from them. The heat of the fire did nothing to calm the nervous chill along his spine.

"This is the most important audience I will ever request," Adam began, his voice low but clear. "And I've never been more certain of anything in my life."

He paused. They waited. The air thickened.

"I love your daughter." He cleared his throat and turned to Waylon. "Your sister."

Lord Fielding's expression didn't shift, but Waylon's brows rose slightly.

Adam continued, "And I believe I always have. Even when I didn't allow myself to know it. Even when my family's expectations, and yours, pointed me elsewhere. I thought Charlene was meant for David." He swallowed hard. "That was my mistake. One I'll regret all my life. But I'd like to make up for my past failures."

Waylon leaned forward slightly. "But she wasn't meant for him. She was never meant to be anyone's second choice—or a prize traded between families."

His father's jaw flexed, but he said nothing.

"I've waited a year," Adam said, his voice tightening. "Respected her space. I've seen her strength. Her kindness. How she survived that night—and the silence that followed. She didn't crumble. She endured."

Now Lord Fielding sat straighter. Not cold, but alert. "She nearly crumbled because of you and your brother."

Heat rose to Adam's head as if he were a green boy speaking to the school's principal. "I come to you today," Adam said, "not because I deserve her, but because I would spend every day trying to."

A beat of silence passed. The clock ticked. The fire snapped.

"She's still healing," Waylon said carefully. "You know that."

"Yes," Adam said immediately. "And I will never demand more than she's ready to give. But I want her to know—when she is ready—I'll be there. As her husband, with your blessing. Her friend. Her equal."

He drew a breath. "So I've come to ask. Not just for her hand, but for your trust."

Waylon shifted, and for a moment Adam thought he might

protest. But then the elder Fielding lifted a hand.

"My daughter has always been strong," he said. "But since last year, she's grown into something even more remarkable. You're not wrong. She survived. But it's left a mark. You saw it."

Adam nodded once. "Every day since."

"And you still want to marry her." It wasn't a question. It was a test.

Adam's answer was immediate. "Yes. More than ever."

Lord Fielding studied him, and then asked, "What would you do if she said no?"

Adam didn't hesitate. "I'd respect it. And still love her. And never let another man touch her name without consequence."

Waylon let out a soft breath, almost a laugh. "I believe him."

Lord Fielding turned toward his son, eyes narrowed slightly, and then back to Adam. "And David?"

Adam's jaw tightened. "Gone. I sent him away—to an estate far enough that he can do no more harm. He will never step foot in England again if I have anything to do with it."

The fire cracked again, almost, seemingly, louder this time. Was this what purgatory felt like?

"He betrayed her," Adam said quietly. "And me. And everything our father stood for. That's a wound I cannot forget. But I won't let his filthy character near her again."

Lord Fielding's expression softened, but only a fraction.

"Charlene will have the final say," he said at last. "But as her father, I'll tell you this: I've never heard a man speak with more conviction about my daughter. And I've never seen her look at a man the way she looks at you."

Adam closed his eyes briefly. The approval, the tentative trust—it meant more than he expected.

"You have my blessing," Fielding said.

Waylon clapped him on the shoulder. "Just don't break her heart, Rotheworth. Or else I'll remove yours."

Adam smiled for the first time. "Never."

As he stood, his knees nearly gave out from the relief. He

bowed low to both men, then glanced toward the doorway—where, one day soon, Charlene would walk in and everything would begin anew.

He didn't have her yet. But he had this.

And it was a starting signal to begin the rest of their lives.

HE HADN'T TOLD her yet but Waylon had. Charlene had gotten it out of her brother.

Not about the conversation with her father and the way her brother's hand had clapped his shoulder with quiet approval.

She only knew one thing—he needed to see her, and she couldn't wait anymore to see him, when Charlene stood amidst her beloved greenhouse, her hands lightly brushing the delicate fronds of a maidenhair fern. The damp, earthy scent of the room wrapped around them like an unwilling witness, protective yet quiet. Adam watched her from the doorway, his presence stark against the verdant oasis she called her sanctuary.

"You should not have come," Charlene said without turning, her voice tight as she busied herself trimming a healthy bloom.

"I should not have stayed away all year," Adam replied, his steady voice carrying over the space between them. "You were hiding here all that time, in pain, and I was useless…" He reached into his waistcoat. "I couldn't even give you this meagre apology that I knew you deserved all along. You deserve better than me, than any of this. And yet, if you allow me, I'd like to work all of my life to live up to all you ought to have."

She turned then, her green eyes sharp, though misted with something she tried desperately to hide. "Staying away does not suit you. You're the duke! Orchids are not built for retreat."

Adam froze, the faintest line of confusion crossing his features. "What?"

"You heard me," Charlene huffed, crossing her arms. "You've

always been an orchid. A magnificent bloom demanding the brightest sun, tall and pristine for all the world to admire. Meanwhile…" She trailed off, looking away, her lips trembling before she managed, "Meanwhile, I am a fern. Something small, tucked under the canopy, needing shade, hiding because I have no choice!"

"That's what you think?" Adam stepped closer, his boots crunching on the gravel pathway. "That I've stood tall simply to hold my head high while you've suffered, all alone?" His voice cracked slightly, the pain in his tone unmistakable.

"What *am* I supposed to think?" Her voice rose, and she blinked back tears. "No one understands! Not truly. Not like you, and yet here you are, day after day, keeping the weight of the world steady on your shoulders as if I am some… some responsibility!"

"Charlene, you are not my responsibility," he said firmly.

You are my love! My heart! My everything!

Her breath hitched, and for a fleeting moment, hope flickered across her face, only to be crushed by heavy resignation. "What, then?" she whispered, biting her lip. "Why else would you have shielded me from scandal? Why else but to preserve me for your own convenience?"

Adam stared at her, disbelief warring with indignation. "For my convenience?" The edges of his voice softened, and his gaze bored into hers. "Do you truly believe I would waste my efforts keeping the wolves at bay for something as selfish as that?"

"You did not deny it," she countered, her voice breaking. A tear slipped down her cheek, and she turned her face away, as though too ashamed to look at him.

Adam closed the distance between them, his hand reaching tenderly for her chin, forcing her eyes back to his. "I didn't deny it," he murmured, his voice low like the rumble of distant thunder, "because I've been waiting for you to trust me enough to see the truth."

Charlene's breath caught, her tears now unbridled. "And

what is the truth, Adam? Tell me, because I'm so tired. I'm so tired of not knowing what I can trust."

He cupped her face in his hands, his thumb brushing against the delicate trail of tears on her cheeks. "The truth, dearest Charlene, is that I have only acted for one reason. Because I admire you. Your strength. Your fire. And, yes, your ability to hide in the shadows when the world grows too cruel." His voice turned softer, utterly vulnerable. "Charlene, you are no fern because you are fragile. You are a fern because of what they are at their core. Ferns uncurl slowly from their tight, snail-like buds, as if they are testing the world one careful inch at a time. They endure, Charlene. They stay green through driving rain, cold winds, and all the cruelty nature can offer. When orchids fade in their damp little environments, ferns remain steadfast, faithful." He stepped closer, his voice softening, yet filled with conviction. "That's what I admire most about you. Your resilience. You know what is true. What is worth protecting. That is beauty, Charlene. That is what the Ton will never understand. And that is why you're the woman this duke needs at his side."

Her tears fell faster now, and Adam leaned in, pressing his lips to the wetness streaming down her skin. He kissed her tears away, one by one, until his lips hovered just a breath from hers.

"Say you'll believe me," he whispered, his voice like a string about to snap. "Say you'll see what has been clear to me from the very beginning—that you are my everything, and I have never wished to be a savior. Just a man worthy of standing at your side."

Charlene's trembling fingers reached for him, folding into the lapels of his coat, as though anchoring herself to the promise he laid bare before her. "I've misunderstood you, then?" she whispered, her voice cracking.

"Look at me now," he murmured. "Do you see *me*, Charlene? Adam, who helped you fill this raised bed with soil. Who gave you seeds for your thirteenth birthday because that was what you truly wanted, not ribbons and watercolors."

"That was you," she whispered.

"That *is* me!"

Her gaze lifted slowly to his, and in the green depths of her eyes, reflected in the soft glow of the sunlight filtering through the greenhouse glass, Adam saw it. Belief. Her lips brushed against his, tentative and trembling, yet soft as a sigh.

"Yes," she breathed, "I see you now."

Adam's arms wrapped around her then, pulling her flush against him as the walls she'd built crumbled around them both. Their kiss deepened, their breaths mingling, and for the first time, Charlene felt truly seen—not as the ruin the world called her, but as the woman Adam cherished beyond reason.

And somehow a fern and an orchid managed to come together.

Chapter Twenty-Nine

Headline: The Rotheworth Affair Reaches Its Climax! Scandal, Betrayal, and a Duchess in the Making?

Dearest readers, what a whirlwind of intrigue has swept through our fair society like a tempest in a teacup! It is with quivering pen and a heavy heart that I, your faithful purveyor of truth, must relay the final chapter (or is it merely the beginning?) of the sordid tale of the Cross family. Gather close, for the scandal I must report beggars belief and reeks of betrayal most foul.

The Duke of Rotheworth, that once-proud beacon of dignity and propriety, has turned against his very blood! Yes, dear reader, word has reached this author of how His Grace leveled threats against his twin brother, David Cross, forcing him into ignoble exile under the heavy hand of blackmail.

By the close of the week, the spare to the heir was gone from England as if a brother could be dismissed from the duke's family entirely. They had left him no choice, cutting his stipends and seeing him to the docks himself. Whispers claimed Miss Martin had lost her place in polite company by virtue of mere association with the exiled brother. To society, they were both footnotes in a scandal that never quite bloomed. To the duke they were a wound—family and betrayal bound up in one—but a wound he would not let fester in life.

And why, you may ask, would a noble duke take such dras-

tic measures? Why, to make his daring escape with none other than Lady Charlene Fielding, the demure beauty who has proven herself, by all accounts, anything but demure.

'Twas Lady Charlene, whose name drips from every tongue like honey laced with arsenic. We have it on unimpeachable authority that her dalliance with the Cross family was no accident, no twist of Cupid's bow. No, my dear readers! Rumor has it the lady in question meant to play one twin against the other from the very start. Her supposed innocence? A well-crafted charade, designed to earn the Dowager Duchess's misplaced sympathy and secure her slippery ascent up society's glittering ladder. From the "spare," as cruel society labels the younger son, to the heir apparent, Lady Charlene has allegedly charmed her way to the pinnacle of ambition.

But do not shed tears for the Cross men just yet. It appears folly runs thick in that family, for what man of principle would allow himself to be led so willingly astray? His Grace's actions have left the family in tatters, the bonds of brotherhood irrevocably broken. He is now rarely seen apart from Lady Charlene, and tongues wag that he has abandoned his responsibility to the House of Rotheworth in favor of her coy smiles. A love story, some might say, but others see it as the treachery of a woman with no title, no fortune, and, it seems, no remorse.

And what of this very publication, your humble yet tenacious source of truth? Ah, dear readers, it pains me to say it, but Lady Charlene Fielding has delivered the final blow. Women like her, with their cunning ways and duplicitous hearts, have silenced this sheet's noble pursuit of the truth. For more than a year, we have followed the trails of deceit, betrayal, and greed that cling to her like perfume. But now, we must close our pages, our quill stilled by the storm she has wrought.

And so, dear friends, I bid you farewell. The duke may have his duchess, but his soul? Ah, his soul is lost to scandal, and the whispered secrets of drawing rooms and banquet halls will forever taint his legacy. Rest assured, history will remember the names of Rotheworth and Fielding not for their love, but for their infamous fall.

Yours in scandal (if not silence),
The M-Press

"This is not just preposterous fabrication but also quite sad," Ashley said, setting the teapot down with a soft clink.

"And it's two weeks old news. Nobody cares anymore."

The warm air of the greenhouse carried the faint scent of citrus, mingling with the delicate sweetness of tea. Charlene sat at the small wrought-iron table near the orange tree, her gloved fingers tracing the rim of her porcelain teacup. Across from her, Ashley poured herself another cup with an unhurried grace that belied the sharpness of her words.

"Indeed," Maddie added, her sharp eyes drifting to the orange blossoms clustering among the glossy leaves overhead. "Will you be harvesting any of the blossoms this season?"

Charlene shook her head, brushing a loose strand of hair back into place. "No, you may use them for your potions."

"Perfumes," Maddie corrected, her tone light but pointed.

Charlene managed a faint smile, though her gaze flickered to the door once more. He ought to be back by now, she thought. Her stomach churned softly, the uncertainty nearly unbearable.

"Call it what you will," Ashley interjected, stirring her tea idly, "but you won't find a tonic for the emptiness left by betrayal. It's the very antithesis of trust and love. I feel terribly for Adam."

"I'm sure Adam applies himself more than adequately without your sympathy," Charlene replied, adding yet another spoonful of sugar to her already sweetened tea. The room felt suddenly stifling, and she wasn't certain if it was her friends' probing words or her own unease that pressed against her chest.

"And now you've five spoons of sugar in that poor cup," Maddie remarked, her quirked brow hovering between teasing and concern. "I've made many things over the years, but alas, I've yet to concoct a remedy for apathy."

"She's not apathetic nor pathetic," Ashley said with a subtle smile, cresting the edge of playful. "She's hoping for validation."

Before Charlene could respond, the murmur of men's voices reached them from the hallway. Her heart leapt, and she set her teacup down carefully, willing her hands not to tremble. She rose, smoothing her skirts in reflex, as both Ashley and Maddie followed suit.

The door opened to reveal her brother, Waylon, striding in with his usual air of determination. Behind him came Mr. Grafton. Both men offered polite nods to the ladies.

"Well, Ashley will soon be countess. Sera is a princess. And you're the new duchess," Maddie said. "And I have my flowers."

"You'll catch the wedding fever and find the right man, it won't be long now," Ashley said with a wink.

"Ladies," Waylon greeted, straight-backed and formal.

"So," Charlene said, unable to contain herself, "what did he say?"

"There won't be a duel," Waylon said, the tight line of his mouth softening slightly.

"I won't be serving as second," Henry added, a touch of humor lifting his otherwise serious demeanor.

Charlene's relief came in the form of a deep inhale, her shoulders easing from where they had been locked in tension. For the first time that afternoon, a flicker of weight lifted from her chest. Still, her heart raced, her thoughts scrambling for answers. "Where is he?" she asked, her voice steadier than she'd expected it to be.

"We left him just a moment ago," Waylon replied, glancing toward the hallway as her father's voice echoed faintly from the direction they'd come.

"She's in here," came her father's call, and with those words, Adam stepped through the doorway.

He wore his triumph plainly, his black hair catching the light from the wide windows above. His smile radiated something so pure and certain that for the first time since this entire farce began, Charlene felt truly steady. Hope stirred at the periphery of her doubt.

"Shall we continue to fret, or may I assure you all is well?" Adam teased, glancing at the room as though the gravity of their concerns were a puzzle to unravel. But his gaze stopped on Charlene, warm and sure, and she stepped forward to meet him.

This time, no scandal, no threat, no whispered rumor could intrude. Tomorrow's troubles would come, but for now, Charlene knew they had weathered the storm. And most importantly, she wasn't facing it alone.

Chapter Thirty

Gretna Green, five days later...

THEY WERE MARRIED.

Charlene couldn't believe it.

Even now, with the ring warm on her finger and Adam's coat draped around her shoulders, it still felt like a dream. A beautiful, foolish, miraculous dream she hadn't dared to wish for. She pressed her palm over her chest, as if she could steady her racing heart. But how could anything feel steady when the world had shifted so utterly?

She was his wife.

His duchess.

She'd crossed a country with him, fled propriety, scandal, and all the whispered rules that had once bound her so tightly she could scarcely breathe. Now, five days later, she woke beside him each morning in the tiny chamber tangled in linen sheets and the deep quiet of happiness. There were no carriages here, no prying eyes, no parlors full of watchers. Just them.

And it was bliss.

The decisive words from the modest ceremony echoed still in her ears: "By the laws of Scotland, and witnessed by those present, I declare you husband and wife." So plain. So final. And somehow, more powerful than any ballgown, any diamond, any royal decree.

She remembered the press of Adam's lips to her knuckles after he slid the ring into place. The slight tremble in his hands as he'd held hers, and the way his gaze had locked onto hers like she was the only thing keeping him upright.

It had been quick. Simple. Imperfect.

And utterly theirs.

Now, seated beside him at a humble table set with a warm meal and wholehearted joy, Charlene let her eyes drift across the glow of the firelight on his face. Her husband. The man who had once stepped between her and shame, who had asked her father for her hand like a knight from the books she used to devour in secret. She would never be the same again.

And she didn't want to be.

The fire crackled in the modest hearth, the scent of woodsmoke mingling with warm spices and roasted vegetables. Shadows flickered on the rough-hewn walls of the cottage, and Adam couldn't keep the smile off his face as he looked around. The family who'd taken them in had welcomed them with open arms, their sheer joy so pure and untainted it humbled him. They didn't know who he was. To them, he wasn't a duke. Charlene wasn't a newly-minted duchess. They were simply two people in love, and in this tiny home in Gretna Green, labels and titles disappeared like mist burned off by the sun.

The mother, her dark hair streaked with silver, set a steaming dish on the table before motioning for them to sit. With a lean build and weathered hands from years of hard labor, the father folded his palms together and gave a short blessing in Spanish. Adam might not have understood every word, but the sentiment was clear. Gratitude. Unity. Love.

"This is a feast," the father declared with pride, motioning to the simple yet lovingly prepared meal on the table: fresh-baked bread, a hearty stew of potatoes and herbs, and a modest chicken roasted to golden perfection. Adam and Charlene exchanged a glance, their smiles touching with shared understanding. Modesty offered with such generosity had transformed into grandeur in this little home.

Charlene reached for Adam's hand under the table, and the warmth of her fingers curled into his made his heart beat a little faster. Their host family chattered in a mix of Spanish and broken English, laughter punctuating their words. Adam could only taste gratitude on his tongue, sprinkled with the wonder of being here, in this place, with her. The meal itself was exquisite—not for its culinary perfection, but for the laughter shared between mouthfuls, for the way Charlene's eyes danced when she tried to mimic the little son's mixed Spanish and English.

Would their children be this happy?

Adam hoped so. With Charlene, how could they not be?

When the dishes were cleared away, Adam leaned back in his chair, cradling a cup of mulled wine. The children darted across the room, bright bursts of energy, unconcerned with decorum, while Charlene sat beside him, her hair tumbling over one shoulder. She was beautiful. He could stare at her forever and never get used to the way she took his breath away.

Then the father rose, disappearing into another room only to return with a guitar. His weathered hands picked expertly at the strings, filling the air with lively, soulful music. The boy, who couldn't have been older than nine, joined with a small drum, his hands beating a rhythm that had every fiber in the room vibrating. The mother's laughter carried through the music as she tossed her apron aside and grabbed a pair of castanets, clicking out a cheerful, staccato rhythm that flowed with the music.

Adam straightened in surprise as the woman suddenly burst into song, her voice rich, low, filled with stories he had no words for but could feel in the marrow of his bones. The music poured effortlessly into the room, filling every empty corner. Charlene started to clap, completely captivated, her soft palms finding the beat instantly. Finally, the little girl, no older than six, tugged on Adam's sleeve with an insistent grin.

"Bailamos! Dance! Together!" she exclaimed, her determination leaving no room for argument.

Adam laughed before looking helplessly at Charlene, who was already bursting with mirth. Rising, he allowed the little girl to lead him to the center of the room. He followed her lead as best he could, keeping time to the rhythm as she twirled in carefree abandon.

Then the boy approached Charlene. "*Señorita*, dance with me?" he asked with an exaggerated bow.

Charlene's face lit up, and with an air of mock regal dignity, she offered her hand to the lad. Adam folded his arms and watched as his wife whirled in the arms of a boy barely tall enough to reach her waist. Laughter bubbled from her lips, the radiant sound brightening the room in an instant.

Soon, the father and the mother joined, and the tiny space turned into a blur of clapping hands, spinning skirts, and stamping shoes.

Adam couldn't help but clap along until the mother pulled Charlene toward him, her castanets clicking as she laughed. "Your bride, *señor*. Dance with her!"

Their eyes met. Charlene's cheeks blossomed pink from the exertion, her hair wild, her lips curved in a wide, breathless smile. Adam stepped forward and took her hand, sliding his arm around her waist with a confidence that turned the playful claps of those watching into cheers.

He wasn't sure what he was doing, not really, but Charlene didn't hesitate. She moved in perfect sync with him as if their bodies spoke a language beyond words. Her skirt swirled around her legs, brushing his trousers as they spun in rhythm. The beat coursed up from the floor, into his blood, and through his limbs. He moved more freely than he had in years, the rigidity shed like a second skin.

The rhythm wasn't just in the music; it was in her. She was his rhythm. His anchor. His compass. She laughed as he spun her, her eyes alight, and in that moment, Adam felt something he could only call perfection.

She stumbled slightly on a turn but fell into his arms with a gasp and another laugh. He held her close, ignoring everything else, as cheers mixed with the music around them. Her hands rested lightly on his chest, and he dipped his head close.

The music softened, slowing to something tender as the guitar strings hummed a gentle melody. Adam's hand moved to her cheek, his thumb brushing over her delicate skin.

"How did I get so lucky?" he murmured, his voice low but rich with meaning.

Charlene's lips curved into a soft smile, and she reached up to brush her thumb over his jawline. "Maybe I should be the one asking that," she whispered, her gaze fixed on his.

He shook his head slightly, his voice thick with emotion. "No. It's me. You're my rhythm, my clarity, my dance partner."

She started to reply, but he kissed her, gently at first, then deeply, uncaring of their audience. The cheers rose around them again as the music swelled into jubilant energy, the room bursting at its seams with love, laughter, and joy.

And as Adam looked at her, his bride, his love, he didn't care who he was or wasn't to the world outside. He had all he needed right here—with her.

Epilogue

THE CARRIAGE WHEELS hummed steadily against the cobbled streets, the rhythm a gentle undercurrent to the warmth that filled the small, enclosed space. Adam leaned back against the plush squabs, his gaze on Charlene as she adjusted the lace trim of her bonnet, though she hardly needed the fuss. Her cheeks were flushed, her lips curved in a smile she seemed to be hiding and failing spectacularly to contain.

"So, he just gave his blessing?" Charlene asked, her voice half incredulous, half amused.

Adam allowed himself a modest smile. "He had no choice. What father can do much else after his daughter marries in Gretna Green?"

"You didn't exactly give him time to ponder the matter too deeply," she teased, raising a brow.

"No," Adam agreed, leaning slightly forward. His tone dipped to something softer, more intimate. "What's a man to do when his marriage is… consummated?"

"For two weeks?" she said with a laugh, and the sound of it wrapped around him like sunlight breaking through shadow.

"For years," Adam said smoothly, unwilling to be outdone. "I'm not finished." The seriousness in his tone only barely masked the playfulness underneath.

Charlene tilted her head, studying him with mock suspicion. "Oh, you're not finished, are you?"

"Not even close," he murmured, then he leaned forward fully, capturing her mouth with his own. "The papers said you seduced a duke this autumn, but they don't know what's happening next." Her breath hitched against his lips in surprise, but she melted into him almost immediately, her fingers curling softly against the lapel of his jacket. A kiss that started as playful deepened into something unspoken but understood between them, and when they broke apart, her green eyes sparkled with something that stole his breath more effectively than the kiss itself.

"My dear duchess," Adam whispered, trailing a kiss along the line of her jaw to her neck, where the fragrance of her skin was soft and tantalizing. "This is only the beginning." She giggled, that unmistakable sound of her joy sparking against his resolve like flint. He lifted his head to meet her gaze again.

"You're relentless, Your Grace," she said, trying for seriousness, but her smile betrayed her.

"And yet, you seem quite content," he said, sliding his hand over hers where it rested on the bench. "I'll have no objections to my determination, I hope."

"None at all," she replied, eyes gleaming. "Though I do hope Cavendish wasn't offended we left the celebration so soon."

Adam grinned. Not Jack. "Cavendish left town this morning. He was rather mysterious about his sudden departure."

"Seems just like your friend."

Her fingers laced with his in quiet acceptance, and she gave the faintest squeeze that felt to him like a vow of its own. The carriage slowed, and he noticed the shadow of the Rotheworth residence looming outside the window. The high arched windows that spoke of legacy and history now felt like a promise for something new. Together.

"This is our home for now," Adam said quietly, his thumb brushing against her knuckles, "but only for now."

Her brow furrowed slightly, curious. "What do you mean?"

Adam smiled, leaning forward, pressing a kiss to the tips of her fingers. "Because where you are, my duchess, is home. And no matter where the road takes us, I intend to spend every last day reminding you of that."

He saw the faint glint of tears in her eyes then, though her smile never faltered. The carriage door opened, the cool air of the London evening rushing in, but its chill couldn't touch either of them. Adam stepped out first, turning to help her down with a clarity humming in his chest. This was not merely an ending to their uncertain past but the irrevocable start of a future together.

As they ascended the steps of the Rotheworth residence together, her arm firmly in his, Adam thought that for the first time in his life, he understood what it meant to wholly belong. To love, and to be loved. And for once, the future seemed not a burden to shoulder but a gift to unwrap, day by day, with Charlene by his side.

Yes, this was only the beginning. And he very much hoped his Charlene would seduce him every day of the year, every season, and for as long as he lived.

The *Wedding Fever* series heats up as Maddie takes center stage in *Ways to Kiss a Marquess this Winter*. Will her sparks lead to a love story as unforgettable as the dreamy winter wedding of Ashley and Thomas from *Dare to Tempt an Earl this Spring*?

Don't miss the grand finale! All four friends—Charlene, Maddie, Ashley, and Sera—reunite for one last instalment where romance, friendship, and fate intertwine. Hearts will race, secrets will unfold, and with all the main characters returning, anything is possible.

Prepare for the ultimate culmination of love, laughter, and happily-ever-afters. Are you ready to see how it all ends?

About the Authors

Sara Adrien

Bestselling author Sara Adrien writes hot and heart-melting Regency romance with a Jewish twist. As a law professor-turned-author, she writes about clandestine identities, whims of fate, and sizzling seduction. If you like unique and intelligent characters, deliciously sexy scenes, and the nostalgia of afternoon tea, then you'll adore Sara Adrien's tender tear-jerkers.

For more information and exclusive sneak peeks, new releases, and more books, sign up for Sara Adrien's newsletter at www.SaraAdrien.com.

Tanya Wilde

Award-Winning and International Bestselling author Tanya Wilde developed a passion for reading when she had nothing better to do than lurk in the library during her lunch breaks. Her love affair with pen and paper soon followed, after she devoured all their historical romance books! When she's not meddling in the lives of her characters or pondering names for her imaginary big, white greyhound, she's off on adventures with her partner in crime.

Wilde lives in a town at the foot of the Outeniqua Mountains, South Africa. You can read a bit more about her at www.authortanyawilde.com.

9 781969 349430